All rights reserved by the author. All contents and corrections are the responsibility of the author.
Kindle direct 2022

Disclaimer

Any resemblance to a person either living or dead is purely coincidental.

Any information which is written that could possibly be considered to hold a medical or educational overview is purely fictional. It may bear resemblance to life situations but should be discarded and not taken seriously.

Other work by Beatrice Finn

The Value of Hindsight.	1996
Eileen a Mayo girl.	2014
Erin Go Braugh	2015
Old Ireland left behind.	2015
Full circle for the Toweys.	2016
The circle of life.	2016
Secrets lies and deceit	2017
Let's be friends	2017
Whispers from Cloontia	2018
Revenge is sweet	2019
Jacintha an Irish Emigrant	2020
Coventry to Indiana.	2020
Jacintha part Three -The Trilogy.	2021

Beatrice Finn

Simply Moira

The Russian Experience

Acknowledgements

To everyone in my life who has offered encouragement and support, I want to say "Thank you." You all know who you are! without your much-appreciated help I could not have continued on this journey.

The tribute to my parents, 'Pakie Finn and Mary Ann Forkin' from Derrinabroock, Cloontia, Mayo West Ireland, which was written in my first novel 'Eileen a Mayo Girl,' continues to be a tribute to them today. Without their love their support and their encouragement throughout my life, I would not have the ability or the confidence to be the person which I am and do what I enjoy doing so very much.

Hope you all enjoy the read as much as I enjoyed the work.

Much love to you all

Table of contents

The beauty of Enniskerry.	P 09
Shock and Surprise	30
Religious discrimination.	61
The value of hindsight.	72
New beginnings for Moira.	85
Revelations from Michael and Moira.	103
The foster child.	112
New Spanish friends	130
Another surprise	148
Diagnosis they didn't want.	169
Helen showing gratitude.	189
Deceit in its lowest form.	206
Blast from the past.	245
New adventures for the Kearns family.	259
Dilemma for Helen	281
Further Revelations.	306

Character Reference

Gerald Kearns – Father to Michael	Born 1937
Bridget Kearns- Mother to Michael.	Born 1937
Padraig Riley- Father to Moira.	Born 1939
Grace Riley- Mother to Moira.	Born 1939
Michael Kearns	Born. 1959
Moira Kearns.	Born 1960
Helen Kearns. - Daughter	Born. 1988
Dominic Kearns - Son	Born 1991
Alice -Moiras cousin	Born 1950

John McGinty -	Farming neighbours
Eileen McGinty -	Wife to John
Marissa Geary -	Foster child
Jessica Geary -	Marissa's mother
Frank Geary -	Marissa's Father
Rodrigo -	Spanish shop assistant.
Gabriella -	Spanish lady
Akim-	Boyfriend to Helen
Martina Kearns –	Sister to Michael and story narrator.

Introduction

This is a fictional story based on some facts. Set in Ireland in the late 1970s with new characters being added and eventually going forward to a Russian setting. Life in Ireland was very strict between the different religions, with each not wanting to engage with the other. We can't help who we fall in love with. Moira Riley who was raised as a strict Catholic found herself in one such situation. The man who caused her heart to miss a beat was not a Catholic. She was involved however she was sensible. Breaking off their relationship after almost one year of seeing each other broke both of their hearts.

Moira continued with her life at college and that's where she met the next man who stole her heart. Going down through the years, Moira experienced a good life on many levels but some hardships too. Becoming the mother of two beautiful children who each brought something different to her days she felt content. She upheld her parents views on mixed marriages, in so far as religion or any other matter was concerned. Eventually moving away from the suburbs of Dublin to live in a small village in county Wicklow, Moira had felt that as a family they had it all. They were then to discover how their first born was wired up a bit differently, to that which is accepted as the regular human brain for anyone to have. As you will see this difference did not prevent their daughter Helen from having a very fulfilled life. Helen too found herself in a mixed relationship. Knowing her parents' feelings, well her mother's really, about those matters, she had some degree of anxiety about introducing her boyfriend to Moira and Michael. One or two more hurdles for the family to overcome highlighted their level of resilience.

The beauty of Enniskerry

Moira Riley was born to Padraig and Grace Riley in a small terraced house in the leafy suburbs of Dublin city. Being the middle child in a working-class family, she had often felt somewhat out of place. She had so many times been on the defence due to those feelings of displacement. Ploughing her way through school life and the many aggravations which that had brought to her, Moira was delighted when the final school day arrived. Delighted to have completed her upper school education, she released her joy in a very inappropriate manner. Ripping up her school shirts the girl squealed with delight.

"It's done mom. I'm done. I've finished at last."
Grace Riley was not impressed. Quite rare for her she had some very strong tone in her voice.

"You can't go around tearing up clothes. Someone else could have used those shirts. Its wasteful Moira and that's not like you to be wasteful."

Moira understood. She readily took her mom's point on the chin and for a change she didn't give any backchat. She was subdued. The Riley house was unusually very quiet that evening. Older one had gone out with some friends and the younger one was a little upset. Many young children would cry or throw a tantrum or do something psychical when they *feel upset. The Riley children usually did throw tantrums but on that particular evening they didn't. Quietly going to their bedrooms, they remained there almost in virtual silence. Padraig getting home from the town couldn't help but notice the sullen atmosphere in the house.*

   "What's happened Grace what's wrong.? You could cut it with a knife."

Guessing it had all stemmed from Moira ripping up her school shirts, Grace assured her husband it was dealt with. Knowing the younger one would be upset to hear her raised voice, the woman decided that would have to be enough of the shouting. She reminded her husband how the younger one would need to toughen up. She would need to be prepared for the world rolling out in front of her as would the older ones too. Grace had always told her children that this wasn't and isn't the nicest of worlds to live in. Sadly, she was not wrong.

   Commencing the next stage of her education held some great excitement for Moira Riley. How different it would be by comparison to the school days when she had to wear uniform. She didn't like the dark green uniform at all. Always thinking how drab looking it was on her slender body and how it didn't match her long red hair either. Neither did she like being so thin. Standing just over five feet tall she would have liked a bit more meat on her bones. Choosing her three favourite subjects would progress Moira to the start of her University days, should she ever choose to go to University. Padraig and Grace never pressured her either way.

   "Well it's not for everyone Moira so we'll have to see when the time comes."

Moira scratched her head with a look of confusion. She had inherited her mother's independent gene. She really didn't like anyone attempting to have a view on her future. What did her mother mean by 'we'll have to see?' Whose decision did her mom think this was going to be? Clearly it appeared to Moira that Grace thought she would have a say in what should happen next. Grace Riley perhaps should have known her daughter better. Only she would decide about her further education or the lack of it.

Being almost eighteen was so mature and so grown up through the eyes of Moira Riley. She was starting to crave some real freedom from the clutch of her parents. She often stressed whilst trying not to. Everything in her head was so hard for Moira at that time. How was she ever going to get through life with parents like hers? Everyone would be going to the rave except her. Just about everyone! A head count of almost two hundred was what she had been told to date. Injustice beyond reason was what she felt she was now faced with. She would have to find a way to overcome her dilemma. Heightened levels of anxiety with almost despair etched their way across Moiras face. She had on some occasions been heard telling her parents Padraig and Grace Riley, how they at times would change their view in order to fit their desire of her behaviour. Her mom and dad would on some occasions be open to persuasion, leaving Moira with feelings of elation.

"Well, all right then Moira you can go just this once but remember the coming home time and don't be late."
Would she and should she remind Padraig and Grace of those occasions. She did not like bringing up events from the past. She was in turmoil but maybe she should remind her parents. Wasn't anything worth a try?

With her head yet again buried in her hands Moira wished her mother could make up her mind. Calling out sharply to Grace in her often-impatient manner, brought hope of quite a positive reaction this time.

"You're doing it again mom. Your telling me that as I'm almost eighteen that I'm old enough to know better. Yet, when I want to do something you don't approve of, you tell me I'm just seventeen therefore I'm too young. You're so confusing and so annoying. I am almost eighteen and I want to go to the rave."

Grace Riley had not been open to persuasion where the rave was concerned. She remained silent. She had no comment to make back to their daughter. Smiling sweetly in response to Moira's annoyance was not a great decision. The resulting hole in the wall caused more damage than the slight bruising to Moiras knuckles. Having the knowledge, that it would be pointless approaching her father, also gave Moira the clue it was maybe time to give up the fight or was it? There were options. Lying wasn't a great option yet 'needs must' was starting to be Moiras motto. Already having lied to her parents regarding the boyfriend, this would now be her way forward for the rave and for many other situations too. Yes, at last getting away from that awful 'no win' with the parent's situation, could be and would be achievable for her. A Life which had felt very unfair to Moira on so very many occasions, had suddenly now begun to turn over a new page. She smiled sweetly.

Struggling at times to understand her mom and dad's controlling motives, Moira would speak to the boyfriend who was her very biggest secret at that time. Having thought of him as being quite a level- headed sort of young man, she always felt he would know what to do. His advice usually was, that Padraig and Grace are simply being protective as parents often are.

   "You don't have too much of a choice Moira and maybe they're right. Often there's potential hazards which we don't see as teenagers, yet our parents at times seem to have radar vision. It's like they can see the hazards see what we can't see quite clearly."

Impressed yet not impressed she spat out the words.

   "Darn your maturity Charlie Cunningham but I do love you."

They embraced. Charlie being quite tall standing around six feet with dark brown hair, Moira was proud to have such a very handsome young man on her arm. Him being her secret boyfriend was one of her 'needs must' situations. She had found some devious ways to throw her parents off the scent. Charlie Cunningham was raised as a very strict protestant. The same religion applied to his parents and to his extended family. Moira was raised as a strict Roman Catholic as were her parents and her extended family. Rules which had to be very strictly adhered to between the two religions were that basically never the twain should meet. There lay the life time problem for Moira and for her boyfriend Charlie Cunningham. Neither were too keen on the idea of making war in the name of religion.

   Charlies levels of understanding usually made Moira feel better, alongside the thoughts of he was just her age and not a million years older. Moira often wondered how did he ever get to be so sensible and so very mature and very grown up for his age? Having met each other properly in their last year at secondary school they had dated very many times. That was a very secretive behaviour which Moira kept well out of ear shot of Padraig and Grace and in fact from the whole family. The titles of parents or mom and dad were ones which Moira often choose not to use. They made her feel a little inferior. Addressing her parents by their given birth names helped her feel a little more on an equal platform with them. Being from a new generation with both having a mutual respect for god and for all religions, Charlie and Moira had both felt that the out-dated view of their parents was wrong. They did however for their family's sake and for the sake of peace adhere to the rules, hence their relationship being kept a secret. Close friends with the same thinking process as the young couple, were the only ones aware and were happy to provide alibis should the need arise. It often did.

The letter arrived at the house in Dublin for Moira when she was seventeen years of age, well if we're splitting hairs she was actually closer to eighteen. The white hand-written envelope told her it wasn't the usual official stuff, which she had always found so boring. Could this be the day of a turning point in her life she wondered. Mail arriving at her parents' home address very rarely in fact almost never contained her name. Maybe the odd thing or two from school or from the local college but that was it. Never anything which had a hand-written name and address, which might have brought her any tiny degree of excitement or meaning, was ever addressed to Moira. Seeing her name right there on that small white envelope almost gave her an adrenalin rush. Muttering to herself, as she considered what an uneventful life she otherwise had, she looked pensively at the envelope. Deciding that her life had to be uneventful if something in the mail box gave her that much excitement she promptly put the envelope down on the mantle shelf. That's where it would remain until she was ready to open it. Taking herself off out to the woods for a walk and sensing spirituality all around her, she had a great sense of pleasure from all of the wildlife which resided there.

Returning back home through the busy streets of Dublin city, Moira was reminiscing. Wondering about the envelope and its contents brought a smile to her face. Using the small green public phone booth situated at the end of their road, she was assured of her privacy. She called her boyfriend with a plan to share news about the letter. On a lot of occasions Moira had called Charlie from the privacy of the outdoors. Changing her mind, she then choose not to tell him about the letter. Deciding she didn't know its content then what would she have to tell him. That bit of news was put on hold till the next time.

Teasing herself about some of life situations had become quite habit forming for Moira Riley. This time would not be any different. Her eyebrows were raised a few times as she looked at it and ahead of her slowly pulling the envelope apart. She had waited and then waited some more before opening it up to find out what its contents might be. Eventually having made the decision to do it, she pulled out the sheet of white plain paper. Much to Moira's surprise the paper had been neatly folded in half and then in half again. Feeling curious as to why anyone would fold a letter that way, she began to open it up. She was quite bemused by the content of the letter which was by all accounts extremely brief. There was however no doubting its clarity.

*M*oira was invited to attend at her mother's 1st cousins' home in Enniskerry for a whole weekend. The specifics were that she should arrive on the Friday evening and stay till the Sunday evening. With or without her parents was included in the request. There was no further news nor was there any further information or instruction given. The letter contained nothing else. No small talk. No how is everyone? Excitement rushed through her body. Staring at the letters content Moira was highly intrigued about the invite. Not knowing her mom's cousin Alice all that well just added to her curiosity. A journey down memory lane of some family events passed didn't help her either. The struggle and the curiosity for Moira Riley to establish what the invitation might be in aid of continued.

*T*aking the stairs two by two Moira raced at some speed to find her mother. Surely, she would have some answers. Grace Riley was always a busy woman but was especially so at that time. Hanging new curtains in one of her spare bedrooms she turned to see what the noise was all about. Bursting into the bedroom the words were already slipping out off of Moiras tongue.

"There's a letter for me from your cousin Alice out in Enniskerry. It's all very odd mom that she's asking me to go out there to visit for a whole weekend. She's your cousin. You have any ideas why she might do that or what it might be that she wants to see me about?"
Grace Riley's concentration was mainly focused on herself not falling off of the ladders.
"Give me a minute Moira then I'll be down from here and see what it is that you're talking about and will you stop

running like that on the stairs. You're like an accident waiting to happen."

Knowing her mother as well as she did Moira was very aware there was no point in her trying to push things. Leaving the spare room momentarily she told Grace she would be back in an instant. Sharing her view of the letter and her question with her mother did not enlighten Moira very much at all. The woman shrugged her shoulders as she told her daughter.

   "It's anyone's guess Moira! You want to go? And if yes you want to go alone or with us. Your choice given to you by Alice so now it's your decision?"

 Grace had held a very strong desire to see her child become a little more independent in life, in ways and situations which would meet the approval of herself and of Moiras father Padraig Riley. She was hoping for more personal reasons that Moira would do this visit to see Alice by herself. Grace much to her delight was not disappointed.

   $\mathcal{D}$eciding how she was almost a grown up at that point Moira did choose to go to her cousins home alone. She would show Padraig and Grace just how independent and how very mature she was. Show them how wrong they were when at times they would be treating her as though she were a child.

   "It'll all be fine mom. I'll call Alice and then I'll look into the bus service going out there. I'm feeling excited already and that's before I even know what this letter is all about."

Quietly slipping out of the bedroom and clearly being a young woman who did not always listen to her mother's advice, Moira once again hurriedly took the stairs two by two back down to the kitchen. Hearing her mother's voice yet again call out to her the safety on the stairs warning, did not seem to penetrate Moiras ears enough to make anything of a difference. It did not seem to register with her. She was behaving a little hyper almost dizzy with curiosity. Hands trembling, she picked up the phone to call her mother's cousin Alice. She would hopefully be able to visit out at Enniskerry the following weekend.

Having decided that she would attempt some small talk with Alice, she waited as the rings echoed out quite loudly in her ear. Eventually after what had appeared to be taking forever to Moira, the phone was picked up. Quite a distinguished sounding voice at the other end of the phone, gave her what Moira considered to be something of a rather tiresome greeting.

"Who is it?"

Moira had a slightly nervous quiver in her voice. It showed in her response despite her attempts of a cover up. There was no hiding it.

"Alice it's me Moira Riley- Graces daughter, how are you?"

At least the girl had remembered to be polite. Alice would have appreciated that in a teenager, even if she didn't always acknowledge her appreciation. The woman was on this occasion totally dismissive of Moiras question. She cut to the chase. She went direct to the point of the visit. Alice whilst overall, was considered by those who knew her to be a very nice lady, she could also be a bit direct and Moira had yet to find that out.

"Will you be coming over to stay Moira and would this weekend be convenient?"

The smile which Alice couldn't see had broadened Moiras very pretty looking face.

"Yes, definitely I'll be there. Would around 5pm on Friday evening be any good and should I bring anything or not?"

Alice confirmed that the suggested time would be fine. The offer to bring something was declined. She was to bring just herself or would her parents be coming along too?
Moira was feeling very much like she had wanted her sense of independence. She told her cousin.

"No, it'll just be me. Stretching my wings a bit these days. Trying to become a little more independent of Padraig and Grace. I'm sure you know how it goes."
The ladies bade goodbye.

"Till the weekend then Moira till the weekend."

Replacing the handset of her phone Moira considered how she had often felt better. Wow; she had just addressed her parents by their given names to her mother's cousin. What would Alice make of that. Considering she didn't chastise her for it, Moira felt how that maybe had to be a bonus. Perhaps Alice was thinking of her as being more grown up, than that how Padraig and Grace consider her to be. That would surely have to be a positive in Moiras head. She was then conscious of perhaps having created hurt for Alice by having said the wrong thing. How could Alice possibly know how the parent and teenager thing goes? Not having had any children of their own, would surely have to put her at the back of the line in her understanding of teenagers.

Knowing how their phone chat had been quite short and very to the point, left Moira feeling unsure about how to analyse her cousin. Yes, Moira was definitely into analysing people. Their conversation being very much like the letter which she had received from Alice, it had all felt like a double whammy to her. Trepidation took over in her mind. What if Alice was going to be that brief when they actually meet up and she has to endure that level of quietness for a whole weekend. Should she now maybe be remorseful of her decision making to go out there without her parents? Quickly dismissing those thoughts, Moira put her very positive way of thinking back in action. Convincing herself that it was a short journey to be looked forward to with some enthusiasm, that's exactly what she would do. She would be having a break from city life and would make the most of it.

The smile which broadened her face from ear to ear at the thoughts of having a whole weekend away from home, gave some clues to Moiras innermost feelings. Albeit she would be stopping with family at a cousin's house, it was still a good feeling for Moira Riley. Plans already firmly in place for that weekend she then realised her dilemma. She was now double booked. Momentarily feeling very popular she then realised she would need to disappoint someone. Moira also had held the view that nothing was ever set in stone. Being raised in a household where plans were regularly made then changed at a minute's notice, she knew what she had to do. She would prioritise. There was little hesitation in her decision making.

Having a strong sense of curiosity about her cousin and the motives for her summons from Alice, her mind was quite easily made up. Moira knew how the trip out to Enniskerry to see Alice in her farm house would have to be her priority. She hoped that her boyfriend Charlie Cunningham would show some understanding, yet knew he probably would not. Moira knew that she could and would deal with whatever reaction Charlie would present to her. She would deal with any lack of understanding from him; She affirmed to herself that yes, she would have to deal with it. Charlie would have to wait until *another time. He would have to understand. She would have to make him understand. Not certain how she would proceed with that cancellation, she had some thinking time ahead of her before she would approach Charlie.*

An almost sleepless night showed Moira that she was more concerned than she had realised. Having to face Charlie was not going to be the easy task she had initially thought it may be. Time spent alone in her bedroom gave her opportunity for some meditation. Always finding that practice to be helpful in clearing her mind, she hoped this time would be no different. It allowed Moira to see that she would need to avoid meeting up to tell him face to face. That potential meeting no longer came into the equation for her. She knew Charlie pretty well. Moira was very aware of the serious attempts of persuasion he would make, in his attempt to try to persuade her to have a change of mind. She felt how it was quite likely that he may even attempt to accompany her out to Enniskerry.

That would be a risk she felt was not worth taking. Moira's mind was made up that she would just call him. Yes, that would be the easiest and the safest plan. She could work the excuse to be to her best advantage. In general terms Moira did not like to be a devious or a manipulative sort of person. She was now going to break her own rule on that. She saw her deviousness as a necessity rather than through any strong desire to be either of those things. Recalling how she had lied to Padraig and Grace regarding the rave and the many times she lied to them regards Charlie, for those times she lay the blame on her parents old fashioned and outdated attitudes. Moira adding one more white lie to her now very extensive list, she decided it would be well within the realms of acceptability. Plans which were already in place to see her boyfriend would at that time be duly cancelled.

Choosing her moment very carefully she knew just when would be best to disturb Charlie. Not only was she going to lie to her boyfriend, but now she had planned to be somewhat devious too. Moira would call him at a time when she was aware he would be engrossed in some football on the television. He hopefully would then want to get back to the sporting event making her job all so much easier for her. Manipulation, telling lies and being devious it appeared were all strategies which were becoming Moira's game in life. She thought about how very cunning she was behaving and didn't altogether like that trait in herself. However, on that occasion cunning or not cunning she would go right ahead. Recalling the needs must phrase to her mind was Moiras way of finding a degree of forgiveness for herself.

Listening to the echo in her ear she was willing him to hurry and pick up the phone. She wanted this job over and done with. Eventually he picked it up.

"Where have you been Charlie it's taken ages for you to get to the phone?"

Sounding a little apologetic but in a hurry at the same time was just what she had hoped for. Moira was quite relieved. Her plan so far appeared to be working out very well. She was direct to the point and willing him not to ask any questions.

"I'm sorry Charlie but we need to re schedule our date for this weekend. It's not a biggie. We can meet the following weekend instead or maybe one night in the week."

Having given him choices assured her that the cancellation would be less painful to him. She held her breath whilst waiting for a response. His response wasn't quite what she had expected or what she had hoped for.

Silence and then an attempt at persuasion coming from the other end of the phone, confirmed Moiras previous thoughts to her. It confirmed that her decision to call Charlie was favourable to the face to face option. She wanted to and she would and did prioritise her time. Charlie would simply have to try harder to understand, even if he found that concept difficult. Insecurities in her boyfriend's head which she had not been aware of, were evident to Moira at that time. She would give reassurance but nothing else. Her mind was firmly made up. Finding out the reason for the totally unexpected request of a visit out to Enniskerry, just had to be a priority for Moira. A brief explanation of that given to her boyfriend, with a lot of reluctance from him he eventually accepted. They then rescheduled for the following weekend. Moira continued to remain very curious with what she had considered to be something of an enigma. The week had felt like a month to her, with one day feeling as though it was longer than the previous. Eventually the day for her travelling out to her cousin's place in Enniskerry arrived.

Preening herself ahead of saying goodbye To Padraig and Grace, Moira Riley packed a weekend bag and took a bus out to Enniskerry and to the home of her second cousin Alice. There were lots of areas of interest and beauty to be seen as she went through the countryside. The journey was no longer than maybe thirty-five minutes, yet had felt as though it was taking for ever. Isn't that the thing with buses. Always going around the houses to get from one destination to another. That can seem to be especially the case when you just want the journey to get to its end, as Moira surely did on that occasion.

*A*rriving at the bus stop closest to the farm house, Moira was in awe of all which she could see. Disembarking from the bus she quickly began to breathe in some fresh country air. She had a great sense of appreciation for all of it. Her mind was racing almost as fast as her heartbeat. She opened the gate and slowly begun to walk up the long Borreen. The house standing in front of her looked stunningly beautiful in so many ways, yet a little in need of tender loving care at the same time. Tall bushes and trees were growing at one side of the house and some around the back too. She could see them towering above the house roof. Sunshine was seen glistening through their branches. Being still for a few more moments Moira wanted to absorb the ambience of that which she was now surrounded by. The sound of dogs barking quite loudly felt very welcoming to Moira. She was a dog lover and had grown up with dogs. Pushing the buzzer situated next to the front door, she heard some footsteps approaching down the hallway. It had to be her cousin Alice. Moiras hands perspired reminding her to breathe. Deep breathing had always helped when she was feeling a little nervous or a little anxious.

*A*lice appeared to be somewhat warmer in person than Moira had anticipated she might be. The briefness of her letter followed up with a very brief and quite to the point phone call, had sent out a certain type of message to Moira. Depicting Alice in a particular way the message appeared as *though it was wrong. Arms outstretched she greeted the girl with a hug and a quietness in her voice.*

"It's great to see you again Moira. My, how you've grown since we last met. It has to be a few years now. Anyhow what am I like keeping you standing there in the doorway. C'mon on in girleen and your welcome back to Enniskerry again."

Quite a nervous Moira reciprocated the message of it was good to see Alice again. She liked being called girleen. The word she thought had an affectionate tone to it, reminding her of her childhood days when her grandma would address her as girleen. Alice trying to figure out how long since their last meeting was unable to do so with any degree of accuracy.

"I'm kind of guessing around four years. I've been thinking about this and remember how it was the Christmas before you went up to Secondary school."

Moira knew the estimation was inaccurate, however, she was not going to commence her weekend visit with the correction of her aunt.

"Alice; can I call you Alice or should I be traditional or be more formal and call you cousin Alice?"

Thinking how astute the girleen was Alice laughed. It was loud. So loud and infectious it made Moira laugh too.

"Been called much worse things in my life, so whatever feels right for you girleen I will be happy with. You asked if it could be just Alice so maybe we will stick with that shall we?"

Moira nodded quickly.

"Yep that'll do it for me."

Already Moira was starting to feel quite relaxed in her cousins' company. Alice had made an impression by calling her girleen and by their chat, regarding how she Alice would like to be addressed. Accepting that nothing is ever perfect in this world for anyone, Moira found herself secretly wishing that Alice might be just a little bit more communicative or even a lot more communicative. That thought would remain for her ears only. The feeling of slight awkwardness between them was something which Moira didn't very much like. Knowing how it probably was awkward for Alice too, she then felt annoyed with herself. Whilst wanting her independence Moira decided she should not have allowed herself to have got as worked up and stressed out, about the visit out to Enniskerry as she had done. Reminding herself of how this could be a life lesson for any future events which may feel daunting to her, she almost felt a little silly. She would keep thoughts of the reality of how it turned out, opposed to how she thought it might turn out firmly placed in her mind.

Despite the awful level of quietness shown by Alice the reality was still much better than the expectation which Moira had held as a possibility. Yes, she would make some mental notes of all of that. Moira felt like she should be kind to her cousin. She was guessing that receiving kindness might bring out some more of the warmth in Alice. She had hoped not to be proved wrong. Moira was quite a good communicator. The words which she had carefully chosen then rolled naturally off of her tongue. Sitting back on the chair in a relaxed fashion and with a happy smiley looking face, Moira told her cousin.

  "I remember you with such fondness Alice. You were the one who always came bearing gifts. Mom hardly ever let us have sweets but you made sure we did on your visits. I'm especially remembering the mint humbugs. They were always

my favourite. The problem was that they were everyone's favourite so you can imagine the fights behind your back. Oh, they were great days and some great times too."

Her cousin nodded and smiled back. That was it! Not fully the response which the girleen had hoped for. It was however a start. Moira was secretly wishing and hoping that the woman might brighten up a little and might say a little more. Thinking how otherwise their weekend together was going to be a pretty tense one she wasn't ready to give up the fight just yet. She wasn't ready for a failure in the communication stakes. Her kind comment to her cousin had not brought the desired response. It had not done the trick with Alice. However, Moira was a resourceful young woman. She was not one to be ridden roughshod over, as she was analysing the situation to be. She would consider another plan if the need arose.

Moiras eyes were opened wide. Being in total awe of the surroundings in which she had just found herself was almost a little overwhelming for her. Being a townie girl and coming from the leafy suburbs slightly outside the very hectic city of Dublin, being in the countryside was feeling blissful to Moira. Her cousins place in Enniskerry by comparison to the city, was feeling and looking like a little bit of heaven here on earth to her. Sharing those thoughts with her cousin Alice, they were met with a smile and nothing else. Failure number two was how she saw the situation. Having to rethink her approach she decided not to do anything different. Be true to herself and surely it would all come good in the end.

Alice showed the young woman to her room. Despite Alice having what appeared to be a very quiet demeanour, Moira had felt very welcomed. She was still no closer to and so very curious, regards knowing why she was out there in the first instance. Knowing just how rude it would appear to be had she asked Alice the direct question, she had chosen not to do that. She was aware that she would have to wait to be told. Wait till Alice was ready to share that information. She would have to practice being patient. Moira knew and appreciated how that could only be good for her in all aspects of her life. The ladies later that evening dined out in a very small local restaurant. Everything on the menu she was told was organic and had been locally sourced. Moira was impressed.

The meal out was a lovely treat from Alice to her young cousin. The woman was very clear with her guest that for the whole of the weekend in whatever they did, it would be her treat.

"I did not invite you out here Moira in order for you to spend your money. I'm sure you find plenty of ways to do that back home in a city as big as Dublin is."

Moira was feeling as though she was being looked after and in some ways being treated as though she was royalty. She joked with her cousin whilst hoping that Alice might have a sense of humour.

"You'll have to courtesy to me at this rate Alice but thank you I appreciate this so much."

The woman did have a great sense of humour but it wasn't yet ready to take an outing at that time. Alice smiled what Moira considered to be a half smile. She otherwise remained quite silent. It was almost as though she would only have the *desire to communicate when and if she had something quite important to say.*

Moira whilst she was feeling very welcomed by Alice on the one hand, on the other hand she was almost feeling used in some bizarre sort of way. Feeling the strong urge which had by now become almost a need to call her mom, she recalled her own developing sense of independence. She was wanting to share with Grace what she had by now considered to be the weirdness of her cousin. She fought against that urge. Not making the phone call to her mother felt good. Often having talks with and to herself it was now the right time for another one. Thoughts of how calling her mom, would not be very conducive to her being independent in that situation, was the catalyst for her decision making of not to make the phone call home.

Resting on a sun lounger tucked away under a bush for shade, was something of a favourite and regular activity for Alice. Watching her cousin through the upstairs bathroom window, Moira had tried very hard to recall her from years gone by. Memories of a quite demur woman floated around in Moiras mind. Ideas of that maybe being a false identity and relating to another aside from Alice, were also in her head. She was uncertain. She decided to end her speculation. Choosing to join her cousin in the garden, with the hope that maybe a chat about nature would give them some common ground, wasn't altogether very effective either. She had hoped as she saw the situation, that it might liven Alice up a little. It didn't!

Shock and surprise

Moira Riley deliberated some more to herself, about the quietness and what appeared to also be the serenity which surrounded her cousin Alice. It was as though her cousin was perhaps preoccupied with something, which was far more important and far more serious than the spending of a few Irish pounds, or as they were then known as 'the punt'. Being raised well with good standards, Moira had been taught by her parents that she should never to be a user. She had therefore brought some of her own money to Enniskerry for the weekend. She decided that she might be able to buy a small gift for Alice, ahead of her return back home to Dublin. Wondering again about her boyfriend Charlie Cunningham, there were many thoughts in Moiras head. Realising that despite her solo adventure out to Enniskerry, that she had also thought about Charlie quite a lot, gave her a clear but unspoken message.

Missing seeing Charlie that weekend and much more so than she had anticipated she would, Moira's thoughts and feelings about her boyfriend took her by surprise. Giving her the signals that perhaps Charlie was more important to her, than she had anticipated or cared to admit to, she was now a little worried for their future. Wondering if he might have *settled down from his obvious disappointment, her deepest wish was that he would have done so. Knowing how Charlie had considered her to be somewhat mean for cancelling on him, she knew that for her that the weekend in Enniskerry had to take priority. Moira hoped that deep down he had realised and understood that too. She smiled sweetly to herself. Moira thought about how she would look forward to seeing Charlie again the following weekend. She realised that she was falling in love with the man. She did not especially want for that to be the case. She knew that it would become a painful journey without a happy ending for both herself and for Charlie Cunningham.*

The weekend out at the farm house in Enniskerry on the whole went very well. Alice escorting her cousin around the village and giving introductions to many of her neighbours and friends, gave the woman some great pleasure. Having expressed her joy from doing that to Moira gave Moira some pleasure too. She was beyond delighted to eventually see the more communicative side of her cousin. Alice shared with her how some of the villagers were very self-sufficient. Being farmers, they looked out for and looked after each other too. She shared how their produce was often grown in abundance to their needs. They would then supply local shops and the local restaurants too. Moira also learned how the village had many local attractions and was in quite close proximity to the Wicklow mountains. Discovering from Alice how the overall population of Enniskerry was under 2,000 occupants, it was feeling like the most wonderful place on earth to Moira Riley. However, she had kept those thoughts to herself at that point. Having become aware that Alice was appearing to be something of a no fuss type of person, Moira did not wish to project any unwanted vision or unwanted image of herself.

The weekend being almost at its close and still no mention of why she had been summoned out to Enniskerry felt a bit odd for Moira. In fact, it was quite confusing for her. The whole scenario left her wondering over and over in her mind, if she would actually have to ask her cousin for the reason why she was invited out there. She did not feel very relaxed or very comfortable, at the idea of having to ask what she considered Alice might perceive as pertinent questions. That total uncertainty of her cousins' motives for bringing her out to Enniskerry, was for Moira becoming somewhat weirder by the minute. She felt quite proud of herself for sustaining her curiosity and for her display of patience to that point. She did however feel some cracks in her patience were beginning to immerge. Her levels of staying in the dark were maybe going to have to change.

The idea of her asking Alice what it was all about, whilst seeming like a rude idea, would now have to be a priority to her regardless of its perception. She could not and would not return back home to Dublin, in the absence of any depth of knowledge regarding why the weekend had happened. She knew there had to be a reason why she was summoned out there. She felt that perhaps Alice had changed her mind in regards to sharing it. Watching Alice as they prepared their Sunday lunch together, Moira considered that whilst Alice could be a little bit on the sharp and abrupt.

  "let's cut out the middle man and get to the point side." She also thought how equally what a lovely person her cousin appeared to be. At that point Moira had very little idea just

how lovely Alice was. No idea what the future held in store for either of them. She was however shortly going to make that discovery and the discovery of some other information which would impact her family too. It was going to be a very testing time for both women to hold onto their emotions, but perhaps more so for Moira as she was still so much in the dark. Alice in all respects was holding the advantage card in terms of why Moira was out there.

The table being duly laid for lunch the ladies sat down together almost in silence. Moira was leaving her cousin to take the lead then she would follow. Feeling the tension rising a little and being very aware that her cousin was holding the advantage card, she quietly considered blurting out to Alice the unfairness of it all as she was still holding the upper hand. She did not do that. Deciding again to remain silent, Moira was obviously aware that Alice knew why she had brought her to the farm house that weekend. Her struggle to try to understand her cousins motive became more of a struggle for Moira. She once again found herself silently wishing that Alice would share that information. Alice as we will discover was not yet ready to share her information- well not ready at that specific time in any case.

Enjoying a very traditional Irish dinner of boiled bacon with cabbage, some potatoes boiled and served in their skins, with swede added as a side dish, Moira was very impressed. She complimented her cousins' culinary skills. She was in the hope those compliments might generate some conversation from Alice. She was yet again to be disappointed as her plan failed miserably. Alice simply nodded her head in affirmation of the compliment. A very frustrated Moira excused herself from the table. Not wishing to let her frustration be known she didn't trust herself at that moment. On her return back to the kitchen table she hoped to try to generate some chit chat of some description again. Finding the whole scenario very hard work, Moira simply sat and took in some deep breaths for the moment.

Suddenly and perhaps quite abruptly breaking her silence Alice spoke out almost in a whisper.

"Well now that you've had a whole weekend here, what do you think to my house then Moira and what do you think of the area and the village of Enniskerry?"

Moira had no hesitation. Being very relieved with something coming from Alice she was quick with her response.

"Oh my god it's all so beautiful Alice. Your house is just so beautiful and so is Enniskerry. I'm absolutely green with envy. The idea of a life in the countryside is way beyond my wildest dreams. Yes, your very lucky indeed to be living out here in such a beautiful place."

A wide and beaming smile spread across her cousin's face as she heard those comments. She thought about how mature and how very sensible Moira's reaction was. Alice was by now aware that she had beyond doubt made the very best decision. Finishing off their lunch of boiled bacon with all the trimmings, Alice produced a homemade apple pie.

"Custard or cream or maybe just with a cup of tea?"

The ladies enjoyed a large slice each with some hot sweet tea.

Moira was yet again very impressed by her cousins' culinary skills. She expressed her thoughts with some enthusiasm.

"Wow that's yummy Alice you make great apple pie."

Accepting the compliment this time and the pots washed and put away, Alice then took herself outside to the garden. At her request, she was Joined there by Moira. That's where they sat once again in almost silence. Deciding to return back inside the house alone, Alice wanted some privacy in order to prepare herself for the hard conversation which was about to follow.

"I'm going to the bathroom. Stay there I'll be back out shortly."

She wasn't. Moira however followed her cousin's instruction and simply waited. Thinking how Alice was taking forever in the bathroom, in reality she realised it probably wasn't all that long.

Eventually Calling Moira through to their living area Alice told her.

"I've really enjoyed spending the weekend with you Moira. I'm sure you have been wondering why I asked you to come out here out of the blue, yet you've held onto your patience with amazing resilience. I like resilience in a person."
Moira smiled.

"Yes, I have been wondering Alice. I really struggled at times not to ask you."
Alice took in a deep breath.

"Well you're going to find out now and I don't want you to be sad. I want you to be brave and to be the strong young woman you can be. You hear me girleen there's to be no sad face?"

Moira with reluctance nodded her affirmation of no sad face. At the same time her mind was running on overdrive. What was she going to hear from her cousin? Screwing up her face and intaking a deep breath in preparation for whatever it was that she was about to hear, Moira then suggested to Alice that she should continue.

Proceeding to remind Moira how her husband Mikey had died some two years previous and how they were a childless couple, Alice had a sense of relief that at last her painful story to be shared with Moira had begun. Remembering Mikey with a great deal of fondness, was a good feeling for both women. Moira was quick to acknowledge to her cousin, the part which Mikey had played in her life whilst she grew up in Dublin. Telling Alice how she had often felt that Mikey was like a second father to her, brought untold joy to Alice. The smile which beamed across her face was glowing.

"That thought makes me full of warmth, comfort and joy. Thank you for sharing that with me Moira."

The women both acknowledged how they had wished and hoped, that Mikey's life after this earth would be a peaceful one. Sharing their thoughts about the kind hearted and good person whom Mikey was whilst he was here on this earth, they considered how this would have made him very worthy of some peace in his next life. Alice took in quite a deep breath and then was direct to the point. Telling Moira how she herself had a terminal illness, she had a sense of relief after getting the words out. Sharing how she had a lifespan of no more than four to perhaps six months of survival, she watched Moiras face for a reaction. Her own face she knew just had to be drained looking. Making that disclosure to her cousin and having the knowledge of what would be coming next in their conversation, Alice once again attempted to gather her composure. Breathing in deeply she told her cousin

"Give me a minute Moira and get me a drink of water please. There's a good girleen"

Moira was beyond happy to oblige with the wish she could do something more useful than fetch a glass of water.

"There's nothing more you can do at the minute girleen. Let's wait till the end of our conversation. Then we'll see if there's anything else you can do."

Roles had temporarily reversed. Now Moira was the one with almost nothing to say. Just a nod of her affirmation that yes, she would wait.

Despite her fervent promise of no sad face Moira could not hide her shock or hide her emotions. Neither did she wish to hide her feelings away. Leaning forward in the chair her eyes had popped wide open. She stood up to walk towards her cousin but was quickly rebuffed. Alice was very aware that keeping their emotions under control was going to be quite a struggle for both of them. Nevertheless, that had to happen! The barriers were up! She was quite firm in her tone!

"No sit-down Moira, we have to discuss this with very clear minds. There can be no head space for unwanted emotions as this is strictly business now."

The girl or girleen as Alice fondly addressed her however lost some control. Her thoughts compelled her to express her feelings of bewilderment, feelings of sadness and of shock.

"Oh my god Alice that's so awful. I'm so sad to hear that. I obviously didn't have a clue as you've hidden it all so very well. I'm so confused too. It's just such a lot to absorb. What can we do for you? How can we help you?"

Her cousin was quite matter of fact and almost cold some might say in her response. Moira guessed how that was perhaps the only way which Alice could deal with her awful situation and still function with some sense of normality on a day to day basis.

"It's more about what I can do for you Moira. I think you've done all which you can do for me. When I've gone I want this house to be cared for with love, the way it's been cared for over the past three hundred years or so. Your reactions this weekend to the house, to Enniskerry and to all within it which I have shown to you, is confirmation to me that I have made the very best possible decision."

Stopping for a quick breath Alice herself felt a little unable to control her emotions and it showed. Quickly wiping her tears away, she apologised to Moira for that lapse in her strength. She had said it all out loud to a family member perhaps for the first time ever. She clearly knew that her illness was real and her life time was limited, however sharing her news and all of that information with Moira, had made it feel even more real and more final if that could ever be a possibility.

Waiting with baited breath for her cousin Alice to continue which she eventually did, the girleen as Alice loved to call her shuffled back on the chair. Sweaty palms were the give away to how she was feeling. Only a give away to those who knew so that didn't feel so bad. She was relieved that Alice did not know. Moira was fearful of what she was going to hear next. Thinking whilst still being under the age of eighteen years, how this was an awful lot of news and information for her to absorb and to deal with. Thinking about that silence which she had previously had from Alice, she decided that it was in many ways more preferable to what she was now trying to absorb.

*R*egrets *for not asking her parents to attend the weekend in Enniskerry with her, were now spinning in Moiras head. She wished Alice had invited her parents too or at least her mom. Moira then remembered that yes, she had the choice to go alone or to bring a parent or two. Alice would have known how hard it would be for the girleen to hear of her fate. She was however happy she had chosen the route of independence. Smiling broadly Alice shared with her cousin how she had pre-empted the farmhouse situation. She had seen a solicitor who by now had completed her will. Despite knowing how the news was very hard for such a young woman to take on board- Alice did continue. As she wanted to have this deal secured ahead of Moiras return home, she felt there was no choice other than to continue. How ever painful it was for Moira she would have to hear all which her cousin had to say.*

"Upon my imminent departure from this pretty rotten world, the farm house together with all of the land will be inherited by you Moira."

*S*tanding *up and pacing through the room in circles, Moira was beside herself with such a huge turmoil of emotions. Two shocks in one day was feeling a little too much for her. She repeatedly told her cousin through tears which she could not control.*

"Jesus Alice are you crazy? I cannot accept this I just can't. It's just too much."
Despite their situation Alice with determination was holding on to her sense of humour.
 "No girleen not crazy just dying."

Alice acknowledged that yes it was a lot of information for the girleen to take in. However, the woman's dearest wish at that time, was that Moira would hopefully and graciously accept what she had just been told. The only conditions from Alice were, that Moira would duly inform her parents of her forth coming inheritance, in order for there to be discussion around it. She had her own private reasons for that request. Alice requested that Moira together with her parents might execute the final arrangements for her, when the time was upon them. She was clear that her final journey was already fully financed. Moiras head continued to be in a spin. Saying it had felt as though she was on a merry go round at the funfair, Alice did not look overly impressed and she was not feeling impressed. With a slightly raised tone to her voice she told her cousin.

"Get a grip girleen. This is hard for me too you know but we have to do it. We need to finish this conversation."

Explaining how everything regarding that final journey was carefully documented and placed in a folder in her bedroom, Alice then requested a change of topic in their conversation. Moira wasn't feeling very ready for that. She understandably shed some more heartfelt tears despite being told not to be sad. She was in absolute awe of her cousin Alice. Extending her arms and expressing her gratitude Alice received her cousin warmly this time.

"So that's it then Moira the deals done and I can relax. Now I know I can be happy leaving this world. I know the family home will be taken great care of."
Can we please change the conversation now and let's enjoy the remaining time having you here with me?

*S*miling broadly Moira nodded her head in agreement. The women reminisced. Alice raised many memories of times gone by, from her visits over to Moiras parents' home in Dublin. Recalling some family visits and some shared day trips to the seaside, kind of rekindled some bits of the past for Moira. She recalled how Alice would at times race her to the beach. The women chatted away as though life was great and nothing was wrong. As though nothing was different for Moira, from the time ahead of her going out to Enniskerry for that weekend. As though Alice would still have a very long life ahead of her. Wasn't it that strong level of resilience which was being shared by both women, which contributed immensely to getting them both, but especially Alice through those tough hours, days, weeks and months. Moira thought about Charlie Cunningham. Thought about how he would possibly react should he ever get to hear the truth, regarding his cancelled date in order to accommodate her trip out to Enniskerry.

*S*tanding suddenly to leave the room Alice had quite a jolly but fake looking smile painted on her face. Trying to forever be the optimist she told her cousin Moira.
"Come on girleen let's go back outside in the garden. Be a shame to let all that sunshine go to waste."
Moira by that time, was still trying desperately hard to hold back the tears. Feelings of pity for her cousin, mingled in with the deepest feelings of admiration had appeared to have taken over her thoughts. Alice despite her having requested a change of conversation, continued to be very clear with Moira, in her explanation of what life would be like for her and what would be happening when the time was getting

closer for her extra needs. Moira was openly receptive and encouraging. She was proud of herself. She did not cry. With a strong and supportive tone, she told her cousin.

"C'mon Alice give me all the information you feel I need to have."

Carefully explaining to Moira how carers would be going into her home. Having her needs dealt with and managed by some professional people was the plan. Continuation of that plan right up to the point of her eventually going into the local hospice, was and would continue to be very important for Alice. She clearly explained how everything was all in order. No further plans were required. Despite Moiras repeated suggestions and her ideas, that she and her parents would be very honoured to care for Alice, the woman's mind was by this time clearly made up.

"No girleen I'm both an independent and a fiercely stubborn woman but thank you all the same. Carers and the hospice all have your parents' phone number. They will inform you when they need to. I'm just so delighted that we have shared this weekend together. All of that has genuinely made me happy knowing the family home will be taken great care of. That is highly important to me so already you have made a dying woman happy."

Alice continued to share how her final will and testament together with a spare set of house keys, were both with her solicitors. Giving Moira a letter containing details of her carers, details of the hospice and her solicitor's details, Alice decided it was time for her cousin to go home. She was tired. She knew her own body well. She did not wish for Moira to see her at any low ebb.

"I've had one of the best weekends of my life Moira and that's down to you so thank you for that. It's time for me to rest now."

Moira with her head still swimming in a daze was now the one who was almost speechless. She managed a short but polite response. She was sure to put care and compassion in her tone

"Me too Alice. Me too"

"Come visit if you like whenever you like and your parents too, but not as the end draws near."

Moira was determined not to be weak at that point. Again, she wiped a tear away from her eye. She heard how Alice had lived quite a solitary life since Edward died and that's how she had wanted it and how she had liked it. Alice again was firm in her tone.

"Your young girleen but know this much- Death is a journey on which we are all travelling. There's nothing to be frightened of. I'm not frightened so go home with as peaceful mind as you possibly can do. I know that all of this has been tough for you to hear but its life and that's how we have to look at it."

Despite her emotions and some feelings of great sadness, Moira was very aware that it was time to give up the fight. Secretly thinking of her total admiration for her cousin and wanting to explode with expletives and profanities, regarding the unfairness of her illness, she knew that it would not be accepted very well if she was to express any of those words. The needs of Alice had to be the priority. Regardless of however Moira was feeling, she had to and would keep that to herself. The ladies fondly embraced once more ahead of saying their goodbyes. Moira took in her last breaths of fresh *country air as she headed off on her way down the Borreen and back to the bedlam of Dublin city. Closing the Borreen gates behind her she turned to wave. A smiling Alice stood in the doorway. Shouting out to her cousin she told her.*

"Well go on then girleen and hurry up else you'll miss that bus. You're not resident here yet you know and then Alice laughed."

Struggling to understand how her cousin could be so flippant about life in the situation she is faced with, Moira was over flowing with admiration for her. She waved again shouting

"See you soon the wonderful woman you are."

Alice gently shut the door. Taking a well-deserved rest, she retired to her bedroom for a short period of relaxation. Friends would be calling over later. Time sitting in the garden with people she had known for many years was precious to Alice. Her illness had been kept secret from them too. Now she had shared with Moira she felt perhaps it was also time to give the news to her friends. Perhaps not that evening though. Recover a little from the emotional weekend she had been through first. An evening of consuming some nibbles and a glass or two of red was enjoyed by Alice and her many guests. Hearing compliments about her arable farming and her gardening skills felt good. Time going by too fast- Alice bade goodbye to her guests. Her decision was that she would call a gathering the following evening. That's when she would share the news concerning her own demise and the moving forward plan of Moira Riley taking over.

The bus journey back home to Dublin felt as though it was taking forever more, giving Moira Riley too much free time for thinking. She struggled to remove thoughts of Alice and

her imminent demise from her head. Contemplating how and when she would share that news with her parents only added further to Moira's anxiety. The hands were confirming those feelings to her. Pulling some tissue paper from her pocket she kept hold of it tightly. If she could not feel the sweat dripping from her hands, she could convince herself that her anxiety attack was pretty much under control.

Eventually arriving back home she breathed a deep sigh of relief. The door closing behind her was the clue to Padraig and Grace that their daughter was once again back home. With open arms Grace Riley embraced their child. Moira wiped her eyes and then heard the words which confused her from her mother.

"You survived it then Moira; you survived the quietness of Alice, the weekend and all which you have discovered." Looking questioningly at her mother Moiras brain had gone into overdrive.

"You know about it? Has Alice just called you?"

"No Moira she has not."

Grace and Padraig Riley both smiled a very knowing smile.

"You knew before I went out to Enniskerry?"

"Yes, we knew."

"Mom why? Why throw me in the den? It was awful finding out about what awaits Alice from her mouth. It was so hard for me to stay in control of my emotions. And why give me the house when I have two other sisters. Why favour me? It doesn't make me feel good and it doesn't make an awful lot of sense to me either."

Padraig shared with her how they had known about the plan for Moira to have the farm house for some time. Not wishing to cause further stress for Moira, he tried to be sensitive in what he said.

"Alice needed to be sure about everything. She needed to see for herself how you felt about the idea of a home in the countryside. In her head you going out there without any knowledge of the situation, was the only way to find out. You might be a little young to understand these motives. I'm sure you will do when your older."

Moira cried in fact she sobbed-This open display of emotion was partly due to what she had experienced and discovered over the weekend. It was partly due to her parents secretively having been a part of the overall plan. The Riley's were also aware that Alice was ill with terminal cancer and the fact that she did not have a huge deal of time left on this earth.

*M*oira being denied any and all of that news ahead of her visit out to the farm house, had the reasons for that denial explained to her again by her father. He told her how It may have influenced her thinking around the farm, around the house and all of that which Enniskerry had to offer to her. Her inevitably deep sadness plus her emotions might have made her want to please Alice. That was everyone's fear and their good reasons for keeping quiet. Padraig was sensitive in his explanation to her, that she herself would never be sure of her reasons for accepting the inheritance, if she had known that Alice was shortly going to die. Reminding Moira how her sister who was seven years older than Moira, was happily married and very financially secure. How they had their own house out in the countryside. Those reminders removed some of Moiras feelings of guilt regards her inheritance. Padraig shared how her younger sister would eventually inherit their parents' home. Giving assurance that the whole situation had been well discussed and well thought through by Alice, Grace and Padraig, left Moira feeling more receptive of her current situation.

Updating Padraig and Grace on some of the events of that weekend and despite them already having all of that news, it was still an emotional time for everyone. Moira shared about her feelings of delight when Alice referred to her as girleen.

"She reminded me of grandma. She always called me girleen."

A look of deep thought then swept across Grace Riley's face. Moiras grandma was mother to Grace. They reminisced for a while.

"We need to get back to the here and now Moira."

Being a first cousin to Alice, Grace was now feeling impacted by what the future held for them as a family. Remembering what a great sense of humour Alice had demonstrated even in her current situation, was now inspiring Moira and her parents too. Moira was deep in thought.

There was no time to be wasted. She promptly decided to put pen to paper. She would bring some more humour to her cousins' life whilst there was still time to do that. Still time for Alice to be able to enjoy. Recalling many joyful and many fun times gone by, when the two families had shared some time together, now brought so much joy to the whole of the Riley family. The letter was duly composed by Moira together with some input from Padraig and Grace. It was soon ready to be dropped off at the local post box. Thinking of the reaction which would be coming from Alice once she pulled open that envelope, gave Moira and her parents some feelings of great excitement. Being a strict and devout Roman Catholic family *the Riley's were all great believers in the power of prayer. They prayed the rosary that night. It was for the happiest and most peaceful outcome possible for their cousin. Receiving a prompt response to their letter back from Alice, had delighted and given much joy to Moira and to her parents too.*

Alice was her usual typically humorous self. There was no indication at all of her imminent demise in the letter content.
"At last you've developed the art of pen to paper Moira. To have been in all of your company on those occasions was an absolute joy and delight for me. I too am remembering those great times and some others too. I'm waiting for the next set of memories from you. Waiting to hear more about the funny times. I'll be watching for the postman."
Moira felt quite accomplished. Having had the achievement of bringing joy and laughter to a lady who was waiting to imminently die, felt quite special to all of the Riley family. Many further letters were regularly exchanged between Moira and Alice.

Finding herself back in education Moira was set on creating a good future for herself. She would no longer be a slave to any mistakes which she may have made in her past. Focusing her mind on a career in childcare, Moira Riley was at that point feeling a little unsure of which aspect of childcare she might pursue. Time for her to meet with her boyfriend Charlie Cunningham Moira knew and did not much like what she had to do. Needing to withhold information from him regarding the inheritance she felt wasn't actually going to be a lie. She had escaped the line of lying usually used with Padraig and Grace. She would share with Charlie the news regarding her cousin's ill health and hope that he wouldn't ask too many questions regarding why she was out there in Enniskerry. Lady luck had favoured Moira at that time. Her boyfriend had appeared to have acceptance of what minimal information she shared with him, regarding Alice and the weekend away in the countryside.

Some five months after Moiras first visit out to Enniskerry, coupled with a few visits from her parents and further visits from Moira too, Padraig and Grace Riley got the quite long-expected phone call. Alice had very peacefully left this world. She had gone to meet her maker sometime earlier that morning. Cancer of the stomach had been her awful enemy. Alice had behaved as how her family would have considered to be very typical of her. She had declined all attempts and offers of chemotherapy treatment putting quality above quantity. Having enjoyed slightly over twelve months of decent quality life, from diagnosis to the need of a hospice bed, had left Alice feeling that she had made the very best decision. Descending the stairs in bright floral colours, Moiras choice of clothing for her cousin's funeral was very seriously questioned by her parents. She was passionate in her response.

"It's exactly what Alice would want me to do. Being in her company that weekend showed me how much she believed in positivity. How she wanted to make headway and had shown fortitude in the face of adversity. That's what I'm planning to do today in her honour as we all celebrate her life."

Padraig and Grace Riley looked silently at their daughter ahead of then dressing themselves in some bright coloured clothing. Knowing how Alice would be proud of the way she impacted her parent's decision making that morning, Moira once again felt quite accomplished. A small and very dignified funeral service took place in her local church and later at the cemetery for burial. Moira choose and liked to believe that her cousin would be watching down over them that day and every day for the duration of their time on this earth. Perhaps she would be keeping check that everything was going ahead just how she would have wanted it to. The glowing smile on Moiras face showed how those thoughts had brought some comfort to her.

By now having the awareness that she was a very rich young woman felt somewhat daunting to Moira. Struggling a little with the comprehension of that fact she almost wished it was not the truth. Confiding in her parents the uncertainty she was feeling seemed sensible to her. Expressing just how unsure she was feeling, about the way in which she had now acquired her inheritance, she talked it through with her parents once more. Padraig and Grace Riley were both quite reassuring in their response to their daughter.

"*Its life Moira. People become unwell and sadly they die. Alice died the happiest she could possibly be. She had the knowledge that you will be taking great care of the home which she has always loved. She knew that you will respect it just like she did.*"

Moira nodded

Laughing their way through the conversation Padraig and Grace continued to tell their daughter.

"*Now go forward and do what it is she wanted you to do, only don't think about moving out there just yet.*"

Acknowledging her parents comment with a smile, Moira assured them that she had no intention of moving out at that time or for the foreseeable future. Her mind began racing going straight to thoughts of her boyfriend Charlie Cunningham. What a surprise all of this would be for him should she change her mind and decide to enlighten him? What would he have to say about her current situation with home ownership? Charlie as we know was the secret love of her life, yet his religious situation was complicating her life as was she complicating his. Moira was starting to reach the sad conclusion, that her relationship with Charlie would be best forgotten and not to continue. She decided that for a variety of reasons it would be best not to share information about her inheritance with Charlie. They would however need to talk at some point soon.

Going together with her parents to the allocated solicitor's office, Moira quietened her mind. She was aware that being on a merry go round is not how Alice would have wanted her to be. She would therefore be calm and attentive to whatever was presented to her whilst at the office. Ahead of the office entrance Padraig suddenly stood still looking at his wife. Then a serious tone to his voice as he addressed their daughter.

"Just listen carefully when you go in there and perhaps it might be better if you go in alone. We can wait in the coffee shop for you."

Without hesitation Moira showed her age and quite a large degree of immaturity. With a well raised and almost panic-stricken tone in her voice, she told her parents.

"You have to be joking. I got set up on the weekend when I went out to Enniskerry to see Alice. You're not doing it to me again. I'm actually feeling a bit anxious and nervous now so we're all going into that office together."

Taking a minute to wipe the sweat from her hands she looked to her parents. With a deep breath in she eventually told them.
 "I'm ready now."

That was the day when Moira Riley became the proud key holder to the farmhouse out in Enniskerry. The owner of the home which had graced their family for such a very long time. There was another quite substantial surprise for everyone at the solicitors. It was a previously unspoken about surprise gift for Moira. There was one each for both of her sisters and one for their parents too. Mr Tomlinson who was the solicitor duly acting for Alice handed Moira an envelope. He then handed a further three envelopes to her parents. Two of those were bearing their other daughters names. There were some very specific instructions from Alice left with Mr Tomlinson. The family were not to open their envelopes whilst in his office. They should go for coffee and lunch if the time of day agreed with that. That's when and where they should pull open their envelopes.

Padraig and Grace Riley were feeling very intrigued with Moira holding the same view. Padraig expressed his opinion quite openly.
  "Let's take bets shall we Moira. Alice always had a great sense of humour. Despite the rollercoaster of a life which she has experienced over the past few years since her husband died, Alice never waned in her spirit or in her sense of humour. I'm sure this is going to be something funny."
  "C'mon dad she wouldn't do that."
Padraig was stuck in his thinking about the envelopes, telling their daughter that yes, Alice would be very likely to do that.

"The content of those envelopes will most likely be some funny incidentals and perhaps some anecdotes from her life. Perhaps we might be included in there too. That however still wouldn't explain, why we need to be consuming food when we make the discovery or would it?"
Moiras thoughts regards her father's comments were, that whatever the envelopes contained, they would be precious memories for all of them to have of Alice and her sense of humour. She reminded her parents how Alice was keeping them amused even after her death.

Saying goodbye to the solicitor who was acting for Alice, the Riley family duly went to a local steak house in the centre of Dublin city. Despite it being around midday the area was relatively quiet. Feeling pleased with their choice of venue a table for three was dressed and duly laid out for the Riley family. Having a table with a window view and being tucked away in a quiet corner, offered the Riley's some much-needed privacy from other clientele. Moira continued in her struggle to hold onto her composure. Having a slight quiver in her voice and a deep breath in she told her parents.

"God it's so hard but we all know what Alice would want and expect from us, so we have to stay strong and keep our spirits up."

Padraig and Grace both nodding in agreement and having placed their orders, they slowly pulled open their envelopes. Everyone's face was aghast with shock. Being speechless and looking at each other they simply swapped envelopes. Three cheques each showing an amount of thirty-five thousand Irish punts were written out for the family. One each for Moiras parents with a separate one for Moira. Having no idea what was in the envelopes for Moiras two sisters they would have to wait. Surprise and shock continued to overwhelm Moira Riley and her parents that day. Now they understood the very clear instruction from Alice to remain in the city. They could whilst in the city place their cheques into their bank accounts, therefore commence receiving interest from the very earliest point. The enclosed notes from Alice said.

"Be like me. Be thrifty. Get this money earning for you straight away."

Moira and her parents fell into laughter. They agreed that how despite her demise, Alice was still there guiding them and telling them what to do.

Calling their other daughters to plan a meeting at the Riley's home that evening, Grace could scarcely get her words out. Telling their girls there's a surprise for them from Alice and how she had left all of them something in her will, they agreed to meet up at the parents' home at six that evening. Having collected the house keys and with lunch now finished, Padraig, Grace and Moira Riley all set off together on their journey out to Enniskerry. Going to what had been their cousins' home and what was now Moiras home was feeling quite surreal. It was painful for all of them but perhaps more so for Moira, to comprehend the situation which they had found themselves in.

Padraig and Grace Riley sat together quietly reminiscing in the rear garden of the farm house in Enniskerry. Thinking about and with admiration for all which Alice had done to the home, those thoughts were expressed by Padraig. Feeling totally overwhelmed by their daughter's inheritance they too struggled to accept the concept. Given her young age her *parents did not wish for Moira to live there at that time. That was a conversation which would need to be had sooner rather than later. Perception and intuition both being quite strong points for Moira, she could see how her parents were thinking. She was effectively reading their minds.*

"Mom, dad I wouldn't dream of moving in here for a very long time and certainly never on my own. So, will you stop worrying."

Returning back to their home in the suburbs of Dublin the Riley family travelled in silence. Everyone was feeling a little on edge waiting for their daughter's arrival that evening. Padraig in particular found himself wishing time away.

"What can we do for the next two hours to calm ourselves? God how I wish it was six now. Maybe we should have a brandy?"

His wife did not look very impressed by his idea and neither did Moira or her younger sister.

Deciding not to as one may well lead to another, the Riley family made themselves busy in the garden. Eventually the sound of their door bell brought a great sense of relief. The Riley girls were anxiously looking forward to whatever they might receive from their cousin Alice. Moira was struggling to contain her emotions, as their father handed the still sealed envelopes- one to each daughter.

Unlike Moira upon receiving the letter from her cousin Alice several months previous, her sisters were eager to open and see the content. Both girls having a look of sheer shock on their face, they looked at each other then at their parents. Being literally speechless they handed their envelopes to their father. He too was almost speechless.

"Oh my god Grace. here look at these."
An amount of thirty-five thousand pounds was written to each girl. There was an enclosed note from Alice to each of the girls.

"It was hard to know how to sort the house out. Moira being the middle child and me knowing something which you girls don't know made my decision making easier. This is why I have left the house to Moira. It's now up to your parents to enlighten you regards what I'm talking about here. Should they choose to do so then don't let there be any feelings of animosity for or towards anyone. Have a good life and spend your money wisely as I know you all will do."

Hearing the words being read out by Padraig Riley, his wife felt as though she was about to collapse. To say that the feelings of devastation had taken over in their minds would be a gross understatement. Both being aware of what Alice was referring to they also had kept that as their secret. There was never a plan in their life to ever discuss or share that information with any of their children. That awful can of worms had now been opened and they were powerless in the decision making. Was Padraig going to close it? Looking to his wife whilst searching for a response from her expression, he knew how it was best for him to remain quiet at that time.

Hoping their daughters would be immersed in some deep thoughts of their inheritance, he could then have chance to speak privately to Grace to consider their plan of disclosure. Padraig struggled to hold onto his composure as they both realised, there really was no choice left to them now. Initially feeling cross with their late cousin Alice, Grace and Padraig did acknowledge that this is what Alice was about. Despite *her agreement to never tell the children she had never felt happy or felt that the decision was the right one.*

"She's given us a choice now Padraig. We can buy ourselves some time and tell the kids we need time to think about this. We could then invent a story."

Padraig wasn't sure and then he was. Knowing they might one day find out through another source, he felt it would be best they enlighten Moira of her biological fathers' identity.

"We really don't have any choice now Grace. Alice has taken care of that decision making and maybe the woman was right by helping us to bring it out in the open."

Grace Riley felt as though she was facing the hardest decision of her life. She did however share her husband's view.

"We'll be as brave and as strong as we can be Padraig. Hope and pray that there won't be too much distress and maybe a lot of understanding."

Considering what a very close relationship their daughters had with each other, Padraig and Grace decided to share the information openly. Moira would then have her sisters for immediate support should she need it. They anticipated that regardless of her strong sense of character, that Moira would need that support.

The meeting that evening at the Riley's home whilst starting well, then developed a degree of tension which could be sliced through with a blunt knife. Having decided between them to be fully honest with their daughters, Padraig's whole body almost trembled as he started the conversation. It was for everyone to hear but addressed to Moira in particular. Asking their daughters to show understanding and with a trembling voice he begun.

"Things out of our control as we all know, can and do at times happen in this life Moira. There's an awfully horrible beginning to this story but it has the most beautiful ending. I'll just get straight to the point as there's no point in trying to sugar coat it. Whilst walking home from work quite late one evening, your mam was very brutally attacked. She was pulled from the foot path and dragged into some bushes. That's where she was then raped. That rape resulted in a pregnancy. Nine months later our beautiful baby girl was born and named Moira Riley."
Moira looked horrified. She could scarcely get her words out.
 "Oh my god Padraig so you're not my dad. I'm the result of violence from another man."
Moira sobbed almost hysterically rejecting offers of comfort from her mam and from her siblings.

*P*adraig looked broken as did his wife Grace. Nevertheless, he continued to share information with the girls. Telling them how the man had handed himself into the Gárdái station the very next morning, was the easiest part of the story for him to tell. The man was a distant relation to Edward who was the husband of our cousin Alice. He was suffering from and was on long term treatment for schizophrenia. Edward is now deceased having wrongly spent his last years in a Dublin jail. Padraig shared how the jail sentence was wrong as the man had been let down badly by Mental health services, or rather the lack of them. Telling his daughters, how Edward and Alice had forever felt the guilt and the responsibility of his cousins' actions. They were not responsible. They should not have felt that way but they did. Those thoughts of what had happened to Grace on that fateful night brought them both untold suffering.

*E*dward and his wife Alice held a shared view that the only way forward in life for them, was the hope that they could one day reward Moira in some way. The farm house in Enniskerry was there absolute pride and Joy. Having been in Alice's mams family for a few hundred years Edwards cousin had never been to visit out there. Alice and her husband had been very reassuring to Padraig and Grace about that fact. Now they wanted the house and the land to be Moiras pride and Joy, with the hope that one day she may get married and have children there. Yes, they would give her the house providing she satisfied Alice, that she would take the best care of it and as we know that transfer of deeds for the house and the land did happen.

*G*race Riley wiped her eyes as the memory of that terrible night came flooding back to her. Moira deep down knew that Padraig had always been her father, regardless of the news she had just heard in terms of the biological aspect of it all. Being the determined and strong-minded young woman, she was, in every aspect of her life, Moira knew that there may well be ups and downs but she would get over herself. She would not allow this awful situation, to cause her behaviour towards Padraig Riley to be in any way different to how it's always been. Moira was aware that there would be ways to discover other aspects of the man's background, should she ever have that desire to do so. Opening up her heart to her parents felt good to her.

"Mam and dad, love you both for the people which you are. Wipe your tears away mam and be proud of each other. You didn't let such an awful experience break you back then. I'm not going to let that knowledge break me either. As for you *dad, well there's many who would not have stepped up to the mark like you did. I love you my forever dad. None of this information matters to me other than for one very important aspect. I will sell the farm house out in Enniskerry and share out the money between all five of us. That way feels fair to me as my sisters will then inherit exactly the same as me, as will you and dad. You more than deserve that.*

*R*eminding the woman how she wasn't thinking straight, her family assured her that there would be no selling of the house. Refusal to allow Moira to make that decision was coming from her two sisters and her parents. They had all felt nothing short of admiration for Moira and for their parents too.

"You will not sell the house Moira. It'll be your home to live in one day just as our cousin Alice has wished it to be. We all have life changing amounts of money and so unexpectedly too."

Glancing towards a photograph of their cousin Alice and her husband Edward the girls smiled and then turning to their sister Moira.

"The house is big. We can visit and stay for sleepovers? Can we never mention this again and just enjoy life as Alice wants all of us to do?"

Padraig and Grace felt very proud of the daughters whom they had raised.

Religious discrimination.

Being a very practical type of young woman Moira Riley had kept her feet firmly placed on the ground. She felt grown up. She hoped how now she had her own house that her parents might treat her more like a grown up. They didn't. Returning back to her studies at Trinity College in Dublin felt like a priority for Moira. Now knowing how she hoped to eventually become a clinical psychologist, she had felt that psychology would perhaps be a very appropriate path to follow with her training. Her other motive for a prompt return to studies was to show her parents how maturely she was behaving. They might then loosen the reins a little she hoped. She decided to tell what she would be doing as opposed to ask if she could. Knowing how Padraig and Grace might or would feel about being told, she knew she was taking a chance.

"It'll be hard work mom but I'm very determined. I'll only be going out on special occasions such as the rave you didn't let me go to a few months back."

Listening out for her mother's reaction Moira was more than a little disappointed. Rightly or wrongly she felt penalised.

"There's going to be no raves for you whilst your living under this roof Moira. I know your turned eighteen now but you have to give the right example here and show the right way to your sister."

*M*oira didn't respond at all. She just turned and quietly and slowly walked away. Back to lying again would have to be her policy. She hated lies but needs must had been her motto for quite some time now. Moira was a smart girl. She had a very active brain and a very active mind. Whilst studying psychology she planned to study sociology alongside of it. She wondered if that might impress Padraig and Grace a little more. She would then hopefully hold two degrees in the time frame of four years, where a lot of people might acquire just one. The future she felt was looking very bright for her. She had not allowed her inheritance of the farm house, or the huge amount of money from her cousin Alice, to change her life plans at all. Neither had she allowed the knowledge of her conception to impact her life in a negative manner.

*H*aving met and fallen in love with a young man ahead of her first year at College, they had both enjoyed some good but very secretive times together. Despite the couple dating for more than a year a joint decision to continue tell lies when needed to had been made by them. Moira hated the lies she shared with her parents and hated Charlie having to lie to his parents. Keeping up the pretence of a night out with friends, or babysitting for a friend of a friend, or whatever excuse she made up in order to cover her tracks played heavily on her mind. Moira Riley and Charlie Cunningham had always known, that their relationship would not be acceptable in the eyes of either of their parents, or in the eyes of their extended families. She and Charlie had never been introduced to each other's respective families. Both knowing how that would be a hopeless situation, they had the agreement right from the start of their friendship. It was a friendship which turned into *something much deeper than that. They had fallen in love with each other.*

Moiras family being very strict and somewhat old-fashioned Catholics and Charlies family being very strict and quite old-fashioned protestants, was where the young couple's problem lay. Both families strongly observed the stern rule of, you always fully avoid those of different denominations. In other words- never the twain shall meet. Discrimination was quite rife between people of different religious categories in Ireland. It was still very alive and very rife even in the late 1970s. Moira Riley and Charlie Cunningham had both felt trapped in many ways through religion. Finding their situation increasingly hard as time went on, they struggled to fight their attraction to each other. Having continued in their relationship Moira was aware that they would now perhaps need to rethink the whole situation again.

Knowing how there would be no exceptions to the never the twain shall meet rule, in the eyes of either her parents or his, they both often questioned the higher moral ground on which that decision making had been based. Was it a generation thing they wondered? Moira and Charlie did not see religion as a barrier to two people falling in love and spending their lives' together. That fact was obvious to all of those who knew Moira and Charlie inside of their friendship circle. Both knowing other young people in their situation, Moira and Charlie concluded that it had to be a generation thing but based on what? It felt like a truly ridiculous situation to them. Moira could be very forthright at times.

"It's truly shocking Charlie that people have the expectation that we don't get together. That the church and its followers *disallow people from different branches of Christianity, to have association which could lead to spending a lifetime together. I'm a bit tired of their rules."*

Charlie was almost non-responsive. His only reaction was a nod of his affirmation that he agreed with what she had to say. Being a bit of a thinker, she knew Charlie would turn it all over in his mind. She knew he would try to find a way forward for them against all of the odds. Kind of wishing he would and kind of wishing he wouldn't she felt quite confused by her own thinking. She was aware of some gypsy families who had successfully had relationships with people who were not gypsies. Some had actually walked down the aisle together and said their vows in marriage. Moira struggled with her religion and the many restrictions which it placed on human nature. She was desperate and would try anything which she felt might make a difference. Maybe a conversation with her parents regarding her gypsy friends and how they had overcome their differences. Then reality came knocking on her door. It would be a pointless waste of time. She knew deep down that her parents' heads were not to be turned.

Moira had a strong awareness that should she pursue her relationship any further with Charlie, how it would ultimately be guilty of causing a strong division in both of their families. Was that something which she was prepared to allow or to let happen? She many times questioned herself around how that might make her feel. Made her think about what she perhaps needed to do, before the relationship stepped up to the next level. She knew that there could be only one answer to her question. That was quite hard for Moira to accept and especially so, when she knew she would have to share that message with her then boyfriend Charlie Cunningham. Pacing herself around the room whilst practising her deep breathing, Moira was trying to prepare her mind and get her thinking process ready for what lay ahead. Knowing how she would need to be emotionally strong in order to execute their awful and dreaded conversation, she dug deep in her thoughts to bring out her strength of character to the fore of her mind. Eventually she felt ready.

Moira could always think somewhat clearer when she was up and about and on the move. She decided how she would put the ball in his court. She would ask Charlie if he felt that things could possibly work out between them. Ask if he could see any way forward for them. Ask him how he felt about his religion and if there might be any margin of hope, for the possibility of him changing and becoming a catholic like she was. Deep down Moira already knew the answer to all of those questions. Changing her mind once more she had the awareness that Charlies religion was of high importance to him too.

Eventually after some more quiet thinking time, she had clearly reached her decision of what to do. Remembering her father's phrase there's no time as good as the present, Moira picked up the phone with very sweaty hands and put it back down again almost instantly. Being nervous and almost consumed with anxiety would not be the time to make that call. Waiting for the anxiety to pass she felt almost nauseous at the thoughts of what was going to happen next. She was ready. Slowly dialling the digits her hands trembled with that sickening feeling in her belly. She paced up and down as she waited for Charlie to pick up. Keeping their conversation quite short but not altogether very sweet and very strictly to the point, felt to Moira as that would be the very best way to handle that situation.

Tears running down her face was not what she wished for whilst making that call. Placing the receiver back down on its charging platform before he got to pick up, Moira ran to the bathroom. Cold water felt harsh against her dry skin. Talking to herself she decided how that made her feel better. She was ready once again to attempt that call to Charlie. Feeling quite heartbroken herself she was now aware that she was about to break Charlies heart too.

"Charlie it's me. Nature called a minute ago so I had to hang up before you answered."
There she was lying again and this time she was lying to her boyfriend. Lying or the stretching of the truth as Moira liked to think of it, was becoming almost like second nature to her. She did not like that feeling. Deciding to come clean with her boyfriend was going to be the best way to help her to get rid of that awful habit.

"Sorry Charlie I just lied to you. Its horrible how easy it's becoming to me to do that. The truth is I was upset and could not make the call but I'm ok now."
"Go on then Moira I can guess what this is about. I've been sensing it all day."

Reminding her boyfriend of the facts which he was already more than aware of, confirmed Charlies intuition regarding where the content of the phone call might be leading to. Moira pointed out how she had initially hoped, that they could maybe continue as they had been regardless of the religious issues between them. Then reality would hit and she knew that could not ever be a possibility for them. He heard from Moira how she had wondered about some other possibilities, of which one was the possibility that maybe he might feel able to change his religion. Then she would be understanding of the facts of how that would not ever work for his family. She then knew there was absolutely nothing left for them. She reminded her boyfriend how religion had come between them and that there lay the end to their beautiful romance. Moira attempted to hide her deep level of distress but was not overly successful in doing that. She wiped away the tears which he could not see yet was aware that they were falling.

Charlie was left feeling quite heartbroken too. He also had realistically held quite a strong awareness of that potential outcome for them both. Charlie with phone in his hand paced up and down the floor a bit like you might on a racing circuit. She could hear him pounding the floorboards and requested he might slow down, actually that he might sit down. He did not do either. He could not calm his mind. Just like Moira he could always think better when on the move. Trying to hide the quiver in his voice he told his girlfriend.

"I know Moira and I do have to agree with you. I knew this conversation was coming at some point but had hoped it might be later rather than sooner. Then I had the feeling it was going to be today and wish it wasn't. You'll always hold a very special place in my heart. I'm hoping that you will always remember that."
Ending the call, they had both wished the other well for and in whatever the future was holding for them. Moira hurriedly went to her bedroom. That's where her very long-time pent-up anger about religion was openly expressed. Using words,

she wasn't aware she had in her vocabulary, the ensuing array of broken belongings created quite a large pile on her bedroom floor. Sobbing till no more tears left she felt slightly better.

Holding her parents somewhat responsible for religious discrimination within their family, Moira wasn't overly sure if she was being fair in doing that. Reality told her how they would have inherited their religious views from their parents and from their grandparents. She hoped that as she progressed through her life that she might be able to make and to see change. That those religious views and situations might change. That little positive voice in her head kept reminding her, that if the religious views didn't change, then perhaps she could be the change in those situations of religious discrimination. That could maybe be one of her life goals. Moiras heart ached. She knew it was the same for Charlie Cunningham. She had a great sense of determination, that religion would never again impact another couple the way in which it had impacted herself and Charlie. Hearing her mother's voice would generally have a calming effect on Moira. Feeling probably, it would not be the case at that time and in that situation, she choose to take a long soak in the bath tub ahead of settling down for the night.

Receiving a return phone call back from Charlie the next evening, found Moira having to be the strictest she could be with both herself and with Charlie too. She had visions of him pacing the floor again as he told her how he would speak to his parents. He was planning to attempt that which he would never achieve. Moira knew that and basically, he knew that too! Requesting a minute to use the bathroom with a promise to return his call immediately, Moira had bought herself a few minutes to gather her composure and to gather the strength required to be firm with him. She was almost cold in her tone.

"Look Charlie it's no good. Deep down your aware that your parents are equally as strict as mine are where religion is concerned. We're both hurting but also, we're both realizing we have to somehow find a way to overcome our feelings for each other. We have to move on Charlie. We will achieve that because people just do. You have to believe it and don't call me again."

Having ended the call Moira took in a deep breath. She knew she had been harsh with Charlie but felt she had no option. She went out to the garden and to the lavender plot. Knowing how some time spent there had never failed to help her feel better, she hoped it would not let her down on this occasion. Writing a short note to Charlie, advising he did the same thing she took a long walk to the post box. Feeling better in the knowledge she had done something positive in an attempt to help Charlie sort himself out, Moira Riley then decided how that was it. That was her sadly but finally done with that part of her life. Taking sometime out for herself in order to recover from the loss of Charlie Cunningham, Moira decided there would be no more romantic liaisons for her for the foreseeable future. Having decided to concentrate on her education she would give it her all. Reminiscing about the house out in Enniskerry and the huge amount of money in her bank, Moira felt very fortunate on many levels. Despite her loss of Charlie Cunningham, she still had many other things of excitement in her life, for which she would be eternally grateful. Takin g a bus ride to the cemetery she paid a visit to

the grave of her cousin Alice. Placing a single rose by the headstone she once again thanked Alice for all which she had done. Letting her know that she now knows who her biological father is, she also thanked the woman for helping to bring that information to light. Assuring Alice that Padraig always had been and always would be her dad, Moira then felt at peace. Walking away slowly from her cousins grave she felt a great sense of peace in her mind.
"Till the next time Alice and yes I will be back."

Having had driving practice in Charlies car Moira had taken to the mechanics of driving very quickly and very well. Deciding to set herself up with some professional lessons she was soon well on the way to being test ready. Padraig and Grace had bought their daughter a small run-around car. Very basic but in good condition for its age. Padraig was forever attempting to offer sensible driving advice.

"You'll get there Moira and when you do just take it steady. Remember you have as much rights to travel the roads as everyone else."

Eventually after three months of professional lessons Moira Riley was the proud owner of her full driving licence. The car would be used in a sensible manner. Taking public transport at times she felt would perhaps be a better plan. Travelling to work placements would be made easier by having her own transport. Moira considered her good fortune and was proud of the fact she had saved up to buy the car. Determination felt by Moira not to touch her inheritance money was still quite strong. Informing Padraig and Grace how she was going out for her first solo drive, gave Moira a great sense of excitement. Gave her parents a great sense of worry. Resisting telling their daughter how to drive they simply wished her enjoyment in the freedom which the open roads would bring to her.

The value of hindsight.

Our Lady's hospital which catered for sick children was situated in Crumlin in the Southside suburb of Dublin. It appeared to be quite an out-dated hospital. It was also one of the places where Moira Riley had been sent to, as part of her training programme. She wasn't initially overly happy with that decision making. Often thinking of ways in which she might be able to influence her superiors in their placement's decision making, Moira would then decide that might be her taking things a step too far. Having a change of heart and mind she would then support herself and others too. She was not the only student who did not appreciate some of their placements for hands on experience. Eventually raising the topic of student placements for their hands-on work experience, sadly for Moira and for her class mates she was not successful.

Having become a matter of do as your told when your told and be grateful for the opportunities availed to you, she was defeated. She did not like that feeling and continued in her quest. Moira would bounce back with some new ideas for student placements at the risk of being reprimanded for her interference. It was to be at that hospital in Crumlin where Moira would hopefully gain some solid hands-on learning. She was keen to make very good progress and to succeed. This hospital experience would then be presented as a small *contribution of her work towards her degree in Psychology. First day there she had thought would be a huge dilemma for her. Looking forward at the same time she quite anxiously did her checklist.*

Moira was a super organised type of person who kept a tick list for almost everything she did in life. Whilst she previously dated Charlie Cunningham she has now let it be known how she had a tick list for him. Can you imagine that and imagine what might have been on that list? Its perhaps best we don't know what she had written there. Everything had its place in Moiras life and everything should be and had to be in its own place. There would be no deviating away from that in her mind. Grace could often through sheer frustration be heard quite seriously telling their daughter.

"Jeez Moira at the rate your going you'll be keeping a tick list for your own getting ready for bed routine soon."

The girl would simply smile with no other response back to her mom. Ticking off all of the requirements for her first day at the hospital in Crumlin, she duly bid farewell to her parents. Feeling a little anxious, she felt quite confident at the same time. Being unable to understand how she could be anxious and confident at the same time rattled her brain. Moira was a little confused. Deciding that the use of public transport would perhaps provide a much less stressful journey for her, she checked out the local timetables. Eliminating the need of finding a parking space could only be seen as a positive by Moira. She loved walking and thought how a brisk walk from home to the nearest bus stop would set her up well for the day. Perhaps get some adrenalin burnt off which was always a bonus for her. Anything, any activity which would help with a reduction in Moiras anxiety levels had to be in her better interest.

That brisk walk of around fifteen minutes from home to the bus stop, helped put a spring in her step. Cursing quietly underneath her breath Moira wished she had left the heels at home. A tiny blister causing so much discomfort if not pain was something she could easily have managed without that morning. The walk, which would need to be repeated at the other end, to get her to what was going to be her place of work, was just what she didn't need at that time. Generally, when her feet were not hurting Moira liked the fitness aspect of walking. She always thought how it gave her some clear-thinking time too. Time to place any anxieties into those little Pidgeon holes in her mind. That being taken care of she could then breathe with ease. On her approach to the hospital on that very first morning she was still a little nervous. Standing tentatively outside the door she had yet another conversation with herself ahead of entering the hospital. She recalled and repeated to herself, the words which she had heard her parents say to her so many times.

  "Come on Moira you can do it. Just like Grace and Padraig have always told you, the world waits for the goodness which you can and will bring to it."
Finding those words very comforting and reassuring Moira smiled to herself.

Thinking about how despite their over protective ways, how very nurturing her parents had always been, left Moira Riley feeling quite blessed. Having grown up in quite a mixed neighbourhood, there were many families in Moira's vicinity, whom she had at times considered to have a lack of nurturing skills. Moira was a deep thinker who did not readily except information at face value. She did wonder if nurturing was more an inbuilt aspect of your personality rather than an experience based acquired skill. Her own nurturing from her parents was paying dividends now as she knew it would get her through those hospital doors. Eventually getting there with very sore and blistered heels Moira had a great sense of relief. She was early therefore she could sit down for a moment once inside. Taking some deep breaths in she frowned deeply at the vision surrounding her. She was not impressed. She thought how awfully grim and sad the whole place was looking. Those very first impressions for Moira were how very dated looking the building was. She wondered how children of any age, might feel in that very old-fashioned and quite dull looking environment.

Discovering from the notice board how the hospital had been built in 1953, Moira then considered how it perhaps wasn't all that old after all. How maybe a fresh lick of paint could and would make the difference, to the dismal and dingy looking walls just inside of the front entrance. Not wishing to start her placement on a bad footing, she considered how it would perhaps be best practice to keep her thoughts to herself. Well for then anyhow! Moira was not very good at staying silent, when she felt strongly about an issue that could be open to change. She would see how she went along and see if it felt appropriate to express her thoughts. She was aware of and knew how to behave in different situations in life, therefore she knew that ultimately, she would be making the best and the right decision.

*S*ettling into her three months placement at the hospital went relatively easy for Moira Riley. She quite quickly discovered what great pleasure she would gain, from working with children and their families. She was quick to make the overall discovery that children who were inpatients at the hospital, had not given even the remotest thought to their surroundings either way. She concluded how they just simply didn't notice these things. Moira rapidly discovered what the children's only interests were. They were in no particular order. What food they would receive? Who was at their beck and call for playtime? When and how soon might they get to go home. Some children were found to be more distressed than others with home being their only interest and their only desire. She thought about how wonderful it was on the whole, to be in the children's world virtually worry-free mind of a child. On reflection to that thought Moira could see that the children's expressed desires were very much their worries.

A lavender scented candle created quite a bright glow on the edge of Moiras desk at the hospital. Having brought it into her office from home on some bad work days she felt the connection with her calming lavender bush. Being tucked away in quite a dark and gloomy looking corner of the room, having a little extra light created there was also helpful for her. Moira loved the scent of lavender. She loved the colour too. She had a great awareness of the healing properties provided from it. She had often wished that more people in the world, would utilise natural products in order to enhance their lives. Having had many discussions and some plans put in place with her previous boyfriend Charlie Cunningham, they had both felt proud of their attempts for healthier living *lifestyles. Having looked at and spoken about how to raise awareness, on how nature can help people to enjoy healthier and better times, Moira quietly wondered if she could now do their well-planned advertising campaign alone. Knowing Charlie as she did she was aware that he would not attempt to do it alone. Some further reflection allowed her to see the enormity of that undertaking for just one person. Sadly, for her the only way forward with that, was to put the plan on the back burner for the then present time. Knowing how she would be able to revisit it in the future should she choose to, helped Moira to feel a little better about its abandonment.*

Despite her young age Moira had come under the umbrella of poor memory retention. Grace and Padraig Riley had both made observations of that fact as she had gone through her childhood years. Despite many appointments and chats with their family doctor a cause for her memory issues was never discovered. It had appeared that this would be a condition which Moira would have to live with and become accepting of through life. Eventually after getting through her younger teenage years she achieved that acceptance. Throughout her younger years it did cause her some stress with anxiety and heartache. She had always been aware that she would have to adjust certain aspects of her life in order that she would be able to accommodate her poor memory.

Keeping that memory issue very much in her mind Moira wrote herself a reminder note. She was to pick up lavender oils on her way back home from the hospital that evening. Momentarily day dreaming, she was in anticipation of the aroma which would burn nicely in her bedroom. Moira was not typically a day dreamer. She was fast brought back to reality as the phone rang out. Taking the call from her office, well maybe not exactly her office, but rather the one which she was now sharing with the psychologist whom she was shadowing. She was in the hopes of discovering if psychology was really the ultimate road for her to travel down. A Tusla children's team manager was on the other end of the phone line. Moira was taken by surprise by what she was hearing. The lady was very well spoken with a strong accent sounding like that of Mayo people.

"*Miss Riley Moira Riley?*"

Giving affirmation that yes, she was Moira Riley, Moira continued to listen. Introducing herself as Karen Gallagher the woman informed Moira of her position within Tusla and the purpose of the phone call.

"*Tusla are continuously recruiting new psychologists. Your details have been passed on to me as perhaps a potential for employment somewhere in the future. We currently have a role for you as part of an assessment team. It's a role which will support your current training programme, potentially working for the better good of us both.*"

Moira continued to hang on every word which she was hearing.

The woman continued to inform Moira how she had been summoned to attend a family meeting, which was scheduled to take place later on that week. Very graciously accepting the offer she managed to bury her reservations and bury the feelings of her own inadequacies. Ahead of ending their call Moira expressed her gratitude to Karen Gallagher for having considered her for the role.

"*Well this is a lovely surprise for me Karen. Thank you feels as though it's not enough, but thank you and goodbye.*"

Replacing the phone Moira Riley punched out and into the air at least three times. Considering her young age and her having the knowledge of so many other people on the same study course as herself, she felt quite privileged to have been chosen for the family assessment conference. Her thoughts were racing as was her heart. Becoming anxious and worried about participation in the assessment after her agreement to do it, Moira felt how she still had ample time to think the whole thing through. Those nagging but brief moments of doubt in her own ability quickly disappeared. Knowing how she could always change her mind should she feel the need to do that, was the overall catalyst which helped to relieve those feelings of anxiety and those worries for her.

The family in question to whom Moira had been allocated were parents to one child under the age of five years. The file presented to her was quite a thick one with entries over a number of years. The file had been signed off by their team Manager Karen Gallagher, the lady who initially drafted Moira into the team for the forth coming meeting. Moira was informed how the family were under the strict and at times considered to be quite dubious, umbrella of Tusla. (Children's social services). Tusla did not have the greatest of reputations throughout Ireland. Moira had during her training to that time, read some articles of the wrong doing of Tusla on more than one occasion. Some less able families had lived in fear of the organisation. Having allowed themselves to be treated with injustice, they often did not have the mental strength to present Tusla with a challenge. Thinking of ways in which she find some help and support for those families, Moira had to see and had to understand how it could never be her role to do that. Quickly changing her mind, she then felt how part of her role in society, was going to be to seek out injustices and have them put right.

*M*oira Riley as we know, had been summoned to do an assessment on one particular family and their young child. Tuslas main interest appeared to be around the generalized capabilities of that childs parents. They would be looking in particular at the abilities of both parents combined with their strengths and desires or the lack of them in caring for their daughter. Accepting the request to join that meeting, Moira had initially as we know felt a little on the edge of being perplexed. It was going to be quite a strong challenge for her yet one which she would need to complete, in order that she should expand on her own knowledge.

*C*oming from a very well-balanced, compassionate, caring and well-adjusted family herself, Moira grappled with her thoughts. Knowing how she was probably going to struggle a little in this new situation, she would pull on some other life experiences to gain strength. She thought about her own and Charlie Cunningham's parents' rules around religion and how that had impacted their lives. Recalling with some fondness the young man who's heart she had simply broken in the name of religion, which in turn broke her own heart too, showed her how strong her character could be when required to be. Moira felt she had already met and dealt with quite a few very strong life challenges. She recalled some other life achievements too. She decided that as she had been strong enough to meet and overcome those challenges, strong enough to end that loving romantic relationship with Charlie Cunningham, despite how it had distressed them both, then she was strong enough to participate in, comment on and do *this assessment. Yes, her mind was made up. She would not try to pull back from the agreement. She would continue to go ahead and do the assessment.*

Always having had the view that her dress attire either gave her confidence or it didn't, Moira would and did choose wisely from her fairly extensive wardrobe. Needing all of the confidence she could muster up, she was very selective on the morning for the scheduled meeting. Reminiscing privately to herself she took ten more minutes, in order to distract her thoughts from the upcoming meeting. Having picked out and now dressed herself in some grey striped trousers, to be matched with a navy-blue shirt, a matching grey blazer and navy-blue shoes, she admired the image which was looking back at her from the mirror. She considered how business like and professional she was looking in addition to looking quite smart. Flicking her long red hair over her shoulders the lady decided she was ready to face her meeting and everyone else within it. In fact, Moira felt as though she was ready to face the world and anything which may present itself to her that day.

Shouting out her goodbye message to her parents Moira shut the door behind her. Signing the cross on her forehead was something which she had grown up with. Making an extra sign that morning with some special prayer too, she hoped might bring her some good luck. Climbing into the car she was very careful, not to catch her trouser leg on that tiny but very annoying piece of metal, which was exposed on the corner of the driver's seat. Many times, Moira had thought about how the seat needed to be repaired. Every time she observed the piece of metal protruding, she was either busy preparing to go somewhere important or busy doing something which was important. She would pass up on the repair aspect and the servicing of the car putting those thoughts and those jobs away for yet another day.

Moira would convince herself how she would call the local garage soon. She would have her car booked in for repair and for whatever else it may require. Problem was that she didn't do that. Now she was having regrets! Turning the key did nothing to fire up the engine. Her foot pressed firmly on the accelerator brought a little noise but nothing more. The cars refusal to start only added to her anxiety and to her worry and frustration. Why did it have to be on that day it let her down? Calling out to her father she had to surrender to her fierce sense of independence.

"It won't start dad can you help?"
Padraig was polite and caring in his response.
"Things are never really a problem Moira providing we learn from them. We all experience the value of hindsight as we go through our life's."

She heard her father's comments but choose to remain silent. In that type of situation you could always be assured that if Moira decided to be quiet, your best option would be to respect that decision without question. Being driven to the hospital allowed her some unwanted thinking time, which wasn't useful to her at all. Her brain had gone into over drive. She could now only see problems. Her father's attempts of distraction by way of mundane conversation was not helpful either. Asking him to be quiet didn't feel great to her but she did it anyhow. Padraig was an understanding man. He was also a man who knew how to quickly raise up the confidence level of his child.

"It's all right Moira I know you want to be quiet, but you need to know that you will be fine. Just be your natural, wonderful, understanding and caring self."

Padraig was a person she would as a child and as a young teenager turn to in times of stress. He could now see that his daughter was growing up and perhaps growing away from himself and Grace.

Eventually upon their arrival at the Crumlin hospital Moira smiled as she waved goodbye to her father. Gathering her composure, she quickly proceeded to the delegated area. The corridor on which the large conference room was situated was bright and airy looking. Scent from the extensive hospital gardens was seeping in through some open windows. Moira breathed in deeply. She adored the scent of flowers of any description, but as we know she especially loved the scent of lavender and petunias. There were lots of Petunias in the recently planted beds. At last, she was standing there outside of the conference room and despite the car problems she was marginally early. Moira was outwardly very well composed. That was not a true reflection of her innermost thoughts.

Moira could hear quite loud chattering coming from behind the closed door, of what she knew to be a very large room. She had been in that room on some previous occasions and didn't especially like its size for a meeting. For a moment she froze on the spot with heightened anxiety levels too. She was aware of the potential of cctv cameras which were placed in random areas throughout the hospital. She was conscious of the strong possibility of being monitored. Pretending to adjust her blazer buttons in case of being observed, she felt would surely throw people off the track. It would be a good disguise for her anxiety and for her nervous reactions at that time. She didn't want people to see she was nervous. Moira wanted to present as the confident young woman, which she was more than capable of being. She took yet another breath before knocking that door and then entering through it.

New beginnings for Moira.

She was in the room and with all eyes upon her Moira was thinking that maybe the hardest part was now behind her. Pulling out a chair she had taken the only seat which was left around that large table. Ahead of formal introductions and in attempts to boost her self-confidence, Moira silently and repeatedly told herself how this would be fine. How it was all going to work out just as she would like it too. She wondered quietly to herself about the pros and the cons of being the first to arrive, as set against being the last to arrive as she had been. She continued to feel all eyes in the room upon her. She shuffled her way through her briefcase for the necessary paperwork. Perhaps people's eyes were not upon her but it's how it had felt to Moira. It was time for introductions. She listened with great care as they went anti clockwise around that huge table. There were people from so many different and varied professions in the room. A high level of education which was demonstrated by their professions felt a little intimidating to Moira. Being not too far into her own course of studying psychology, had in her mind put her on quite a different and somewhat lower level to everyone else.

Her eyes briefly meeting with those of the young man sat across the table from her, Moira froze just for a moment. She heard his introduction of himself as a trainee paediatrician whose name was Michael Kearns. She blushed to a colour of crimson red. Her cheeks beginning to warm up a little Moira quickly turned her gaze to the next person around the table. A definite connection had just occurred between herself and the handsome young doctor. Struggling not to wonder if he had felt it too she quickly dismissed her thoughts. She began focusing more on the reason why she was there in the first instance. Eventually it was Moiras turn. Introducing herself to the room her gaze returned back to Michael Kearns. Looking for an attempt to distract people's thoughts from her gaze towards the young doctor, she shuffled a little on the chair. Uttering some comment about not being very comfortable, in the hopes that would be sufficient distraction for all in the room, it was. Some joined in with a repetition of, the seating feeling as though you were sitting on a concrete slab. Moira had yet again proven to herself what a very quick thinker she could be, when and if that skill was required. She had always maintained, that whilst many would not consider quick thinking to be a skill- she would always see it that way.

Colour appearing on her cheeks yet again highlighted her level of frustration and her immense sense of embarrassment with herself, for having given that gaze which was almost a locking of eyes. Michael had smiled too as their eyes had met across the table once again. Moira was quickly reminded by the chairperson within the meeting, of exactly what her role would be with the family in question. The room was informed that the childs parents would be joining them, for the second part of the meeting. A period of approximately one and a half hours, had been allocated towards the end of the meeting for the parents Frank and Jessica Geary. Expressing her view of appreciation to whoever was responsible for allocating the time frames, the whole room was taken by surprise by Moiras comments. Chairperson leading the Geary's family meeting namely Karen Gallagher, expressed her quite obvious delight for having invited Moira to attend.

"Your sounding like a breath of fresh air in this room Moira. I'm simply delighted that we choose you to be the student present. I'm guessing that your planning to inject lots of positivity, with respect for both the child and her parents into this meeting. You've clearly got those parents' wishes and their needs in your heart, in addition to those of their daughter Marissa. Well done!"
Moira welcomed and appreciated the managers comments.

"Oh, wow thank you Karen. Praise of the highest standard. Hope I live up to your expectations."

*M*oira then smiled as she had recognised and accepted the compliment which she had just been given. She surprised herself by the impact her presence had made. That was all ahead of the meeting starting or of any input from her. It would be in that family meeting when everyone would yet again hear the opinions of Jessica and Frank Geary. It was already known by those in the room who had previously met the Geary's, that their views and their opinions on their family situation, would be quite different to that which Moira had been advised was the case by Tusla. It had the makings of a very difficult and very sad situation which they were all there to address.

*T*he whole situation was by now feeling and sounding very real and very formal to Moira Riley. She was in new territory and ready to give it her best shot. Her thoughts occasionally diverted to the young doctor in the room and how very handsome she considered him to be. There appeared to be *many and varied issues within the Geary family. Their child was already in the foster care system, having been removed from her parents three weeks prior to this meeting. Jessica and Frank Geary were fighting to get their daughter returned back to their care. They would be saying that Tusla had no real concrete basis for removing her in the first instance. They had previously shared with social workers, how they were and would be prepared to take Tusla to court if that's what became a necessity. They wanted their daughter back and nothing or no one would be allowed to stop that happening. Moira whilst keeping the thought private to herself, she had felt quite a strong sense of admiration for Frank and Jessica Geary's determination.*

Hearing and absorbing all of the relevant information from the professional perspective of everyone in that room, Moira felt slightly more confident in following through her own role. Her interest in discovering more background information on the parents, was the catalyst for her making further plans and appointments to have meetings with some professionals involved. She also arranged to meet with the childs parents at their home, for some more psychological assessments to take place. Meeting the parents within that conference room was a totally new experience for Moira Riley. She had heard lots of information from the professional's perspective and now she was hearing quite a different story from the young childs parents. Moira felt confused and questioned herself about that feeling. She had on some previous occasions heard a few stories about Tusla and how they were taking children into care, in some very unfair and very wrong circumstances. That information had worried Moira. She had no way of knowing if it was truthful or not. Being a person who had always considered that no one would, could or ever should be above the law she was keeping a very open mind.

Moira considered how in her opinion based on what the parents had said in the conference, that this family were quite possibly fitting into that category of wrong doing by Tusla. She could see that despite all which had been shared about them, all of the accusations which they had faced and were still facing, that Frank and Jessica Geary were mentally quite strong people. They were on a mission to have put right, the awful wrong doing which they had felt their family and especially their daughter Marissa, had endured and was still enduring. Deciding to sit tight with her thoughts, whilst taking space to reconsider all of that which she had heard in that room, Moira felt would perhaps be quite a sensible decision. Questioning herself regarding her possible intention, to question the decision making of a group of highly trained and highly qualified professional people, again Moira decided to hold on tightly to those thoughts.

Wrapping up the meeting everyone then dispersed back out and down that long corridor towards the exit. Moiras head was still back in the conference room, with a strong feeling of empathy towards Frank and Jessica Geary. Reminding herself of her promise to herself that she would leave work behind her at the office door, Moira felt she was failing in doing that. She struggled in her attempts to divert her thoughts about Tusla and the Geary family. Deciding she would perhaps grab a coffee ahead of calling her father to collect her, felt like quite a decent plan to Moira. Eventually being outside of the hospital and walking towards the coffee shop near the car park, she felt a gentle tap on her shoulder. To her surprise it was the young doctor whose eyes she had connected with across the conference room table. He was sociable, pleasant and very complimentary.

"Whoa you did well in there Moira. It can be very scary and intimidating the first time we sit in on those meetings don't you think?"

Her heart missed a beat as their eyes were locked once more. Despite being pleasantly surprised to be chatting with the young doctor, her anxiety levels began to rise. Rubbing her palms against the inside of her blazer pocket she hoped he wouldn't be aware of her anxiety. She wondered to herself if he had any idea how his presence was impacting on her, how it was making her feel. She was quickly to find out how he was feeling. Thanking the man for his kind comments and her attempting to say goodbye, brought the response of.

"Do you have time to grab a coffee ahead of you heading off home."

"Well yes that would be very nice Michael. It is Michael isn't it?"

She wasn't quite sure why she had said that as she knew it was Michael. Perhaps her not wanting him to know she had taken such a strong interest in him, felt like a possible reason for asking the question she already had the answer for. Confirming that yes, his name was Michael, they strolled and chatted together to the Costa coffee shop, located not too far from the hospital car park. Relaxing at a small window table the view outside could have been somewhat better. They both felt how some parts of Dublin was suffering from serious neglect. This was certainly one of these parts. Enjoying her favourite coffee which was a latte, they chatted about their positions within the conference room and how far they both were on their training journeys. Feeling it was perhaps time she was moving on she told him.

"It's been great chatting Michael. Thank you and thank you for the coffee too!

Standing up promptly whilst returning the compliment he then suggested.

"I'll walk you back to the car."
Reaching inside her handbag to pull out her phone to call her father, Moira explained the car situation to the young doctor.

"Don't call your father yet. Where do you live? Maybe I could drop you off at home?"
Knowing she wasn't too far away from home, Moira didn't feel it would be too much to allow him to do that.

"Thank you, Michael, or perhaps I should call you doctor Kearn's."
He laughed out loud whilst flicking his fingers through his hair before adjusting the knot on his tie. Seeing his eye twitching Moira considered that her new friend was feeling somewhat restless or nervous or maybe both. Keeping her thoughts to herself she too laughed out loud as he returned the compliment- Not being sure if it was even a compliment, kind of highlighted Moiras insecurity in her ability at that moment.

"You've a great sense of humour Moira. Do remember - when and not if you qualify as a psychologist, then you too will have the doctor title."
Smiling at his comments she told Michael.

"it's not far to my parent's house. I very much appreciate your kindness. Dad will also appreciate not having to come out in peak time traffic to collect me."
Momentarily thinking about her home life and how she had so often had to lie to Padraig and Grace, she nevertheless felt

very blessed. Having parents who would always be there for their children despite their reluctance to loosen the reins, she felt was something to be grateful for.

*T*he car journey back to her parents' home was informative for both Moira and Michael. With no sense of awkwardness being felt between them at all, they laughed and joked about some life experiences. Having enjoyed each other's company Michael extended a further invitation. It was a request to go out to dinner with him the following week. Moira being delighted to accept the invitation hoped her enthusiasm was not too obvious. Both having quite busy work life's, it was a struggle to find an evening which would be convenient to them both. Monday evening appearing to work better for both of their diaries, the deal was done and a date was put in place. Fidgeting with her hair Moira suddenly blurted out the words.

 "I'd invite you in for a coffee only dad would fuss. He's like that. He's overly protective and was the same with my older sister and is with the younger one too."
Michael showed understanding stating his parents were very similar in nature.

 "Can barely go to the bathroom Moira without mine asking intrusive questions. Yep maybe that's a slight exaggeration but I'm sure you get what I mean."

*S*he laughed. She then whilst saying goodbye outside of her parents' home, did the traditional safe journey home speech. Waiting for Michael to almost disappear from her view, she waved him off as he turned out of their street. Due to Moiras quite hectic work schedule, the week went by very fast from her perspective. She felt as though she was flying. She *wondered quietly to herself, if that might ever be within the realms of possibility for mankind. Realistically Moira was more than aware of the answer to her question, yet felt there's no harm in dreaming. Having thought a lot about her previous boyfriend Charlie Cunningham that week caused her a degree of confusion. Wondering if she was ready to start dating again, Moira realised she would only know the answer once she had spent time out with Michael. Eventually it was Monday- the evening of their date was upon her.*

*D*eciding that perhaps a little self-pampering could be in order she checked the time. Knowing herself well and how she gets almost totally immersed in the pampering business, there was a need for her to know what her time frame was. Promptly running herself a bath, she then allowed her mind to wander again. Seeing herself as one day being the wife of this young man, she had to with some haste take control of her thoughts. Moira Riley was a young woman with a very big heart. She had as we know thought lots about her previous boyfriend Charlie Cunningham. Despite still having feelings for Charlie, the fact that some outside influence being the church had placed them apart, Moira was aware and clearly knew how that situation could never change for them. She did quietly wonder how Charlie was doing in life and if he was perhaps dating again. She hoped that he would be. She wanted him to be happy.

*R*eminding herself how their different religions had driven them apart, Moira decided how she would like to think, that she would never be like that with or towards any children which she may ever have. Having quite a raised awareness that religious discrimination would perhaps be something she would need to work on one day, she would be prepared to do that work should it ever be required. Quickly bringing her thoughts right back to her own date that evening, Moira had developed that feeling of a butterfly flapping around in her tummy. Taking a little extra relaxation time, she then decided to get herself ready for her big date with Michael Kearns. Knowing how she would no longer need to lie to her parents regards her where abouts felt good to Moira. Equally she did not blame herself for her previous telling of lies

Moira Riley was not a vain or an especially conceited type of young woman. She was quite moderate in her outlook and of her opinion of herself. She had chosen to wear for her date night, a plain red skirt with a floral lacey black top and slightly heeled black shoes. Looking at her reflection in the mirror she thought about how she looked quite nice, yet not feeling overly confident in her appearance. The smell of chilli-con-carne wafting out from the kitchen and through the whole of the house was very appetizing. Spending some time getting herself ready for her date, Moira suddenly realised how she hadn't told her mother that she would not be eating at home that evening. Going down from the bedroom she shared that information with Grace and Padraig.

"Mam I'm really sorry. Forgot to tell you I'm going out to eat tonight. I'm sure it'll keep in the fridge I can reheat and eat it tomorrow. It smells great."

Grace and Padraig Riley could be people with quite good levels of understanding in many situations. They were and are tolerant of most situations in most aspects of their life's. They however would never be tolerant of the careless wastage of food. High up in the thoughts of both of them were the facts that there's many starving people, both adults and children throughout this world. They had instilled that way of thinking into all of their family members, including into their daughter Moira. Their daughters offer to reheat dinner the following day pleased them both a lot. Always letting their children know when happy with their decision-making, her mother promptly told her.

"You're a good girl Moira with good principles. It warms our hearts to see you're not wasteful. Yes, it'll be fine tomorrow night. In fact, it might be better. Dishes like this one are often better when they're left a day or two to ferment."

Moira smiled at her mother's chosen word. Wondering how she ever thought that a dinner could ferment, she kept her thoughts well to herself. Not correcting her mother for fear of causing any unwanted embarrassment, Moira acknowledged what she had been told. She returned back to her bedroom.

Sticky clammy feeling hands, showed Moira how she had broken out in a sweat yet again. Always being very aware of the association of her sweaty hands to her anxiety, she found some ways to calm herself down. The butterfly sensation in her tummy had signalled her feelings of excitement, for the upcoming date night with Michael Kearns. Eventually saying goodbye to Padraig and Grace, Moira set off on the journey into town. Remembering her day dreaming episode earlier that evening, she took some deep breaths in and focused. Hoping car parking wouldn't be too much of an issue she had left extra early just in case. She always set off for every event in her life, with the plan to be early as opposed to being on time or being late. To her delight she was a little early on this occasion too. Some spare time for checking out her reflection in the car mirror pleased Moira. She tweaked her hair a little. She applied a little more lipstick ahead of stepping out of the car to stretch her legs.

Some minutes later Moira took a deep breath in. The sight of Michael Kearns stepping out from his car, had caused a slight flush in her body temperature, resulting once again in sweaty palms. Wiping them gently on the inside of her coat pockets, she quickly gathered her composure. He too was a little early for their date. Watching him stroll across the car park she thought about how handsome he looked, in his dark brown suit with white shirt, brown tie and brogue type brown shoes. Michael was complimentary to his date as was she to him. Moira is the type of woman who generally speaking does not hold back very much with her thoughts.

Considering the nature of employment which she was hoping to pursue, I'm thinking it's debatable if that was a good point or not. There surely has to be some occasions in our life time, when its best to perhaps keep our thoughts to ourselves, or 'under your hat' as my parents always told me. Moira was clear with me that she had a very good awareness of the need to keep work matters on a need to know basis and always would practice that. Sharing with me that more generally speaking in life, that she didn't always have a filter between her brain and her mouth, had created another area of reflection and discussion between us. Walking together side by side with her date across the car park that evening, Moira thought about how fortunate she was feeling. Again, having thoughts of her previous boyfriend Charlie and how very devastated she had felt at the time of their parting, she would not have believed at that time, that she could ever be feeling this happy again. This was her first date since Charlie.

She wanted him to be happy. She hoped that by now that he would be dating too.

$\mathcal{T}$heir chosen restaurant almost went beyond living up to their expectations. Being shown to their table by a French speaking waiter felt good for Michael and Moira. The waiter expressed his surprise to the couple, in favour of their ability to speak the French language quite fluently.

"It's a rarity here in Dublin to find young Irish people with French as a second language. I'm impressed."
Accepting the compliment graciously they both showed their appreciation. They complemented his ability to speak English so well. Sitting by a window ledge looking out onto a stream with pleasant gardens, was in their opinion the perfect spot to enjoy their evening together. Having made their choice from the extensive menu, they both enjoyed Salmon En Croute followed by a generous portion of chocolate hazelnut meringue cake. A bottle of French white wine accompanied their meal. Putting Moiras head a little up in the clouds she wondered if maybe she'd had too much wine. Being something of a non-seasoned drinker the wine had impacted her rather a lot. She thought about how chilled out looking her date was too. Suddenly and without any notice he left the table with little to no explanation. Nothing said other than.

"Back in a minute."

$\mathcal{F}$eeling curious and perhaps just a little unsure of herself at that point, the sweaty and clammy hands returned to Moira. She wondered if maybe she had caused Michael some upset or had she said something inappropriate. Going over the last few minutes of their conversation in her head didn't bring any answers, however she was aware that she could be a little inappropriate at times. Maybe even a little forthright. Moira hoped this wasn't one of those times as she anxiously waited for his return. Michael soon returned back to their table. He was clutching a smallish sized bottle together with two brandy glasses. Smiling broadly, he told her.

"The nights still young Moira. Let's make the most of It."

With a deep sense of relief she simply smiled.

$\mathcal{A}$ strong sense of well-being suddenly washed over her as she realised she had done nothing wrong. Slowly sipping from their brandy glasses for the next two hours, they were discovering many aspects of their chosen careers. Moira and Michaels evening out ended with some black coffee ahead of setting off back to their respective cars. Feeling perhaps a bit light headed as they walked the couple considered their car situation. Wanting to ensure they were still within the driving limits; they realised that they were not. With an exchange of phone numbers and a further date put in place, Moira had the hope that this *was going to be the beginning of what would be a very beautiful romance for herself and Michael Kearns.* Their decision to leave both cars in the car park overnight had been made. Moira called her father. It was now her turn to return the offer of transport. Michael graciously accepted.

$\mathcal{T}$hat date leading into another and many more thereafter, the young couple had begun to discover many new things about each other's life's. Michael most certainly was an avid Elvis Presley fan as was Moira. They both spoke about having a desire almost a longing to maybe one day go to Memphis. Neither being especially well travelled, a trip to the Deep

South of America held lots of excitement and appeal for them both. That plan however would have to be fulfilled further on down the line. Six more months of Michael Kearns and Moira Riley dating, found there was an interest between them in meeting each other's family. That would be a get together but in something of a formal fashion. Plans were duly put in place for that meeting to occur. The Kearns and the Riley parents were excited and looking forward. Knowing how their young adult children would not have made those plans lightly, had given both families great assurance that there was some degree of seriousness to the young couple's relationship.

Work for Michael usually challenged him to his limits.

Watching children suffer was now becoming a little stressful for him. His appreciation for Moira Riley grew deeper. The situation had developed into her being his go to person when things got a bit tough on the wards. Being always able to soothe him either with her words or her actions, Michael was feeling quite blessed to have her in his life. Feeling at times as though he wanted to burst into an outpouring of romance towards Moira, he would have to carefully choose the time. He was now very aware that the moment of his inability to contain those feelings any longer was fairly imminent. He could no longer and did not want to supress those emotions. Knowing himself well, he was too aware of the possibility of letting his thoughts just roll off his tongue in an uncontrolled fashion. He had many times rehearsed what he might say and how he might say it. Planned situations like this one however, had never really worked out too well for Michael. He could only hope for the best possible outcome in this circumstance.

𝒜head of the meeting with their respective parents and family, he did it! He burst out and expressed those emotions to his girlfriend and then he proposed to Moira. Not in the fashion or in the conventional manner which you might expect, say perhaps after or during a romantic evening out at a good restaurant and with the presentation of a carefully thought out speech accompanied by a ring. That had kind of been Michaels plan. Being quite impulsive in many areas of his life, was something which Michael Kearns has had to deal with for many years. This situation too would be an impulsive one. It was not going to be any different to the many other situations in his life, which he felt he had quite badly messed up. Walking together back to the car park after a busy day at the hospital, in his eyes he let himself down. Michael quite suddenly and very unexpectedly as he had worried might be the case, let the words roll off of his tongue. A moment lapse of self-control, lapse of some self-discipline and the words were out. They were spoken loud and clear.

"Marry me Moira"

𝒯ugging at his arm to bring them both to a complete halt, Moira wondered if she had heard with accuracy, that which her boyfriend had just said to her. Requesting that he might repeat the question again he did that. Her hands beginning to feel sweaty, Moira was instantly aware that she had to take some control of her anxiety ahead of her response. Taking in some deep breaths was a practice which never failed her. His eyes piercing hers as he waited anxiously for a reply he told her.

"Moira I'm aware that the proposal was impulsive. I have however been thinking about this for a long time. You would make me the happiest man on earth if you say yes."
Eventually she was calm enough to respond. Michael got his answer. You could see the love in her eyes as she told him.

"To be your wife would be the biggest honour anyone could ever bestow on me. Yes, Michael Kearns I will marry you."

The couple embraced then they hugged and kissed some more right there in the car park. Wanting to scream their news from the roof tops they didn't! Saying goodbye at that point didn't feel right for either of them. Moira as was so often the case, was the sensible one and the strong one too. She didn't want him to feel rejected. She thought her words through with great caution before very gently saying them.

"Go on then Michael get in the car and get home. Prepare yourself for your exams tomorrow. I've got lots to do too. See you in the morning."

Placing a soft kiss on her lips he then turned towards his car. Moira held back the tears of joy she could feel starting to drop from her eyes. Waving their last goodbye of the evening to each other, they promptly left the car park together. Finding it quite difficult to apply herself and to concentrate back home that evening, Moira picked up the phone. Very quickly changing her mind in the knowledge that an intended five-minute phone call, would most likely become an hour at least, she put it back down again. Neither had an hour to spare away from their studies that evening. Rapidly changing her mind, she reminded herself how self-discipline would be crucial for both of them in their chosen employment. She should practice it now - they should practice it now. This could be their given opportunity to do just that. Calling Michael, she Reminded him how they were seriously time limited. Adhering to the five-minute rule he still appreciated the call.

"Till tomorrow Moira till tomorrow you have my love." Despite her being the strongest one out of the two of them, Moira still struggled to adhere to the five minutes rule. She did however much to her delight manage to overcome that struggle.

Revelations from Michael and Moira

Michael Kearns proposal of marriage, had come ahead of him having any knowledge or any idea of what a rich woman Moira Riley already was. She had not considered any wrong doing in their relationship by withholding from Michael all information regarding her inheritance. She had her reasons for doing that. What a shock and absolute surprise lay ahead of him. Her inheritance of both the farm house, the land and the enormous amount of cash which was still untouched, was all information which she now planned to share with Michael. Her cash payment was clearly gathering up some interest as time passed by.

Planning out their future in his head, Michael had visions of them renting out a one bedroom flat, in the initial stages of their marriage. He had planned to have that discussion with Moira after their family meeting. Deciding how they could look at and consider which area around Dublin city might be best suited for them both, gave Michael a great deal of pleasure. They would officially meet each other's family first. Yes, Michael confirmed to himself that after their meeting with their respective parents, would be the time to begin planning. It would be a good time to have their living plans discussion. There would be lots for them both to consider in making that decision.

The Crooked Glen at Nutts corner circuit, was the chosen place for everyone to meet up. Both families having been there separately on previous occasions they were happy with the venue. Gerald and Bridget Kearns had arrived quite early. They were together with their son Michael. This being a first meeting between Michaels parents and Moira, she was quick to realise she did not need to be nervous. Bridget and Gerald appeared to be nice warm people. She felt quite comfortable in their company. Their greeting to her which was almost in stereo quickly put her at ease.

"It's great to meet you Moira. You look like a real Irish colleen with your lovely red hair. C'mon girleen give me a hug."

The ladies embraced. Moira had a warm feeling inside of her. Bridget Kearns comments and being called girleen, reminded her of her own grandma and of her cousin Alice. She would share that thought when the moment became appropriate.

*P*adraig and Grace Riley arrived a little late. That was not very typical of them and was much to the annoyance of their daughter. Moira had travelled separately from her parents and was now pleased she had done that. Her apologies for Padraig and Grace being late to the people who were to be her intended in-laws, (only they didn't know that yet) were very graciously accepted. Having previously met Padraig Riley, Michael duly expressed his delight to be in Padraig's company for a whole evening. He expressed his delight to meet Grace Riley too. He complimented the appearance of both of her parents.

"You live up to everything which Moira has told me about you both and that's lots. Your both looking so well too."

$\mathcal{T}$hinking what a nice young man Michael was appearing to be, they returned the compliment with a smile. Introductions over and done with, the two families duly sat down for their evening meal. Michael had thought how very beautiful his bride to be was looking that night. Almost having a butterfly tummy Michael had learned how deep breathing can be helpful in those situations. Excusing himself from the dining table, he took himself away to a quiet area for a few moments' reflection, whilst he got his anxiety under control. Meanwhile a huge smile had spread across and graced Moiras face. The smile had been pre-empted, by the thoughts of her sharing the exciting news of her inheritance with Michael. With good imagination of his reaction her decision was finally made. The best time to make her revelation she decided, would have to be at the then present time. She would share the news with all present during their family gathering.

$\mathcal{E}$veryone feeling very much within their comfort zone their orders were placed. Picking something from the grill menu was most people's choice. Moira and Michael not being overly keen on steak they choose from the curry section. The hotter the better was what suited them both. Steaks with all the trimmings together with two bottles of the finest red, set the evening off very nicely for both sets of parents. Raising a toast to their meeting they had no idea what else they would be toasting before the night was done. Conversation flowed at ease between the two families as the evening progressed. Despite not previously knowing each other, their parents were discovering how they had so much in common. Not the least that they were both hard working-class families, whose *hopes for their children always had been, that they might secure quite a good education with good careers. Hopefully one day their children might take a step up that ladder of success and class, was high up on their list of wishes for their children.*

Discussing how both Michael and Moira were now pursuing professional careers, the Kearns and Riley parents could see how their children were taking their education for granted. It almost felt as a given that Michael and Moira would both eventually reach that achievement, which had been desired and hoped for by their parent's. Looking deep into the eyes of the young man she considered to be her very handsome boyfriend, Moira asked if he was ready to share their news. Michael had been waiting very patiently and now he was more than ready. With him what you saw was generally what you got. With no airs and graces, Michael simply told the table.

"Were getting hitched and we're hoping that's going to be good news for all of you."

That wasn't quite how Moira had imagined him sharing their news, however she did on the other hand appreciate his down to earth outlook on life. A slightly worrying silence had momentarily fell around the table causing Moiras hands to perspire once again. Then almost in stereo their parents exclaimed their feelings of deep joy. To see their child become settled in life was the best long-term desire they had held for them. Congratulations offered with a toast raised to their future, Moira then made her best attempt to make her own announcement. Anxiety which she occasionally suffered from was once again her enemy. Trembling and sweaty hands was something which she was familiar with in those types of situations. Flinching for a second or two she then had a sense of relief as that feeling of calmness swept over her.

The look on Michaels face showed his level of curiosity. He was quite observant too. Having noticed her hand trembling, he quickly took hold of it. Moira found that action somewhat comforting. Michael too was becoming a little anxious. That was obvious to people at the table from the twitch on his eye lid for which he had no control. Wondering what it was Moira was going to share with the group being the cause for his anxiety, he secretly wished she would hurry up and make her disclosure. Wondering quietly if Moira might be carrying his child was quite an unnerving thought for him? He was unsure how to think or what he should think. Michael considered that if she was pregnant, how that would not be the place or time for such an announcement. Taking her to one side for privacy he shared his concern with her. Laughing initially and then reassuring him that no she was not pregnant, yet she refused to enlighten him any further at that point.

"C'mon Michael they'll be wondering where we are." They returned back to their place at the table.

Moira went from a sitting to a standing up position as she gathered her composure. She then with some more anxiety and apprehension in her voice, sat down again before she told everyone.

"Padraig and Grace are already aware of what I'm going to share, so I'm asking you both now if I should go ahead and tell everyone together, or should I tell Michael privately first?"

Looking to each other Padraig and Grace had known each other for so long, they could anticipate what the other was thinking.
Padraig told their daughter.
   "Yes, on such a beautiful evening where we have heard news of your forthcoming marriage, now would be the perfect time to share your news with Michael and with his parents too."
Moira glanced towards everyone at the table then addressed Michael directly.
   "I know you'll wonder why I've not already shared this with you previous to today Michael. The answer to that is, that I needed to be sure of your love for me first. I could not feel more sure of you than I do right now. As dad said the time is right and I too just know the time is right!"

Listening to his girlfriend with great care he hung onto her every word. He struggled not to interrupt her in midsentence. Placing his hand over hers was Michaels way of saying.
   "I love you no matter what your going to tell us."
Moira being able to read his hand message took from it a great sense of confidence. Taking a deep breath in she continued.
   "You've already spoken a little bit to me, about which areas we might live in after the wedding. I have the perfect answer to that, providing you also feel its suitable to you and that you might be happy with it."
Michael held back with his comments whilst gesturing to her to go right ahead and share her thoughts. Having some more of his own thoughts and ideas about where they might live which Moira was not especially aware of, he felt how he too would be sharing those in a moment. He waited with

trepidation whilst wondering what his bride to be might have to say.

𝓜oira proceeded without further ado to share about her inheritance some years previous. The fabulous farm house out in Enniskerry, plus the cash amount of thirty thousand Irish punts which had still remained untouched. Gaining interest over the years it would now have a higher monetary value. Michaels parents Bridget and Gerald Kearns were beyond delighted. They were on the edge of being in shock upon hearing that information. Their son Michael whilst making some attempts to raise himself up from the chair, fell back down again almost missing his seat. He was speechless and that was a first ever in his lifetime for Michael. He had quite an array of feelings and emotions to deal with at that time. This was evident in his expressions which ranged from a wry looking smile to a somewhat broad and loud laugh. Being offered understanding from everyone around the table he did eventually become able to gather his composure.

𝓔xpressing how he was feeling absolutely dumb founded yet he was surprised, shocked and delighted all at the same time, Michael struggled yet again to stop laughing. He almost had a quiver in his voice as he turned to her.

"Oh my god Moira Riley you've kept that huge secret so very well hidden. I'm so glad you waited to tell me though. I can never now be accused by anyone of being interested in you, purely due to your financial situation. A situation that's put all of my worries about finance to bed. That's where they're staying too."

He pulled his girlfriend up from the table placing a soft kiss on her lips. They embraced and sat down. Going back for second *helpings the couple kissed and embraced again. That was all ahead of her, explaining the whole story of the inheritance to Michael and his parents. They shared a toast. Raising a glass to the memory of Grace Riley's first cousin Alice, Michael and all at the table, expressed their never-ending gratitude to her memory and to her name. Michael led the toast.*

   "To the lady I've never met or known- You were some woman Alice. You'll never be forgotten."

   Despite their acceptance of and believing all which Moira had told them, Bridget and Gerald Kearns found it quite hard to comprehend the reality of all which they had heard that night. Now knowing that Michael and Moiras financial future was sorted to a very large extent, could only and did bring them a huge sense of relief and deep joy. Bridget struggled to contain her composure as she told them.

   "Oh god Moira, meeting you tonight was more than enough to make any parent happy. It was an absolute joy. To then hear about your marriage to our son put that happiness and joy on another level. Then we hear more exciting news about your inheritance and how your finances are sorted. We're both feeling a bit numb I think and so delighted for you and Michael."

It was decided through open discussion by all present that evening, that the farm house in Enniskerry which was not too far from Dublin city, would very much be the perfect place to raise up any children, which Michael and Moira may have in their future life together.

   Gerald and Bridget Kearns being parents to three children of which Michael was the youngest, had considered how their youngest child had truly landed on his feet. The career, the beautiful wife to be and a farm house with a whole lot of land would set him up very nicely for life. Feeling truly blessed as a family they duly gave thanks to god. Bridget Kearns with such passion in her voice, extended another welcome to Moira into the Kearns family. She expressed her admiration for Moiras tenacity in having kept so quiet about the inheritance and her reasons for doing that. Bridget shared how she felt that their son had made a great choice in life and one which he would never regret. Michaels mom was applauded by everyone at the table. Herself and Gerald were given an open invitation from the Riley parents, to attend at their home at a mutually convenient date which was to be arranged. Graciously accepting their invitation the families bade their goodbyes till the next time.

The foster child

*A*rrival at the office for yet another day brought Moira a day closer to her qualification. Coffee pot on the go and she was all set for the day. Getting nowhere in the absence of her early morning caffeine fix, was a situation which she shared with many others in the office. Having shared responsibility to keep it forever topped up, Moira would regularly bring in her share of supplies. Steam rising up from her cup, it was a reminder for her of seeing her own breath, when walking outdoors on an especially cold morning. The difference being she wasn't cold and the cup was not cold. Her day dreaming was ended abruptly by the loud sound of the phone ringing out. Knowing how she would be immersed into the Geary family file, brought her some mixed feelings of which she was a little unsure of. She wondered if the call may be in relation to the Geary's.

*W*anting to deaden the noise she picked up the phone. To her surprise it was nothing to do with the Geary's. Moira grinned from ear to ear. Listening carefully with respect for the view and advice given by the caller who was a superior clinical psychologist, Moira thanked the young man for his time. She referred to all men as young men regardless of their chronological age. Feeling fortunate to be in the presence of such educated people, she felt that her career *path was strictly being influenced by them. She would most likely seek some employment as a child psychologist once her training was completed. Previously back at the office Moira had spoken to someone higher up the career ladder than she herself was. She had expressed her feelings and thoughts regarding the Geary family and how their young daughter Marissa had already been taken into foster care. Moira felt accomplished as she had been seriously listened to. Plans were then put in place for Moira to meet up with Jessica and Frank Geary again. She wasn't given an actual date but was assured that it would be some time soon.*

She was glad she had not allowed the superiority of the professionals within that conference room, in her initial meeting regarding the Geary's daughter, to tamper with or cloud her thinking. Considering the absolute inferiority of her role in that conference for Marissa Geary, she felt that her standing right by her own thinking, had been quite a big ask for an underdog. Yes, that's how she had seen herself. She was the underdog and no one could change her view on that. However, Moira had followed her gut instincts. She had taken quite a stance. She had taken a risk which now appears to have paid off.

The follow up meeting was planned to be supervised by the childs social worker, together with a new to the Geary case lead psychologist. She was an elderly lady who had come out of retirement in support of Tusla. She had quite recently been allocated the case of the Geary family. A new broom sweeps clean and all that was what Moira was thinking and hoping for. Knowing that the lady was elderly surely there had to be quite a strong possibility, that she had good life experience in addition to her qualification. Moira always thought how a piece of paper showing your qualification, would always be a useful tool to have in your arsenary. She also shared the view that nothing could really match or beat one's life experience. Combine the two and your definitely on a winning streak. Filled with confidence by the knowledge she would have such a person in the meeting with her, Moira looked forward immensely to that day.

That waiting period of just under seventeen weeks before the meeting could go ahead, was already feeling quite wrong and maybe a little stressful too for Moira. Considering the stress levels and placing herself in the shoes of Jessica and Frank Geary, not to mention their daughter Marissa, the whole situation felt quite daunting to her. Moira decided that she could not let this time frame happen. Then reality hit, letting her know she did not have control of the time frame. It was not in her remit either to change it. Being unsettled with that knowledge she wasn't able to leave it.

Speaking to her superiors once again Moira was successful in having the meeting brought forward. It would now occur four weeks from that date. Relaxing at home that evening she revelled in the idea and in the thought of her own persistence. Having the 'never give up attitude' on something which you believe strongly in was helping her to make strides in the work place. She would give all of her focus in the office for the next few weeks to the Geary family file. Scrutinising it with care and caution Moira had made some very unsavoury discoveries. She would hold fire on those findings until after the meeting. That's when she would put a case together.

*B*eing a little anxious about her findings, Moira questioned herself and her ability many times. Needing to talk about her thoughts with someone ahead of the meeting, she almost regretted her decision not to discuss the Geary family case with Michael. She did have an awareness that there would probably be many more cases like the Geary's in the Tusla network. She was aware she would not be able to speak to anyone about those cases, other than on a need to know basis outside of the office. It was a situation she was going to have to learn to deal with and she did deal with it. Keeping that thought in her mind she was quick to console herself, by the fact that this particular case, with Frank, Jessica and Marissa Geary, was going to be a good practice ground for her. Acknowledging to herself that respecting data protection rules, would be an important part of her career in whichever route she choose to go down in life, she felt was some good progress on her part.

*M*oira had prepared herself to the very best of her ability for all which lay in front of her that day. Arriving at Tuslas office slightly ahead of the scheduled meeting time, she was shown into a room away from the childs parents. Having just two other people sitting in there felt much less intimidating for Moira than did so at the previous meeting. A discussion and an overview of the case was held once again, ahead of the parents being brought into the room. Moira shared some of her own thoughts about the Geary parents. Social worker present informed the psychologist of her own attempted intervention with the Geary family. She shared how that had taken place over the past almost two years yet it had never been successful. The woman had a certain edge on her voice *as she spoke about the parents. Moira had the strong feeling that the social worker, most likely had not always acted in a professional manner. She was giving an impression that she did not care too much for Jessica and Frank Geary in a more general sense. There was no compassion evident in her voice towards them or about them. Moira did not feel impressed.*

Having heard how the social worker had found the Geary's but Mrs Geary in particular, to be uncaring and obnoxious felt quite surprising to Moira. She did not express any view or comment or show any facial reaction. She was there only to observe in the first instance and then to speak with Marissa's parents again and for no other reason. She would not be influenced by whatever she heard from the social worker in that meeting. She would draw her own conclusions from her discussion with Frank and Jessica Geary. That may not altogether have been the best plan from the perspective of Tusla. It was however Moiras best plan. Knowing that she too was going to be assessed possibly by the social worker, but definitely by the psychologist in the room, did not give Moira any cause for concern. She was ready for this challenge.

Beginning her interview in a very professional, caring and very easy to follow manner, her plan therefore was to make the couple feel at ease. Knowing how she would be successful in getting more and perhaps better information from them if they felt comfortable with her, she did her best to make that happen. Moira hoped it would work out that way. Firstly, after welcoming Frank and Jessica Geary to the meeting, she acknowledged how this must be feeling quite difficult for them both. Introducing herself plus two other people in the room, she followed that up with an offer of refreshments, a good selection of which was always readily available within that room. The experience of having Refreshments at those meetings had never on any previous occasions, been made available to Bridget and Frank Geary. Jessica looking at her husband spoke out on behalf of both of them.

"Thank you Moira. Water would be very nice please." Jessica and Frank Geary had felt very respected by Moira Riley. They expressed how that was the case. Jessica told the room that perhaps for the first time ever, they were now both being treated respectfully by a member of the Tusla team or anyone of its associates.

"It's very nice to not be made to feel as though we are not beneath everyone in the room. Thank you for that Moira." Proceeding with the meeting, Moira quietly considered to herself how she was getting everything off to a very good start. Informing Marissa's parents that as she had not yet completed her training as a Psychologist, she would need to be over seen and supervised by the other two people present in the room. Moira was then ready to begin her assessment of the family. She had an already well prepared in her mind list of questions to ask and some scenarios to discuss with the Geary's.

The social worker present at that time was well known to the Geary family. She was not especially liked by them and the feeling appeared to be quite mutual. It was Moiras own privately held view that the feeling was quite mutual, as opposed to any acknowledgement of that fact from the social worker. Moira held the strong opinion that when working with a family, that Professionalism had to be and always should be key to everything. Personal opinions of dislike or like of your client should not enter into the equation. The psychologist introduced herself, as being the lead person overlooking and being new to their young daughters' case. Moira made some fervent attempts to put the parents at ease. She used her comments once again of how she could understand just how difficult this had to be for them. Her comments were met with dignity and decorum. Both parents made their acknowledgments.

  "Thanks Moira it's very hard for all three of us. We love Marissa and would never hurt or abuse her and truly never have done either of those things. We would like her to be and want her to be back home with us where she rightfully belongs."

Moira thought about how reasonable both parents were sounding. Making brief notes to that effect in her diary she was ensuring she would recall every detail for her final report. With no intention of attempting to lean towards the Geary family's side, she was attempting to make an accurate, just and fair overall analysis of the situation. She hoped the presentation of herself would show that to professionals in the room. She did not want any misunderstandings to occur.

  Acknowledging Jessica and Frank Geary's comments Moira began by sharing with them, that she was quite interested in and very keen to hear everything from their perspective once again. She requested that they should start at the beginning. The Geary parents who apparently could be quite outspoken, robust and feisty, on this occasion appeared to be very nicely calmed by Moiras voice and by her caring attitude towards them. They spoke very candidly about their parenting of Marissa. Sharing with Moira how they both had always accepted, that perhaps they had not been the best parents in the world at some points in their life, helped Moira to see that they were reflecting with a degree of openness and honesty.

Encouraging them both to continue she heard how things had for quite some time changed drastically in their lifestyles. All unwanted habits of alcohol use had come to an end. They shared with Moira how their daughter Marissa had never been psychically hurt by either of them and how her social workers had been made aware of that fact. Medical records had regularly supported their statements, regarding a lack of psychical injury to their child. They acknowledged how the child had not always been kept clean and perhaps had not always had the latest toys to play with. They expressed some acceptance of how that had possibly being negligence on their part.

Mrs Geary acknowledged that at one point in the childs life, she had no toys to play with and had on some occasions gone to nursery school, with the absence of some items of appropriate clothing. Marissa had however met all of her developmental milestones and was developing health wise at a very age appropriate level too. Jessica and Frank shared how their living arrangements had not always been the most hygienic either. They informed Moira how Tusla had been looking for a long-term foster home for Marissa for almost two years. Jessica shared how throughout that time, social workers were repeatedly verbally threatening them, of taking a full care order on their child.

Sharing that information had brought tears rolling down Jessica's face. Passing the box of paper tissues to Mrs Geary, Moira told her to take a moment to gather her composure.

Moira quietly reminded herself how she must not begin to gather opinions, concerning what the Geary's were sharing with her. How her role there in that room, was purely to listen and perhaps ask some appropriate questions only for the benefit of clarity on the situation. A scribbled on small piece of paper was passed to Moira by the psychologist present.

  "Here Moira some dates for a future meeting in case I forget to tell you. You know the joys of getting older where memory is concerned. The woman laughed and then told Moira to take a minute to digest."
There were no dates on the paper. No indications of any further meetings. It contained a very simple yet poignant inscription.

  "I'm impressed with you Moira. Haven't seen this level of honest compliance from any parents I've encountered over the years. Well done. It's down to you."
Acknowledging she would note the dates in her diary Moira was quick on the uptake. She was aware the woman couldn't have said those words out loud for others to have heard. She gave the psychologist her further response.

  "That's very supportive of you. Thank you. I much appreciate it."

Mrs Geary wiped the tears from her eyes as she explained to Moira, how once they became able to sort a better life for all of them, that they had both felt ashamed of how things had been and ashamed of the sort of parents they had been to Marissa. Moira was thinking how the parents did have a conscience. That surely would have had to be in their favour. She listened, as the couple continued to share, how they had realised how very neglected their young daughter had been by them.

Moira heard how many improvements and many changes had been made in the Geary's lifestyle. Those changes had occurred almost a whole year previous to their daughter Marissa being removed from their care. Mrs Geary shared through her tears, that after many meetings with their social worker at their home, there was still no change in the plan for Marissa. Whilst the home improvements were very visible, with supporting evidence that the parents lifestyles had very much improved Tusla still went ahead and removed their child from them.

Mrs Geary spoke about how very confusing and devastating that experience had been for their young daughter. Moira continued in her strive to be objective, yet could not help herself having the feeling, that Jessica and Frank Geary had very likely and shamefully, been bullied by Tusla and its social worker employees. She would continue, with what was proving itself to be a very stressful meeting for the Geary's and a very enlightening one for herself.

Through some more tears Jessica Geary told Moira that for Marissa's sake they had to let her go. Social workers had stated they would take her forcefully if there was going to be a need. Jessica and Frank did not want their daughter to endure the level of trauma, which would be associated with a forceful removal from the family home, or a removal from nursery school which they were aware was quite a high possibility too. They had simply given up and allowed the action to go ahead without any further trauma to their child.

Moira heard how distressed Marissa had become when the initial move occurred. Being taken by the social worker to her foster home, the child had cried throughout the whole of the car journey. Both parents were tearful at the point of sharing about Marissa's move. Moira quietly wondered to herself why it had been necessary for the social worker to share that information with Jessica and Frank. For Moira it was starting to feel like a punishment of the Geary parents. Moiras hand was scribbling away as she continued to make notes of her own thoughts. Placing an arm on his wife's shoulder Gerald wiped his own tears away.

Moira suggested they might all take a break. Jessica and Frank Geary were then escorted outside of the premises by two security officers. They were directed to a small café shop where they could get some refreshments and snacks. Advice was that they should return in thirty minutes time and to be prompt. There was no sense of respect for them as human beings from the security guards. All of that apparently was demoralising common practice with all parents within the Tusla buildings. Moira struggled to understand why there was any need for two security officers. She was hopefully going to bring change to that situation, of all parents being escorted in and out by security. Understanding that some parents may well present with aggression and attempted violence, she considered how demoralising it must feel to the family who did not pose that threat. Accepting there may be some parents who required that level of security, her view was that Frank and Jessica Geary did not. Sadly, she felt there would potentially be many others who didn't either. Yet families would be made to feel like criminals by the people who allegedly were supporting them. Moira was on a roll in her head. Bringing out the diary she wrote herself some further notes. Her looking into the whole of the security requirement within that building, she decided would have to be on the agenda as her very next challenge in the work place.

*B*ack at the table Moira Riley buried her head in her hands.

That feeling of anxiety and distress which she was familiar with, was starting to almost consume her. She was quite badly impacted by all which she had just heard from Jessica and Frank Geary. Having been out to visit at the Geary's home herself, she could see that all which they had said concerning their living environment was the truth. Mr Geary was employed. He had taken a job at the local supermarket. Paperwork including a short work reference had been shown to the family social worker, which could and did evidence that Mr Geary was now employed. No further financial benefits other than some child allowance were in place for Marissa. That benefit would duly be transferred back to Frank and Jessica Geary, should Marissa ever be returned back to their care. Moira secretly thought how it would be such a travesty if that return home did not happen.

*C*ollecting trolleys from the supermarket carpark, cleaning and some in-store duties, together with some other bits and pieces was Frank Geary's employment. With Franks consent Moira had spoken to his employer ahead of this meeting. He was given a glowing reference. Moira had also spoken to Marissa Geary's nursery school. They informed her how Marissa's parents always had been and still were in regular contact. She had spoken to Marissa's foster carers who had confirmed, that no allegations were ever made by Marissa, to them, against her parents. Scratching her head in confusion Moira looked to her accomplices in the meeting for answers. Politely asking the present social worker the question which was playing havoc with her mind, she wondered how she would be perceived as a student for having the audacity to do that.

"Why has none of this positive information, none of the many life changing events which have occurred within the Geary family, not been documented on the official paperwork for assessments and for capability? Why did I as a student have to work hard and dig very deep in order to find out this information?"

Not receiving what she considered to be a very satisfactory response, especially from the social worker who had been heavily involved with the family, Moira decided that she would have to bite the bullet.

*A*rrival back to the meeting by Frank and Jessica Geary was prompt. Everyone in the room had commented on how calm they were presenting themselves. This appeared to be very much out of character for them. Expressing their desire once again to have Marissa returned back to their care, they were carefully listened to by Moira. Her level of questions were very intrusive into their private life's. She would be leaving no stone unturned. Moira had the gut feeling that Marissa would be given back to her family. Not wanting to proceed leaving any aspect of their life's unexplored, was the catalyst for her deep questions to them.

*M*r and Mrs Geary were once again very polite and very open and candid. Moira thought how the social worker just had to be impressed. How she had to consider the fact that

Tusla had made yet another huge Mistake, or was it another mark of malice against a family whom they could bully. She thought about how Tusla had held and still did hold all of the power. Her sense of determination to change that situation at least for this family had reached new heights. Yes, Moira would challenge her superiors. Bringing the meeting to its end Moira informed the Geary's that someone would be back in touch with them within the next four weeks. Thanking her for her time they stood to leave the room. Being asked to sit back down again for a few minutes by the psychologist in the room, the parents were compliant. The lady was gentle in her tone

"I want to say thank you for the polite manner in which you made your contribution to this meeting today. I would also like to ask have you always been this open and polite in previous meetings?"
The parents spoke separately with both making more or less the same comment.

"Yes, always this open and honest. No not always this polite. Moira speaks to us in a respectful manner and not in a way which would wind up the calmest of people."
Looking at the social worker the Geary's both reminded her of the abusive manner, in which she had spoken to them on virtually all of her visits. The psychologist thanked them both for that input and said her goodbyes.

Social worker present who had sat in on so many other meetings with the Geary's, acknowledged this was a first for them, to ever have shown respect for and to thank a professional who was working on their childs case. Moira had that look of success on her face. Only she knew about the look so no incrimination for it. She kept her thoughts private.

She didn't feel it would be in her better interest, to tell the social worker that respect needs to be earned. The lead psychologist commented how the change with Mr and Mrs Geary, was partially due to their changed lifestyle and partially due to the respectful way in which Moira Riley was handling them.

Moira was commended for her role and for her input with the Geary family. She was given an assurance by the social worker present at that meeting, that her view of the case would be taken to a higher level. As Moira was leaving no stone unturned she had decided not to leave anything to chance. She herself would be taking her notes and her input to a higher level. She simply did not have any sense of trust in the social worker. A new appointment date to meet with Mr and Mrs Geary was scheduled. It was to be three weeks ahead of that day.

Moira having had some commitments for the chosen day she would need to prioritise. Prioritising getting a child returned back to the love of its parents, was number one on her list. She would cancel her appointment and then do the training day next time it became available. Moira had also made a commitment to herself, that in her own time she would firstly challenge the service manager, about the operational practices which she had just experienced with the Geary family. She would then with his approval, investigate other families who had expressed the same complaints as did the Geary's. Feeling that some people within Tusla had been and perhaps still were operating in an abusive and corrupt manner, she was planning to make it her mission to uncover and root out any such people.

Marissa Geary was duly allocated a new social worker as were her parents. Evidence which was demonstrated by Moira in her meeting with a service manager was thoroughly investigated. Higher level workers did unannounced visits to the Geary's home. No one person could find any hint of a good reason, to persuade them of the need to continue with the plan for a full care order of the child. Information from those visits, together with some other internal office meetings was shared with Moira Riley. Meeting up with Mr and Mrs Geary at the pre-planned meeting together with the new social workers, Tuslas decision regarding Marissa Geary was eventually finalised in favour of Frank and Jessica Geary.

The child would be returned back to the care of her parents by the end of that meeting. Moiras own recommendation was that receiving an acknowledgement in writing, that an injustice had been served upon them as a family, was the very least the Geary family were deserving of and should receive from Tusla. The room thanked Moira for her skilful observations and her determination to stand by what she believed in. The Geary parents thanked Moira too telling her they would be forever in her debt. They had done their own set of investigations. Calmly telling the social workers that their solicitors would be in touch with Tusla, due to a case of wrongful decision making, the Geary's somehow felt quite accomplished at that moment. That charge being made by Frank and Jessica Geary, would be in addition to some other charges relating to the trauma endured by the child and by the parents. They shared that a complaint to that effect would be drawn up against Tusla. People present in the room thanked the parents for their attendance at that and all other *meetings which they had attended. Moira could not help but smile at her own thoughts. Tusla were in trouble and now they appeared to be grovelling. She could only hope that lessons would be learned and that potential staff would be more thoroughly vetted in the future.*

A very small playroom down the corridor was where young Marissa Geary had been held. Unknowingly to her she was awaiting the outcome of the case. The child had no idea or knowledge, that the meeting with her parents was taking place that day. She was heavily engrossed with her foster carer and with her own imagination. Marissa was quite a delightful child who thankfully appeared not to be too damaged by her family separation. That was largely due to the skills of the family she had been placed with and the strong understanding and encouragement shown to her, by her parents on their supervised contact sessions.

Watching the child run to the arms of her parents was more than enough reward for Moira Riley. Knowing how she had been proactive in making that happen was a good feeling. Sitting back in the office chair she recalled her apprehension and her anxiety on the day of her first meeting. Now she felt very accomplished. Back at the office some days later, the summons to a service managers office came as a surprise for Moira. Hearing the quite flattering news that she had been awarded a commendation was a pleasant surprise. It was for her level of astuteness and determination to do the right thing, whilst working on the case of the Geary family. The scenario left her feeling speechless. The manager was quite brief in his words.

"You'll be a great psychologist and a huge asset to whoever you work for Moira. Don't ever let familiarity set in as it only breeds contempt."
Acknowledging the managers comments with gratitude, she thanked him whilst also informing him how she didn't feel she had done anything special.

"And that's the beauty of it all Moira. To do a job well is second nature to you."
Returning back to her desk Moira began analysing the man's statement. She promised herself that she would look at every case assigned to her with eyes wide open giving it her best attention. Never having confirmation of the Geary family's long-term social workers dismissal, gut instinct told Moira how that would have happened.

New Spanish friends.

Holding the keys for that lovely house out in Enniskerry, at times felt quite unreal to Moira. She would on occasions bring her fiancé Michael Kearns out there. Plans in place for how they might modernise the house a little further, were frequently in their thoughts and in their discussions. Moira knew how her mom's first cousin Alice had felt and how she would be happy to see any positive changes which might be made to the house. Her cousins last wish as we know had been that Moira would treat the house with tender loving care in abundance. That wish was being honoured by them both and they would continue to honour it.

Planning of their wedding was also in the thoughts of Moira Riley and Michael Kearns. Being so much for the couple to think about, the future was starting to feel a bit stressful for them both. Moira and Michael decided to take some time out to be alone. Forgetting all about the house and about all of their marriage plans they would simply be. That stillness of mind was going to hopefully set their minds free of worry if only for a short period of time. Both having qualified by now in their chosen professions, they could consider how they could share more time together. A holiday in the sunshine was high up on their agenda. A careful and very well thought *through plan for two weeks in the Spanish Islands, would in Michaels head be just what the doctor ordered for them. The humorous side of that comment was of course, the fact that by this time they were both now doctors. Michael being a medical doctor and Moira being a doctor of psychology. Michael was pretty forthright in his comment. Believing in his own thoughts he hoped that Moira would do so too.*

"It's what we need Moira. Come back home with fresh and relaxed minds. Nothing will seem like an issue or like a problem to us then. Let's do it. Let's go to Spain maybe?"

Moira initially being somewhat unsure of the idea quickly came around to her fiancé's way of thinking.

"Yep your right Michael we both could use a break. I'll pick up some holiday brochures tomorrow after work. I finish at four. Ill go to Cassidy travel on Liffey street near the half 'penny bridge and see what they've got."

Michaels nod of approval was all she required. Being a little on the quiet side at times, he hoped that she would approve of and understand his need to be that way. Moira could readily deal with peoples differing personalities. Michaels was not an issue to her at all.

Feeling a little excited already by the thoughts of two weeks basking in the sunshine, with no demands for their time being made on either of them, sounded like perfection to Michael and Moira. Together they looked through the brochures, flipping over the many pages which held no interest for either of them. Eventually picking out a holiday resort in a secluded part of Benidorm, left them feeling relieved that their search was over. That was especially so for Moira, as she had always struggled with decision making where holidays were concerned. Some hotels being for families only felt the most suitable. They then had a change of mind regarding their accommodation. Benidorm had a reputation which neither of them were overly keen on. The cost however was the enticing part. Moira felt very proud. Having enough money to take a holiday wherever they wished to regardless of cost, she, well they both had agreed not to use the inheritance money from Alice. To pay for their holiday from their regular monthly income, was what would perhaps be the most comfortable to them both. Sharing their holiday details with their parents was a little tricky. Moira once again had to stretch the truth. An evening at her parents' home was enjoyed by Michaels parents too. They were delighted to hear how their children were travelling to Spain, with each having their own room at their chosen hotel.

Setting out for Dublin airport by taxi in the early hours of the morning, Michael and Moira took a flight over to Alicante. Hitting the warm Spanish sunshine for them was the feeling of almost being in another life. In many ways they were in another life albeit on a temporary basis. The small coach transferring from airport to resort, weaved its way through the many windy roads and small villages. Admiration for the scenic views surrounding them on route was expressed by many. Driving those airports to resort customer coaches was something which Manuel had done for a vast number of years. Sharing of local information with tourists always gave him great joy. This would especially be the case for Manuel, if his passengers were interested in the history of the places they were travelling through. This particular trip gave Manuel more pleasure than usual, as Michael and Moira had shown a very keen interest in all which he spoke about. Eventually they reached their destination. Michael and Moira had hired out an olde worldly type of cottage. Whitewashed on the outside it was situated part way up quite a steep hill on a very narrow-cobbled road. The road was leading up to the mountains and was at the side of a fishing harbour. Taking in some stunning sea and land views which were now their new surroundings, Michael and Moira considered what a great life it could possibly be for people who were living there.

A small fishing boat could be seen at a distance way out in the harbour. The local shop down the road was to be where Michael and Moira would find their supplies for the following two weeks. The young man standing behind the counter was speaking English quite fluently. Introducing himself to Moira and Michael as Rodrigo, Moira was quick to compliment his name.

"A beautiful name. Many of our Irish names are traditional to our country. I'm guessing yours is traditionally Spanish." Having an interest in her home country Rodrigo informed the couple, how he had studied some Irish history in school. The Easter Rising of 1916 was something which came quickly to his mind. He spoke of the sadness of the loss of many men in their attempts to overthrow British rule in Ireland. Rodrigo had compassion for all life's which had been lost in that war. He had admiration for the way in which Irish people then got behind the rebels in order to form a Republic and from that the removal of British power.

Michael and Moira neither of whom had previously had any particular view of the Rebellion, were now quite immersed in that information shared with them by Rodrigo. Their new Spanish friend was a talented man. Inviting them through to the back of his shop, he shared his vast knowledge of Grace Gifford and Joseph Plunkett. Michael was astounded to hear him speak of how Grace and Joseph married in Kilmainham gaol, hours before Joseph was executed by firing squad for his part in the Easter Rising. Finishing his welcome to the Irish couple, Rodrigo in his very friendly, compassionate and talented way, treated Michael and Moira to him singing the song Grace. Tears welled up in Moiras eyes. Knowing how their Irish history was being taught in foreign lands and being so well respected by non-Irish people, she made a promise to herself and Michael.

"When we're back home Michael I'm going to study the history of Ireland. In many ways we owe that to the men who gave their lives for our freedom from British rule and to the women who lost their husbands for our cause."
Michael vowed he would do likewise. Both having learned Irish history in their school days, it was now a distant memory to them. They would with some degree of enthusiasm arm themselves with reading material. They would demonstrate their levels of respect for all which had gone before.

Rodrigo talked about the elderly fishermen who went out to sea almost daily. Usually looking to feed their families and to hopefully have some fish left over to sell in the shops and markets. The young couple considered how very blessed and fortunate they and their families were. Considered what great life's they both have by comparison to the people who live in that small Spanish village. Having paid for their groceries they then stood waiting to receive them. They were promptly told by the young shop assistant.

"My mother Gabriella will bring your supplies to the cottage for you. It's what she likes to do."

Protesting against that comment achieved absolutely nothing for Michael and Moira. The young Spanish man was very insistent. Feeling rather pampered by the shop assistant and his insistence regarding his mother and their groceries, they both eventually accepted and expressed their gratitude.

"It's hard on some levels to understand why your mother would want to do that. On the other hand, if doing so gives her pleasure and puts a purpose in her day, then thank you to both of you."

Moira and Michael spent their days in Spain with quite mixed activities. Some time was spent basking in the sunshine and other times they would be found sitting in the shade. A large orange tree stood proudly in one corner of the cottage garden. Next to the orange tree was a small contained and covered area which provided people with ample respite from the blazing sun. That's where Michael and Moira spent quite a lot of their time. Being away from the hustle bustle and the business end of the city of Benidorm, yet being able to access it without too much difficulty, felt just like the best solution to them both. Michael was the one who generally speaking made all of the plans. He had sought out a time table for the local small train. It travelled from the bottom of their hill into the main parts of Benidorm.

"Evening time tomorrow when the sun has gone down we should take a train to Benidorm centre. Take a look at some shops and maybe have a stroll on the beach."
She was quite receptive to his suggestions.

"Sounds like a good plan Michael."

Calling out in astonishment as they watched quite a frail looking elderly lady climb the hill, Michael went forward to offer some help and support. It was the lady from the shop with their groceries. Being greeted in Spanish he had no idea what it was the lady was trying to communicate to him. He assumed she was asking him to take hold of the bags. They looked heavy. He thought about how they had to be heavy. She wasn't asking for help or support at all. That was shown by the way which she fiercely pulled back at his first attempt. Michael was discovering just how independent this lady could be would be and was. Being astounded by the woman's reaction he was also helpless. Knowing that short of forcefully taking the bags from her there was absolutely nothing he could do. He thought about how she was some woman. Feeling frustrated that he could not communicate with her, Michael decided to simply walk with her to the cottage.

A further visit to their local store the young man informed Michael and Moira, that his mother does that climb every day and that she's a very independent lady. Rodrigo shared how the cottage belongs to her and her family. Sharing how she goes there even when its empty for the purpose of rest and meditation, he wondered if meditation was something which might interest their guests and yes it was. The young couple who previously considered they had done well, to travel from Dublin City to that small village in Spain, were now feeling very humbled and almost ashamed of their thoughts. They were in awe of the Spanish lady and her daily achievements. Plans were made for Michael and Moira to participate in their next session of meditation. It would be held in the small garden behind the cottage and would be very easily accessed through an elderly English-speaking interpreter.

*M*editation proved itself to be a major highlight of their holiday. Having enjoyed their train ride as it travelled its way through an area laden with some orange trees, eventually they disembarked from the train by a stretch of the Benidorm beach. A young woman waiting to greet people off the train was handing out some free oranges. Being dressed in a traditional Spanish costume gave a beautiful ambience to the whole area. Michael and Moira complimented the woman's appearance. She explained in broken English how that it was a tradition to welcome foreign tourists. Having spent their evening visiting a few small shops on the sea front, Michael and Moira had seen very little else of Alicante or of Benidorm, or whatever else those places may have had to offer for the tourist. That almost seclusion in many ways was part of what had made it the perfect holiday for them. All too soon it was time for them to return back home.

*P*reparing for their return back to Irish soil and with some belongings packed up and ready to go, the couple made their final visit down to the local store. Two weeks holiday in Spain had gone by very quickly. it was time to say goodbye to their shop assistant and his mother, both of whom Michael and Moira had by now considered to be their new friends. Moira was passionate about how she felt.

"Sometimes we just connect on a certain level with people regardless of circumstances. Don't you agree?"
Michael did agree that he too had made that connection.
"It's a bizarre feeling Moira but I feel like I've known them forever."
Despite the families living around nine hundred miles apart, they knew their friendship would grow and would survive the

passage of time. Having been told that neither the mother or her son had ever left their city, let alone left their country, the young Irish couple could not imagine what restrictions that must have placed upon them.

Thoughtfulness, together with heaps of compassion were two blessings which were bestowed upon Michael and Moira. Placing an envelope onto the young man's hand Moira told him it contained an invitation. It was an invitation for himself and for his mother to attend at their wedding in Ireland the following year. A full week's worth of accommodation, return travel from their city to the airport with return air tickets, plus all travel expenses in Ireland, would all be included in the package. There was a separate note included in the envelope. It had been written by Michael. It was saying that the gesture of the invitation had come from Moira and that he was in full support of it. A look of surprise confusion and shock was now sweeping over the young man's face. Rodrigo was speechless. Gathering his thoughts and his composure he managed to ask the question why?

Moira was very quick to explain about her own wonderful inheritance from Alice and the great uplift which her cousin's kindness had given to her life. She shared with the young shop assistant how very much more important to her than the money, was the fact that someone cared enough to do something nice for her. She now wished to do something nice for people she felt would be very worthy of her actions. It was as simple as that. The young Spanish man struggling to hold back his tears, said he would be delighted to accompany his mother on that trip. A full postal address was taken by Moira as a reference of where to send their final details. They duly bade farewell. A short embrace a handshake and then.

"Till the next time and thank you so much both of you."

*M*ichael and Moira promptly packed up the remainder of their belongings and left their rented cottage in Spain behind them. Handing the keys back to Rodrigo and his mother they waited patiently for the airport coach. Their return coach to airport journey felt quite sober and serious. No joviality like they had experienced on their arrival in Spain. Taking their flight from Alicante airport back home to Dublin city, Michael and Moira reminisced over all which they had done whilst in Spain. Laden with a few small gifts for family and friends they were both delighted to be back on Irish soil and back in their respective places of work. The couple's parents who by now had a strong affinity for each other, had been sharing some quality time together over the previous months.

*R*eminiscing over their families past and looking forward to and planning for their future, they were delighted to at least have the wedding date arranged. Acknowledging that in so many different ways, how their own life's dreams were now coming to fruition. This was occurring through their children and gave them feelings of deep joy. The parents had felt quite accomplished on that level. They could now see how Michael and Moira were having a better education and a better standard of life than they personally had experienced, brought some further feelings of deep joy to both families. Knowing how that high level of education would help them climb their chosen career ladders, the Kearns and the Riley parents raised many toasts to their respective children over the following months.

Wedding venues now chosen with every detail attended to, Michael and Moira were quite happy and felt able to relax a little. A further evening out with both sets of parents brought some more feelings of joy and feelings of pride for everyone. Moira explained to their parents how the Spanish lady and her son Rodrigo were both invited to their wedding. Being proud of the children they had raised, there were other stories shared around the table too. Understanding what a challenge travelling to another country would pose for the Spanish people, Michael and Moira still held out a hope that they might perhaps attend. They held a hope that Gabriella and her son Rodrigo just might decide to be brave. Decide to explore the world a little bit and to accept their wedding invitation. Their evening bringing some sadness and turmoil too, highlighted to both the Kearns and the Riley families, just how quickly situations can and often do change.

The journey back home that night was something of a painful one. Inclement weather had created very hazardous driving conditions. Michael did not anticipate the severity of the upcoming bend. Travelling to the other side of the road going direct into a speeding oncoming vehicle, he brought the car to a halt. Screeching of brakes combined with skidding of tyres, all in addition to himself and Moira screaming, would have been more than good volume competition, to a large children's noisy Christmas party. Head on crashes in Ireland and especially around Dublin city often ended badly. Michael and Moira were on this occasion very blessed by lady luck, as were all occupants of the other vehicle. Other car occupants were observed by Michael moving around outside of their vehicle. There was blood on their foreheads and some on their hands too. Whilst taking care of Moira Michael did not attempt to leave his own vehicle. Calling out telling them he was a doctor and giving some advice to sit down to the other car occupants, his comments were ignored. Very much to Michaels delight the arrival of an ambulance for each family was quickly on the scene.

*T*aken to the local hospital and after initial triage by the nurse, all involved in the crash had a substantial wait in their accident and emergency department. Everyone involved in the crash had sustained some degree of injury, with Moira having sustained the most severe. Having it confirmed to her that she had sustained a broken right shoulder plus a broken left leg, she felt a strange sense of relief. In many ways she had a strong feeling of gratitude for that being the worst of their injuries. Michael had suffered some cuts and bruising but nothing too serious. Nothing which would require very much treatment.

*D*espite him being known to and by some colleagues in the accident and emergency department Michael was not able to establish with any degree of accuracy, exactly the severity of injuries which had been suffered by the other passengers. He was left feeling quite hopeless. Sharing his thoughts about data protection and confidentiality with Moira, they could now see and appreciate the annoyance experienced by others, in their own current situation. Knowing how he had seen the other car occupants walking about, they did take comfort from that. It was a good indicator that their injuries perhaps were not too serious. The lesson learned there for Michael was one of, could there possibly be some scope for the sharing of hospital information, when the situation was highlighted to be one of genuine care and concern and for no other reason. He would have that listed on his agenda as a question to be raised, at the next agenda focused meeting within his department.

𝒯hose injuries sustained by Moira had been sufficient enough to put her out of action for quite a lengthy period of time. She felt as though her life had been brought to a complete halt. Being a person who generally speaking was forever active, she found the following weeks something of a challenge. Having a great sense of determination Moira was not prepared to submit to her injuries and to the limitations which they had imposed on her life. She thought about her cousin Alice and how she had fought against her diagnosis of cancer, which effectively had been her life sentence. Moira reminded her fiancé of Alice and her situation.

"She battled against her illness virtually to the end Michael. She was an inspirational woman. Giving up wasn't something which she did. I have to and I will follow her lead and deal with this without complaint."

Placing a comforting arm on her shoulder Michael expressed his admiration for both her cousin Alice and now for Moira too.

"You're a chip off the old block Moira Determination is in your genes."

𝒪ther people who were involved in the car crash on that awful night, eventually made some contact with Michael. Hearing how they had sustained minor cuts and bruises, but nothing too much or too serious for them to be concerned about, the man had felt very relieved. Gardaí had become involved with an ongoing investigation in progress. Michaels only hope would be, that consideration would be given to weather conditions on that night and its potentially heavy implications on his driving. Psychological injury was perhaps going to be the most concerning for all involved in the collision. Everyone involved was advised by the hospital to see their general practioner. Michaels thoughts of hoping to have made the evening memorable were now surely granted to him. Medical knowledge and experience, together with Moiras psychology knowledge and experience, helped them both to understand the importance of taking advice which had been given to them. Moira would be discharged back home quite soon.

The imminently urgent delivery of a hospital bed and all else which would be required, was organised by the hospital. The Riley's living room was transformed into the liking of a hospital at home area. Physiotherapists, district nurses and carers were all put in place. The package appeared to be quite a reasonable one. Everything now being in place meant that Moira could at last be discharged back home. She would return back to the care of her parents, Padraig and Grace Riley to what was effectively going to be hospital at home.

Arrival at her parent's front door in an ambulance chair felt a little awkward for Moira Riley. She wasn't especially good at being looked after. She was generally the care giver and wasn't really going to appreciate this role reversal at all. Knowing how she would need to try to embrace, to live and work with her situation for what it was, Moira took in some deep breaths. Graciously, allowing herself to be transferred from a wheel chair to the ready prepared bed, she thanked the ambulance crew. Exhaustion had taken over and almost consumed her body. The following weeks found Moira working quite hard to regain her mobility. Physiotherapists attended to her daily sometimes twice per day. That space of time saw the Riley's home be converted. It was now looking like what they considered to be and described as a highway. It felt to the Riley family almost as though their home had been opened up to everyman and his dog. Laughing their way through those weeks was everyone's coping mechanism.

*E*ventually after seven weeks and with very much grit and determination, Moira was able to say goodbye to hospital at home equipment and to the therapists too. She had made an amazing full recovery in a surprisingly short period of time. Getting back up on her feet had felt priceless to Moira Riley. Moiras mother Grace Riley had appreciation for having had a close friend who was very helpful for the family at that time. Geraldine was a lady who called in daily. Having an extra pair of hands around the place was an absolute god send. Grace would often be heard reminding Geraldine.

"Moira might be coping Geraldine but I certainly wouldn't. Where would we ever be without our friends. Thank you and yes I'd do it for you too."
The ladies embraced in silence.

*D*riving was something which Michael had considered leaving off of his agenda for the foreseeable future. Having the experience of many flashbacks from that awful evening, was difficult for all of them to process. It was perhaps harder for Michael as he had been the driver. He had spoken to their doctor's surgery on his own behalf and now on behalf of Moira too. Very much to her annoyance, Moira received the news and information about his discussion from the practice councillor.

"Your fiancé has attempted to refer you to me Moira. Are you happy for us to have a chat?"

No, she was not happy and made that fact very clear. Feeling furious with Michael for what she had considered to be his awful interference, she informed the councillor that should she feel the need for his services, that she would get in touch herself. Politely thanking the man for his call and for his time, that's where the phone call came to an abrupt end. Arrival back to the Riley's home from his place of work that evening, Michael very quickly became aware that he had done something to upset Moira.

"I know you well Moira so spit it out."

Thinking how she would disagree with that statement she told him.

"You don't know me that well Michael. If you did you would not have interfered. Don't you think I'm capable of addressing my own psychological issues that's if I decide I have any?"

Understanding how his previous action of what was meant as kindness only, was now backfiring on him he apologised.

"Look it was naive of me. Of course, I know you're an independent and competent woman, but I was there and well all right I give up the fight. There's no excuse really. I'm genuinely sorry."

Accepting Michaels apology Moira gave him an assurance, that at that point in time, she had no issues at all as a result of the awful car accident. Neither of them liking to continue with negative feelings between them they embraced. Wrapping her arms tightly around her fiancé, she could tell he had been drinking and smoking. The smell was strong on his breath and was strong on his clothing too. Understanding the full degree of pressure which he must be feeling due to flashbacks, was not sufficient reason in her view, for him to behave quite so irresponsibly.

"Michael you're a doctor for Christ's sake. What's going on with you? How can you possibly think that putting poison into your body, combined with daytime drinking is the right thing to be doing?"

Being unable to look her directly in the eye Moira was aware of his feeling of inadequacy and perhaps feelings of some shame too. Expressing his deep remorse to her did not impress Moira too much. She flung her arms in the air telling him to save it as she left the room. Then turning to go back almost immediately she told her boyfriend.

"Apologise to yourself Michael not to me."

Sharing with her how he was still suffering from flashbacks on a regular basis and how that was impacting his life so badly, he thought would give her more of an insight into why he turned to alcohol and tobacco. Michael also shared that he was also engaging with the practice councillor. Not happy to know he was still having flashbacks, Moira was delighted to know that he was taking active action in addressing them. She felt that him engaging with a councillor, was quite sensible behaviour. She was impressed.

"Hopefully therapy will help you sort out your head. If it doesn't then talk to me about it again. I might have some ideas but won't interfere now with what your councillor is providing."

Considering her view to be appropriate Michael once again acknowledged his own inappropriateness. Assuring her there would be no further cause for concern, he was clear, simple and straightforward with his explanation.

"No more nicotine and daytime use of alcohol for me. Behaving stupidly is what I generally place at other people's front door. I'm so sorry Moira."

That was a conversation which would never see the light of day again, unless Michael wished to share his feelings in order to gain her support. A line was drawn.

Another surprise.

*E*ventually, with Michael Kearns and Moira Riley being back at their respective work places, life had taken on a sense of normality for them again. Viewing that awful car crash as something which they perhaps had been destined to be involved with as a life experience, was how they now both viewed that whole situation through their spiritual eyes. That was quite deep thinking on my brothers' part. Not being a person who was readily open to new spiritual ideas his view did somewhat surprise me. They had a future to prepare for and would do so with a good degree of family support and enthusiasm. Plans were to be continued for their forth coming marriage. Both practicing the Catholic religion Moira had arranged a meeting with their local priest at Saint John's church on Harrington Street in Dublin.

*B*eing happy to proceed with their wish to be married at that church, the priest then outlined what his expectations of them were and would continue to be. He was an elderly man who had looked after that Parish for almost forty eight years. Being quite rigid in his way of thinking, with little to no space left for ideas which he may not approve of, the couple were cautious with what information they shared with their priest. Michael and Moira being quite strict Catholics themselves were mostly happy to go along with his rules. Attending for *some weekly marital sessions at the church hall over the next six months, was a request which they had both been readily prepared for. Both feeling their private life was and should be just that, they had hoped for no questions regarding their habitation practices. Their plan was made. Despite their total dislike for lies, that would have to be a situation where lying became a necessity. Getting through the weekly sessions was relatively easy for them. They had a great sense of gratitude for the facts that their living arrangements situation never arose.*

Venue chosen and wedding guest list produced it was time for Michael and Moira to relax. Feeling how everything was now going very nicely to plan, there hope was for all of that to continue. Sharing their time between their residence in Dublin and their farm house out in Enniskerry, Padraig and Grace Riley were not feeling overly impressed with that arrangement. Having their view was one matter. Expressing it to Michael was on a whole other level. Choosing their moment was not done with very much discretion either. Driving up to Moiras parents' home Grace and Padraig were outside. They were together with some family members, who had dropped in and were now saying their goodbyes. The broad smile on Michaels face as he stepped out from the car, was quickly wiped away. Moira seeing the annoyance on her mother's face she attempted to intervene. She was too late. Grace blurted out their thoughts.

"I know your sleeping together Michael. I'm not happy neither is Padraig. It's not right."
No response from Michael was met with some more accusations from his mother-in-law to be. Moira came rushing outside bag in hand.

"Back in the car Michael. She's not allowed to speak to you like that."

*G*race Riley felt almost instant remorse for her outburst as she watched Michaels car be driven off without a word from their daughter. Embarrassed family members whose business it had been made by Grace, spoke to her of their feelings of horror by the manner in which she had addressed Michael. She would need to seek forgiveness from him and from Grace and do it fast. Michael and Moira behaving out of character they choose to ignore their phones that evening. Walking out in Enniskerry taking in the beauty of their surroundings, was the therapy required to calm their ruffled feathers. Michael was first to relent as his phone rang out the next morning. It was Padraig Riley.

"She told me what she said Michael. There's no blame on you and Grace for simply driving off. I agree she's entitled to her view as am I to mine, but she was very much out of order in speaking to you in such a rude manner and in front of other family members too."

*M*ichael interrupted. Telling Padraig how it didn't matter as what was done was done, he then requested to speak to Grace. Padraig was left feeling astounded to hear the man's comments.

"You're some man Michael Kearns. Thank you. Ill ask her to come to the phone but fear that she may be feeling a bit too humiliated."

Grace spoke with a quiver in her voice. Appealing to Michael for forgiveness she had a great sense of relief upon hearing his response. She made it very clear to him how she now fully understands, that her views regarding his life with Moira are *not her business. Apologising to Moira too, Grace requested they might be able to draw a line with lessons learned by her. The line was drawn!*

Many months later and with much planning having been put in place, the morning of the wedding day of Michael Kearns to Moira Riley was upon the family. Moira woke up earlier than she had been expected to. Finding her parents already down in the kitchen, her father had prepared her favourite bacon sandwich layered with some fried onions. Planning to give her breakfast in bed on her last morning as Moira Riley, she showed her appreciation to them. Arrival of the bridesmaids and two hairdressers was prompt. The ladies took their turns under the driers. Everyone was in awe of Moiras hairstyle.

"You're looking swell Moira. Michael Kearns is a very lucky man."

She smiled and remained silent.

Arriving traditionally late for the wedding ceremony, Moira had some feelings of anxiety. She cursed under her breath as sweat began to build up on her palms. Using the inner layer of her fathers jacket she wiped both hands fiercely. Taking a deep breath in ahead of walking with her father, she felt all eyes would be on her as they walked up the aisle. Michael too had some anxiety of which not the least, was his concern she might jilt him at the altar. Being deposited by her father at the groom's side, Michael thought how very beautiful his wife to be was looking. Catholic wedding ceremony's traditionally being quite long, this one was no different. In hope of their Spanish friends attending, a Spanish speaking interpreter had been arranged for the benefit of Gabriella. She was the lady who could not understand English. Being dressed in some traditional Spanish costume, the interpreter would be easily visible to their Spanish guests if they attended. Through some discussion with the priest it was agreed the interpreter would stand almost central to the altar. She would relay all which was being said for the benefit of Gabriella. Michael and Moira had planned the whole Spanish aspect very well. They felt proud.

More than one hour later Moira Riley walked down the aisle as Mrs Michael Kearns. To their absolute delight the lady and her son from the shop in the Spanish fishing village, did attend at their wedding. A wedding gift of another much larger cottage in that same fishing village, was given to the newly married couple. They should arrange for themselves and both sets of parents to take a two-week vacation there at a time suitable for their convenience. Tears of joy falling from Moiras eyes she remembered the saying; of how familiarity breeds contempt. She now had a new saying created by herself and Michael. It was that Kindness breeds kindness. Graciously accepting their generous wedding gift, they wished their Spanish friends to have a good time in Ireland. Taking part in the Ceili music and dancing and in anticipation of their guests from Spain arriving, Moira and Michael had sourced some Spanish music too together with a Spanish dancer. To the delight of Rodrigo and his mother Gabriella, they were both invited to share in a dance with the Spanish dancer. That's a precious memory which they have both stated they will never forget. Being the best day of her life to that point, Moira often revels in those memories as does her husband Michael too.

*Sh*aring the same view in terms of their family planning had felt like a bonus to Moira and Michael Kearns. They had agreed they were both wanting children but not for at least a further two years down the line. Sorting out their home and perhaps completing any further training which might be desired by either or both of them, was their priority at that time. Completing those tasks ahead of any ideas of family making was important for both of them. Moira taking the pill had been and would continue to be their preferred method for contraception.

*Wh*ilst both had in general terms enjoyed very good health, tonsillitis had at times been like a plague in Moiras life. She had on occasions endured that awful illness from her early childhood years. Despite her parents having quite a strong preference for natural healing methods, those methods did not always help Moira. She would on some occasions become so debilitated by tonsillitis that relenting was their only way forward. Trying to get Grace to fully understand the pain she was enduring had often fell on deaf ears.

"It'll be fine Moira just give it time."

And then an end to that conversation with no opportunity offered for Moira to express her view. Grace had some strong opinions against conventional medicine. She would only go there once all other avenues had been exhausted. Trips to their local surgery by Grace or Padraig would usually result in them being given antibiotic treatment for their daughter. It was always a very last resort for Grace Riley to go down that road. Her own parents and Padraig's too were always very much in favour of natural remedies. Holding the belief that our cures would come from the earth their minds were not to *be moved on. that subject. That outlook had come down the generations through Padraig's and Graces families. It was passed down to their children too.*

Having grown up with those experiences Moira would now as a young woman, attempt to deal with her health issues in a similar manner. Being a lady who still preferred the natural method for treatment and medication, she would always attempt to find natural remedies for it herself. Having been reared by a set of parents who always avoided conventional medicine if that was possible, their favourite cure for any issues of the throat would be a salt mixed with water-based solution, which would then be used as a gargle. Moira had many times tried that method. She had tried disprin gargles and some other gargles too. Their success would be defined largely by the severity of the illness.

Less than one year into their marriage Moira found herself grimacing, as she attempted to swallow even a tiny drink to moisten her mouth. Gargling of various attempts brought no change to her situation. Nothing appeared to make the slightest difference for her. Resisting her husband's attempts of encouragement to see their doctor, became increasingly hard as her illness took a stronger hold. Three weeks of suffering, in addition to the associated fatigue which can and did come with tonsillitis, caused her to relent. Her visit to their local doctor provided Moira with a seven-day course of penicillin, together with some health supplements containing very high levels of vitamin C and some St John's Wort to aid with her anxiety. Vitamin C she was told was for the purpose of giving a boost to her immune system. Try build it up a little might equate to perhaps less bouts of tonsillitis in the future.

*S*oon she was feeling better again and back to her usual self.

Some weeks after her antibiotic and her vitamin supplements treatment had begun, confusion swept across Moiras face. Her monthly which was always regular and spot on twenty-eight days was now fourteen days late. Trying her best not to panic which Moira found to be quite a difficult task, she did wait a further two weeks. She continued with her daily use of vitamin C. and St John's Wort. Deciding she should perhaps do some research on women and their use of antibiotics and natural remedies whilst taking the contraceptive pill, she was left feeling uncertain of her situation.

*E*stablishing that taking high levels of vitamin C supplement plus St John's Wort, could be conducive to her becoming pregnant, Moira began to panic just a little. Her heart began racing. Sweat building up on her hands was the clue that her anxiety was rising. She did her deep breathing. She was not ready to be pregnant at that time or for a long time still down the line. Pregnancy would not be at all compatible with her and her husband's life plans. Eventually the continued lack of onset of her menstruation, prompted Moira to pay a visit to the local pharmacy. That's where she made the purchase of a pregnancy testing kit. Having feelings of trepidation, she decided to keep the whole situation secret from her husband for the interim period.

*A*fter a further missed monthly Moira prepared herself for a positive pregnancy outcome. Having on previous occasions reminded herself that she was not yet ready to be pregnant, she was now aware of the high possibility that she was. She had to get her mindset right ahead of doing the test. Telling *herself how it would be fine she was surprised how effective that thinking process turned out to be. Michael had left for the hospital. She felt the timing was right to find out one way or the other. Moira nervously did the test. Breathing in deeply in attempts to calm her anxiety whilst she waited for the result, did not appear to help her very much.*

Deciding to leave the testing kit right there in the bathroom for a few more minutes, she went down to the kitchen for a brew then instantly changed her mind. Taking the stairs two by two Moira hurried back to the bathroom and to the small piece of scientific equipment which was waiting there for her. She thought about its many thin layers and tiny holes. Picking it up enthusiastically, she punched the air twice upon seeing the result. Yes, she was pregnant they were going to be new parents. Surprisingly to her she was feeling delighted. Despite this being earlier by more than a year than they had already planned to start a family, she felt very excited and contented at the same time. She checked the testing kit three times ahead of placing it carefully back into its box and then into a small bag in the bathroom. She would save it to show to her husband on his return from his day at the hospital that evening.

She had that knowledge of a precious little Kearns growing inside of her and Michael didn't. She considered that to be a little unfair. She would make the sharing of it with him very special. Calling him at work she wished to clarify his expected arrival at home time that evening.

"Are you straight home or going out somewhere first?" He was a little suspicious.

"You all right Moira? You don't usually call to ask me that question, in fact you have never called me at work to ask me that question."
Somehow holding onto her composure, she told her husband that yes, she was absolutely fine. She was planning to make a dinner which would not reheat very well and didn't want it to spoil. There was a huge element of truth in that statement. She just hadn't told him the whole story. Michael perhaps not convinced that she was being truthful, confirmed how he would be home direct from the hospital. They then said their goodbyes. Thinking how it might be special to cook a replica of the meal they had shared on their first date, Moira would need to go to the fishmongers.

Ending his shift at the hospital Michael took the most direct route home that evening. Arrival at their home place out in Enniskerry, he sensed there was something special going on. To say he was surprised was the best way he could describe his feelings. Seeing how the table had been laid to perfection and to see Moira wearing the same outfit, which she had worn on their very first date night, all put together made him quite curious. He was aware that she had kept that outfit for special occasions only. Feeling compelled to ask he proceeded to do so.

"Am I missing something here Moira? It's not our wedding anniversary or your birthday or something is it?
She was quick with her response.
"Nope- get showered. Dinner will be on the table in thirty minutes."

Michael was left scratching his head for answers. Perhaps she had invited friends over for dinner or maybe even some *colleagues of his, he considered could both be possibilities. Moira was like that. She liked surprising people. Michael held a conversation with himself. That 'll be it he thought. She has set the table for two just to confuse me and do the rest when I'm taking a shower. Knowing his wife as he did Michael was aware that any further probing on his part would be futile. Relaxed from his shower he went down to the dining room with expectation of extra places having been set. They had not. Confused again, he took further instruction from Moira. She requested that he go to their sun room at the back of the house and wait.*

Having set the scene for a nice evening together she called her husband to the table. Salmon En Croute had lovingly been prepared and cooked without the overnight curing. Served with a large side salad plus chips it tasted very flavoursome. Michael had quite a strong feminine side to his character which often helped him through situations. Female intuition was working for him this time or so he thought. Telling him that this was a very special occasion he didn't really need his intuition to figure that out. It was quite obvious something special was going on. Not being birthdays or anniversary in his mind it left just one other thing. It had to be that she had been promoted at work?

"Come on Moira I'm struggling here but I'm guessing too. It's time to put me out of my misery."

Eventually sharing with her husband, the news of her pregnancy Michaels face glowed. His initial reaction which was of pure joy and delight over with, he then wondered how? Thinking how people taking the contraceptive pill are protected from pregnancy Michael continued to be confused.

"You take the pill Moira as we had both agreed for a two year wait."
Sharing the outcome of her research regarding the use of vitamin C and St Johns Wort supplements when taking the pill, gave Michael the chills. Suddenly he had the realisation that there's lots which doctors don't know about medication and supplement impact. He was gracious in his response.

"Perhaps I should have a word with people down at the medical practice? Help them to see that they need to inform women when prescribing supplements for them. Speak to my colleagues at the hospital too. It would be a very different situation for us now had I realised the potential of what could possibly happen."

*D*ecisions to do that agreed between them Michael would call their medical practice, at his first available opportunity. Speaking to colleagues at the hospital proved itself to be a lot easier for him to do. Reminding the obnoxious receptionist at the local practice that she was just a receptionist, and not a medically qualified person, she eventually connected him to a doctor.

"Thank you for sharing that with us Michael. If I had this information I would never have advised Moira to take the supplements but especially not St John's Wort. Looking on the internet as we speak, I can see there have been reports of pregnancy on the pill when St John's Wort has been used."
Whilst being able to reassure the doctor how the pregnancy was very acceptable to himself and to Moira, he made it clear that may not be the case for many others. Hopefully some lessons would be learned all round. Sharing the news of their pregnancy with the Riley and the Kearns families brought great joy to everyone. My own view on the pregnancy was

one of utter delight at the idea of becoming an aunt. Holding Moira tightly I had visions of feeling the baby long before that could be remotely a possibility.

*M*oiras pregnancy was very straight forward. In fact, you'd hardly know she was pregnant if it wasn't for the odd food craving or two. Her husband Michael at times had feelings of shivers down his spine, which were caused by her unusual requests for food. He could be and on occasions was heard questioning her requests.

"You serious Moira you want a banana sandwich with jam?"

Moira smiled at the very thought of what was coming her way. She struggled a little to understand the cravings herself but could not settle until she relieved them.

*T*ime flying by for Michael and Moira at that point in terms of the pregnancy, she was able to reassure her husband, that the cravings would surely be coming to an end in no time at all. A huge smile broadened his face as he let out a fairly quiet squeal from hearing that reminder.

"You have to admit the cravings are a bit weird Moira. Especially the other one of beetroot with your breakfast cereals. Makes me want to heave yet it shows how foods which we would never consider to be compatible certainly can be, or I wonder if they are only compatible when eaten by the pregnant woman?"

*H*aving had a smart way for his question to be answered she was quick with her response. Michael heaved at the very thought of her suggestion for him to take part in his very own experiment. The screwed up twisted look on his face gave her the non-verbal message that it would not be happening. Being a psychologist Moira was a bit into the creation of and conducting experiments. She slouched her shoulders down as if in disappointment phase, as she placed herself slowly down onto the chair. Feeling very disappointed by her husband's response, she was equally smart enough to know, how there would be no point in any attempt to pursue her idea. Michael considered how he was learning quite a bit from his pregnant wife.

"I might be a doctor Moira but isn't this situation the proof that we can all learn from each other."

Michael was working on maternity wards in order to enhance his training. This would give him a great opportunity to share his new-found knowledge with others during their question time. Moira was encouraged to hear his response.

"That's a plan that cannot do any harm Michael."

Eventually the day for which they had waited for was upon them. A gush of water on the bed felt very assuring to Moira that things were starting to happen. Michael was not home. Contractions had scarcely begun however the woman was now starting to panic a little. Michael was the calm collected and cool one in the marriage. His presence was needed at that point. She thought how typical that now she needed him and he wasn't there. Picking up the phone Moira was quite determined to and would soon bring about a change to that situation. Anxiety was now the overriding factor in her voice as he didn't pick up and she expressed herself out loud.

"Come on Michael for Christ's sake where are you when I need you?"

*Re*placing the telephone receiver Moira slowly walked up the length of their garden. She was about to sit down by the lavender bush. Realising instantly what a foolish action that would be, she went straight back inside the house to be near the phone. What had felt to her like hours yet it was just minutes after she had called her husband the phone rang out.

" You called me Moira I was driving. Something up?"
His question she felt needed a humorous response.
"No somethings down and it's my water bag. I'm in labour Michael and I'm frightened. Come home please."
Michael having already arrived at his work place, reminded his wife of what she needed to do next in terms of getting him back home. He was taking control of the home situation.

"Call the hospital Moira. They already have agreed the plan when it becomes required and that's obviously now. Tell them I said to get cover for my shift today and for the next two weeks. I'll be back home in twenty minutes if traffics not too bad. I'm leaving now."

*E*nding the call then burying her head in her hands Moira wasn't sure how to feel. Thinking how she was an educated lady with two degrees up her sleeve, none of that had prepared her for what she was now experiencing. With both arms wrapped around her stomach, Moira began to feel the sensations of her anxiety shoot throughout her body. Quickly giving herself a short lecture on panic situations and how to behave when they occur, she did some more deep breathing and then called the hospital. Following Michaels instruction, she was connected to the secretary's office very quickly. She was given confirmation that his shift would be covered from *that point in time and with time off arranged as per his request.*

Michael was by now on the return journey back home to Enniskerry. Consumed with thoughts of imminently becoming a father, was the catalyst for him losing his focus and his concentration momentarily. History had almost repeated itself in terms of Michaels previous driving accident. A near miss was the only way he could describe what happened next between himself and an oncoming vehicle. Reprimanding himself for what he decided was his awful recklessness, which had almost resulted in a further accident, he was relieved the incident was more than enough to bring his focus back to the roads.

Another call ended with Moira feeling perhaps a little more anxious by now. She repeatedly did her deep breathing in the hopes it might calm her. Considering taking a warm bath she quickly changed her mind, deciding not to just in case. Picking up the phone again this time she called her mother. Anything to fill that space whilst she waited for Michaels return, had to be good from Moiras perspective. Hearing the key turn in the front door she called out to him.

"I'm in the bedroom Michael and I'm too frightened to go down stairs. So glad you've come back home. I know that I'm being a bit on the dramatic side but will you hurry up." Michael and his calm ways of looking at situations was quick to put his wife at ease. Taking hold of her hand he quietly and calmly told her.

"It's fine Moira and it will be fine. Let's go in the garden sit by the lavender tree. It always helps to keep you calm and the weathers beautiful too. I'll bring some breakfast out if you

feel like eating. Keep your strength up for when you need it. You know what I mean?"
Yes, she knew very well want he meant. She had no interest in eating breakfast or eating anything at that time. Trying not to show her impatience to her husband she kept her response very short."
   "No, it's fine."

Sitting by the lavender bush alternated with her walking back and forward in the garden, she managed to stay relaxed and relatively calm. Michael had at times gone back indoors ahead of her contractions having become regular, fast and hard some two hours later. Moira was beginning to grimace.
   "We need to go to the hospital now. This hurts a lot"
Moira had a relatively fast labour from onset to her delivery experience which was virtually problem free. As the midwife presented them with their beautiful daughter Michael could not contain himself.
   "She's just perfect Moira now our lives begin for real. A life to be free from anguish and all which might accompany that."
 Beaming smiles from ear to ear showed some Joy beyond any degree of imagination, on the faces of Michael and his wife.

I have to pinch myself when I think of my brother making that statement. It had to be the ultimate in naivety and him being a children's doctor too. I cannot begin to imagine, just how many stressed out parents he has encountered over the years through his work. You would have thought that those families would have been confirmation for him, that being a parent would never be conducive to a life free from anguish.

Yes, those comments from him were very naïve. I could only imagine Moiras thoughts which she may or may not have shared with her husband. Having already picked out a name for their baby, they both had welcomed Helen Marissa Kearns into this world. Moira had decided on the name Marissa as a middle name for their daughter. Her decision for that was as a mark of respect for the little girl, whose case she had previously worked on and who had been so wrongly taken into foster care. Moira still thought about the Geary family at times and hoped that they were all doing well. Especially remembering them at this time helped Moira to understand, exactly what a huge impact that case had made on her life. Knowing how she should always separate work life from her home and from her private life, somehow this family was one situation where that rule was and would continue to be broken. Moiras behaviour in that respect was suggesting a bond of some description had developed between herself and Frank and Jessica Geary.

A christening day was duly arranged for Helen. It would take place at their local Catholic church and then afterwards back at their home in Enniskerry. Having made some professional enquiries about the Geary family and having been informed that there were no issues concerning them, Moira with her husband's blessings felt it would be nice to pay the family an unofficial visit. Now a mother herself she could not begin to imagine and struggled to understand, just how painful their situation must have been. Moira having just one boundary in her mind, she would share it with the Geary's if there became a need. There would be no mention of anything concerning Marissa's time in foster care or anything else concerning that situation. Her visit would be on a totally personal and sociable level only. Moira felt quite good about herself for being able to do that. She had hoped that the Geary family would appreciate her offer of friendship too.

*M*arissa's parents appeared to be very welcoming and to be very appreciative of Moiras visit. There was no mention of anything regarding Marissa having previously been removed from their care. Moira could see that as being a huge positive in their potential friendship. Feeling very impressed by the fact that despite the Geary's knowing of her and Michaels previous professional involvement, they were still able to and did leave that in the past and outside of their time together, Moira acknowledged their tenacity in doing that.

"It's great and your both quite amazing in your ability to leave the past where it belongs. Long may our friendship last."

Having enjoyed tea and some homemade fruit scones, Moira couldn't help but express her sense of envy. Sharing with the Geary's how having tried so very many times to bake her own scones, she had always miserably failed. She shared how her husband Michael had never held back with his comments. She giggled as she shared with the Geary's what Michaels usual comments regarding her attempts at baking scones were.

"Lovely rock cakes Moira. Hope I don't chip a tooth."

*F*rank and Jessica coming from difficult backgrounds had given Moira a lot of insight. It had helped her to understand, how and possibly why the Geary's had made some quite bad choices in life. What was feeling important now was the fact that they had addressed and turned those choices around. That fact was plain to be seen in their private surroundings. It *could be and was seen in Marissa's behaviour and seen in their own behaviour and appearance. Moira congratulated them on the birth of their baby son. Having always been a lady who did not feel that a person's class status in life made the person, she was happy to consider the Geary family as her and Michaels new friends. The visit between the two families having gone so well, Moira and Michael spoke about the possibility, of sending the family an invitation to their daughter Helens christening.*

Their decision was made very quickly. Putting an invite in the post to the Geary family Michael and Moira had hoped for a positive response. The Geary's very much appreciated their invitation, nevertheless they agreed for a variety of reasons to politely decline by return post. They demonstrated great composure in their response.

"It's lovely of you both Moira. Thank you! Our experiences in life have changed us in many ways for the better, but in some ways we both are still quite introvert when in the company of those we don't especially know very well. On that basis we have to decline. We will however always know that you invited us. We both sincerely appreciate the fact that you did that. No one can take that knowledge away from us ever and who knows what might happen in the future."
Moira had a little sadness in her voice.

"They're not coming Michael the Geary's are not coming to the christening."

Michael was sensible as was usual for him. He was able to help his wife to understand, that as the Geary's had pointed out a lack of their presence was not what mattered, was not what was important. Helping Moira to see that she had done a good thing in her friendship with them, she could then also see how Frank and Jessica had been made to feel good about themselves, due to having received the invite.

"A small boost to the ego and the self-esteem of Jessica and Frank Geary won't do any harm Moira. Despite their refusal they will feel good from the knowledge that we have invited them. That invite will have told them that we are classing them to be our friends."

She felt assured and comforted by her husband's wisdom and by his comment. Acknowledging how correct Michael was and placing a fleeting kiss on his cheek she climbed the stairs to attend to their child. Being the mother of a new born was slightly challenging for Moira. Having seen and known other families with new born babies, had seemed like the picture-perfect scenario to her. She was now discovering how the reality of it all was somewhat different to that which the text book had said. She was nevertheless a very proud and a very happy new mother.

Diagnosis they didn't want

Cooing mixed and mingled in with a whimpering type of crying could be heard quite loudly from across the farm house landing. The house was old with acoustics which were not too great. Moira had many times thought about and considered, how insulation would need to be a top priority in their list of upgrades and maintenance. Feeling draughts from all around the window ledges and from the underside of doors, she knew they would have to do something pretty soon. Hearing their baby daughter cry as she did on that occasion presented Moira with the reminder which she required. It was a timely reminder of the urgency to crack on with some of those pressing home maintenance jobs. She was aware the jobs had been badly neglected. Being aware that finding time for the renovations would impede heavily on both hers and Michaels time, she decided that she was going to speak to him about it again. Knowing how her husband had quite a hectic work schedule at the hospital, she hadn't wanted to place other issues on his mind. This however was now feeling as though it was fairly urgent.

Winter being almost upon them with all of the natural beauty it would bring, combined with all of the problems which it potentially might bring too, was a frightening thought for Moira Kearns. It was also perhaps the catalyst *required to help her realise that they could not keep putting home maintenance off. There were too many areas within their farm house which needed addressing. Understanding how the early and unplanned pregnancy had perhaps messed up their renovation plans, Moira would no longer allow herself to believe that to be their excuse. Some things needed their attention and they needed it at that point. Having been told about and previously seen quite a few advertisements in their local papers gave Moira some clear ideas. The ads had been placed by young men seeking employment. Perhaps that's what they should do. They should employ a tradesman was a thought now circulating in Moiras head. Yes, men would come and go. They would get all of their maintenance and renovations done in an orderly manner and without too much upheaval to herself, to Michael and to the baby.*

Feeling quite happy with her sense of forethought, she loved how she had considered their daughter in all of the upheaval. She thought how perhaps Michael would have to surrender, to his quite strong sense of pride in doing house maintenance himself. Moira knowing her husband well, she wished herself good luck in persuading him to give her his agreement to a tradesman, or more realistically tradesmen. Her mind was made up. She would speak to her husband that night in her attempt for a plan to hopefully be put in place.

Having calmed down quite a bit by the time her mother reached the cot, Helen was quite contented looking. Moira watched closely as their child suckled slowly on a dummy whilst having almost gone back to sleep. Always having promised herself that she would never give dummies to her babies, she had broken her own rule. Broken her own promise to herself. Thinking how maybe she should not have those types of rules where their children would be concerned, now felt like a much better plan to Moira. That was perhaps something else which she was learning whilst travelling down the journey of early parenthood. Her head was full of anxiety regarding why Helen had been whimpering so much and so loudly. Knowing that finding an answer to her own question may almost be a guessing game, she took a deep breath in and relaxed. She would accept the fact that perhaps it's like this for most if not for all new parents. It was a learning curve and something which no mother could possibly be prepared for. Moira was nevertheless a little hard on herself. She did however feel slightly comforted by those thoughts.

Moira consoled herself further by deciding that the child probably had a little colic, which had by that time settled right down. She was very aware that colic had been around for evermore. She was aware that colic pain was a nuisance experienced by many young babies and was not uncommon. Remembering the stories told to her by her own mother, regarding the great asset which gripe water had been to the family when her babies were suffering, Moira knew what she needed to do. She ensured that gripe water would be added to her next shopping list. Thinking how if only she had the time, how she could stay there by the cot watching Helen all day long. She snapped out of her day dream. Swiftly taking herself back down to the kitchen, that's when she prepared her husband's favourite meal. It would be ready to cook in time for his home coming. Knowing she would be attempting to break through his sense of pride, Moira felt how it was a good plan to get their evening off to a good start.

*S*he watched Michaels face intensely for his reaction to her suggestion of a tradesman being employed by them. Moira was not left feeling disappointed. To her amazement the job was much easier than her anticipation had told her it might be. Michael had no hesitation in his response.

"You know what Moira I'm glad you're suggesting that we have people in, to do some of if not all of the maintenance work. Realistically we both know that neither of us have very much spare time and it's not as though money is short. Can I leave it with you to organise something?"

Being somewhat relieved by what she was hearing Moira was reassuring to her husband, that she would take care of the whole situation. She also wondered silently if she knew her husband as well as she had thought she knew him. Deciding that perhaps she did not was a slightly concerning thought for her. Knowing how there were and would continue to be many issues to be dealt with in their life's, she had no desire to complicate things further. She was not about to embark on creating new problems in her own mind. She would leave that thought of how well she did or did not know her husband, right there for the present time.

*T*heir baby daughters christening day quickly fell upon the family. Michael had struggled to secure some time off from the hospital for the event. Going in for the early shift his plan had been to leave his work place mid-morning. Having a colleague cover for him was how he had many times worked in Paediatrics. Yes, Michael was by now a qualified and very well-liked surgical paediatrician in the children's ear nose and throat department of Crumlin hospital in Dublin. Travelling back from the hospital to their home in Enniskerry, Michael *was surprised to see and hear the curlew over on the bogs. He was not a big fan of the curlew especially when they cried out at night time. Living in the countryside had availed him to their sounds, which he associated with either a screaming lady or a screaming baby. Feeling how that was a small price to pay, for the privilege of living in the midst of the beauty of Enniskerry, was the thought which so often consoled Michael. Traditionally returning back to Ireland for the winter season the curlews were quite early that year.*

Back home with lots of time to spare ahead of their planned time at the church Michael was feeling an appreciation for their life's. He sat pensively whilst watching their baby girl as she gurgled away in her pram. Moira getting the wrong idea and being a little on the snappy side, with some attitude in her voice she told him.

"Been at the hospital all morning and now you're looking as though your back there in your head."
Stirring slightly from his solemn position Michael assured her that he was not. He was not quite sure either why she would make that assumption. He nevertheless went right ahead to give her an explanation of his thoughts.

"I'm thinking about how very blessed we are to have such a perfect child. That's all Moira. That's the culmination of what's going off in my head."
Being a little unsure of his explanation Moira accepted it, as it would be the wrong time to challenge him further. She did however recall her previous thoughts of the question mark on how well she knows her husband.

Leaving for the chapel that afternoon Moira had settled their daughter into her carry crib. Gentle whimpers coming from the front of the chapel, was the cue which we all needed, to say that cold water had been poured over Helens head. Other babies whimpered and cried too. Often wondering why, the ritual of cold water has to be a part of the babies christening ceremony, I've never been given an answer which has totally satisfied my curiosity. Never satisfied my never-ending hunger for knowledge of why the catholic church has certain rules. Despite being raised as a Roman Catholic- I do not and probably never will understand or follow, many of the church man made rules and rituals myself. Discrimination occurring between the catholic and the protestant church has never made very much sense to me either.

Helen Marissa Kearns was Michael and Moiras perfect baby but in a slightly different sort of way. She would continue to be perfectly different throughout the whole of her life, only her parents didn't know that yet. Having the baby which they had not planned for, but had dreamt of having one day down the line, they, but more so Michael, were initially oblivious to anything which might make their child anything less than perfect in their eyes. Moira however as was often the case in many aspects of their marriage, had a more realistic take on things. She had the thinking process, she had the idea that no one's lives are ever perfect and free from anguish. Moira had the understanding, that you cannot have a child and enjoy a life which would be problem free. She at times wondered why and how Michael could be quite so naïve.

This was more puzzling for Moira, due to the facts that he was meeting with families who have children who suffer with health and often many other problems on a daily basis. Moira could often be heard telling her husband.

"I'm sure we will have our ups and downs Michael but for now, let's just enjoy the peaceful and perhaps the not so peaceful moments with our beautiful baby girl."

Nodding in agreement with what he had heard from his wife Michael never actually verbally acknowledged what she had said. He could at times be a man of not many words. He was one for the quiet life so would give affirmation, where and when he didn't really mean that which he was affirming. The above was one of those situations. Moira was not aware. In Michaels head there would only be the good times which would always be problem free. Not having the desire to and perhaps not being able to see past that Idyllic life with their daughter, he allowed those thoughts to consume him.

Watching Helen for the first year or so of her life as she met some of her milestones, her father continued to shower her with his praise and encouragement. Moira had become a little suspicious. Considering that everything might not be as she would hope for it to be with their daughter, she made and kept copious notes. At times sharing those thoughts with her husband she had found herself being almost dismissed.

"I'm concerned Michael. Something seems not to be quite right with Helen but I cannot put my finger on it."

Her words grated badly on his sensory nerves. He did not want to hear them. Considering how he should try to be very dismissive of her comment without giving the message he didn't care, he often told her.

"You're like a born analyst Moira."

He would laugh to lighten his comment a little. He hoped that him laughing might bring a little humour to the situation. It often did not bring the desired result.

"By the way It's not a criticism of you just an observation. I'm sure Helen's fine and she will continue to be fine. Stop worrying, will you?"

Despite her husband's attempts at humour Moira would usually see right through him. Sensing that he held the same views as she did, but didn't want to acknowledge them she kept her thoughts to herself. She thought about how men can be and often are in denial of very sensitive family situations. Wondering to herself that as a psychologist might there be any mileage in thinking of the possibility, of bringing change to the male way of thinking. She was aware that it was not just Michael who would be in denial of situations. It would probably be most if not all men. She was also aware, that her thoughts about changing the male thinking process were very naïve thoughts. No one knew better than Moira how the male and female brain are different and that's how it would be.

Deciding that only the female would listen to their intuition, listen to their gut feeling and openly act upon it, Moira knew her thoughts about changing her husband's thinking process were futile. Thinking how the possibility of any change with him would be very remote, she left those thoughts right there in her head. She knew she was analysing their daughter but what else would you do with any child of that age. In her mother's head Helens every movement had to be analysed. How else would people know or realise if their children were meeting their milestones. She wasn't sure if her husband's statement regarding her worrying, was partly a question or was it also an instruction. Eventually she decided that it felt a bit like both and choose not to raise it with him again at that point.

Progressing through her first to second year of life, Helen Kearn's appeared to be developing very well. Being spot on target from a psychical perspective was quite reassuring for her parents. Being the correct height and build for her age, gave Michael the message that everything really was all right when in fact it was not. Helen had a very full head of honey blonde wavy hair with the onset or beginnings of freckles on her face. Moira loved freckles. Often checking her own image in the mirror, she would feel a great sense of disappointment. Her freckles had seemed to have gradually faded throughout her teenage years. Moira wondered if that might be hormone related. She thought about how so many things were often attributed to hormones, so why not add one more to the list - That of disappearing freckles in your teenage years. She giggled to herself. Taking her mind back to Helen, Moira shared with me how she had previously experienced some concerns and had continued to have those concerns.

The Kearns daughter Helen aside from appearing to be developing well in many ways, was otherwise demonstrating some small differences. Things were not occurring for Helen in a way which might be expected for a child of her age. The differences were noticeable to her mother. Some of Helens behaviours had Moira scratching her head for answers. She could be heard crying out at times almost in rage with no obvious trigger for that. She would be seen on many occasions trying to remove the new items of clothing, which her parents had attempted to dress her in. Her outbursts of rage were associated mainly but not always, with times when they would be in quite a noisy environment. Causing both of her parents but perhaps especially Moira a great deal of confusion, they were mostly left without answers.

Michael becoming a little irritated he would be dismissive of his wife's ongoing concern and her worry for their child. Practising her deep breathing skills at those times would be Moiras saving grace. Her frustration with her husband would lessen ensuring that a peaceful time would be experienced between them. Perhaps Helen being a little on the hyper side was another one of those differences. Thinking how accurate documented information would be helpful to the situation, Moira began to keep a private diary in addition to her many copious notes. This would be solid documentation of her very many concerns regarding their daughter. Remorseful of having to keep the diary contents to herself she did risk his rebuff and shared it all with Michael. His reactions were as she considered they might be yet hoped they would not be.

Days spent at their local nursery school had found Helen not wanting to engage in group play at all. When offered encouragement to play in a small group, she would remove herself from the group often running around the room, or perhaps back to the comfort and the security of her mother's arms. She stood out from all other children present. She stood out from the crowd. Moira was very aware of those facts and was many times left feeling a little perplexed in those situations. She was aware she would need to make further attempts with Michael. She would have to find ways to get her husband's attention. She had the need to make him focus on their childs differences. She would try persuading him to acknowledge what she was saying without rebuff, without dismissal or the use of humour. Michael was like that. Always being respectful of his wife and child, but always flippant in his response to Moiras concern about their daughter Helen's differences. Moira felt challenged and not for the first time in her life. She recalled herself challenging the experts in regards to the Geary family and being successful in doing so. This was the thought which she needed to hang onto so far as Michael was concerned. If she had been able as a student to challenge people in higher authority, then she was surely able to be more challenging with her husband and the father of their child.

Children of Moira and Michaels friends coming over to the Kearns family home to play, had always brought the same kind of response from Helen. The very same response as that which was experienced in the nursery school and in any noisy environment. Those things combined raised some further concerns for her mother, giving Moira the prompts required to think a little deeper about their daughter. Grabbing herself one of her favourite coffees Moira sat in the kitchen. Staring at the outside world thinking how wonderful nature was, she also thought about how very cruel it could be at times. Was it going to be cruel to them as a family and to their daughter in particular she wondered? She was becoming acutely aware that Helen was different to other children of the same or of similar age. She feared the answer to her question was going to be a resounding yes.

Moiras husband Michael was initially somewhat dismissive of his wife's suggestions, regarding the possibility of their child being different. Still largely holding that view she saw a small crack in his response. It gave her hope. Speaking to him once more about her concerns for their daughter, there was a hint of concern in his voice on this occasion, which despite his denial Moira had clearly picked it up.

"Kids develop at different stages Moira- I'm not concerned. You're doing it again. You're getting very worried for what is absolutely no good reason."

Despite his reassuring words Moira wasn't wholly convinced. Feeling that as yet she had not sufficiently persuaded her husband of the difficulties, she decided she would have to travel down this road alone for a while longer. Remembering how she had earlier thought she didn't know her husband at all, she now felt that perhaps in some ways, that she knew Michael maybe even better than he knew himself. She was quite confused and had caused her own confusion with her thinking. Situations like this one where she had to endure that level of confusion, Moira would wish that she was less analytical, yet she was highly aware how that would never come to pass. Being a person who analysed her life situations was in her nature. It was part of her character and part of her personality. It was part of what made Moira the person she was and still is.

𝓐rranging to have Helen seen by their family doctor she felt would be a very good starting point. Taking in a deep sigh as she shared that information with her husband, Moira got the anticipated response. She knew how he would not approve and could see he was annoyed by the twitch coming from his left eye. The twitch was Michaels landmark and was something which had happened since he was a very young child. It was much to his annoyance that he could not control it. He was aware that it was a strong give-away sign to those who knew him well. However, her husband's feelings or what she actually considered to be his lack of support at that time, were fading deep down into the background of her mind. Michael would need to deal with his own attitude regarding Helen. He would then need to deal with his regrets at some point down the line. Watching him momentarily gave her a surge of pleasure that at least she could see the differences in their child. She was leaving her thoughts about Michael right there at that time. There were other more important things to be dealt with which required her undivided attention.

Moira knew that she had to prioritise their daughter's life regarding her development. She knew she had to follow her own gut instincts. Sitting quietly close to the lavender bush she repeatedly went over things in her head. Feeling she was quite alone in this situation Moira needed to be certain of the way forward. Deciding that If Michael choose to remain in denial then that would have to be his choice, she struggled with her thoughts. Not wanting to take away the burden of his responsibility from him either Moira realised she could not do that even if she had wished to. She reminded herself again how he would then have to live with any consequences which he probably would experience in the future.

Knowing how Michael had adored their daughter she was aware there would be some painful consequences for him, in relation to his denial of their being an issue with their daughter. She reminded herself again how that could never be her problem. Having more than enough in her head to deal with Moira would simply focus on Helen. Deep-down her gut instincts were quite strong. She felt that the day would come, when Michael would have to accept and acknowledge their child was displaying many differences, to that which you might expect for a child of her given age. Knowing how that acceptance would be a bigger struggle for him than it would be for her, she had to prioritise her thoughts and focus on their child. Michael would in the end have to deal with his own thoughts. Again, reminding herself how that could never and should never be her responsibility, Moira was now ready with a clear head to take the next step.

The doctor's surgery was full to almost overflowing. People coughing, sneezing and generally looking as though they had seen better days, surrounded Moira as she approached the reception desk. She thought about how due to there being no windows to open, how the room just had to be a top breeding ground for germs. She was delighted with herself and for her decision not to bring Helen with her to the surgery at that time. Almost deciding to turn around and leave again she reminded herself of the importance of the reason for her being there. She knew that she owed it to Helen to get her the medical attention which she required and deserved. Yes, she would stay. She would take a risk regarding any potential germs which might be floating around in the air. Moira considered how some people totally lacked social manners. Watching children and their adults coughing and sneezing, whilst offering no protection to where their droplets might end up, only served to annoy her further. Temptation for her to express her awful thoughts at that time by sharing some advice was quite strong. Having more than enough stress in her life she resisted. Considering their lack of social manners which she had just seen, Moira was quite aware she would most likely be verbally attacked should she offer her advice.

The middle-aged woman at the desk had appeared to be very grumpy. Moira made that decision from her judgement of the way the woman was speaking to people. She had quite a sullen look on her face too. She was lacking with the charm and charisma which you might expect, from a person whose job was delegated to serving the public. Moira had seen the woman on a few previous occasions. She had often wondered why she had chosen the job of sitting at a doctor's reception desk. Accepting that we all have our off days; this particular person gave the impression that for her, every day was an off day. She was harsh and sarcastic in her tone to Moira. That was not one of her best decisions.

"So, it's you again Mrs Kearns. Well what can we do for you this time with emphasis on the 'this time'?"
Moira was left feeling insulted and was not especially in the mood for the woman's sarcasm. She wasn't having any more of it and fired on both cylinders. Out of character for her she gave some home truths back to the receptionist and then she managed to remain polite in her request.

"Now could you try doing the job which you get paid to do, with maybe a little, no with a lot more dignity and respect for the doctors' patients who by the way are not your patients. Make me an appointment please for my daughter Helen as soon as one is available."

That line of strong self-defence which was not at all typical of Moira Kearns, caused some raised eyebrows in the room, combined with a shocked facial expression on the lady behind the desk. Moira was thinking how she would like to be able to read the woman's mind at that time. She waited patiently, whilst the woman scrolled through what appeared to be *quite a scruffy and disorganised appointment book of some description. Eventually she was given an appointment to bring Helen into the surgery a week the following Tuesday. Wanting to go somewhere towards redeeming herself for her earlier outburst, politely and with a smiling face she thanked the woman. Thinking how some fresh air would not go amiss in the room, she purposefully trapped the entrance door with a magazine, leaving the door wide open as she walked away from the surgery. A quick glance back over her shoulder she saw the door had promptly been closed again. Thinking how some people were their own worst enemies she continued on her journey back home to the farm.*

This would be the fourth visit from Moira to see a doctor with and about their daughter Helen. With much persuasion and some further visits to the doctor's surgery together with their child, she felt how at last she had accomplished something. She recalled from her training days how she had been told that perseverance would always pay off. For her it now had. The diagnostic process had been eventually agreed. Some weeks later their childs appointment letter arrived. Assessments would shortly begin for and on Helen Kearns. It was going to be quite a long and detailed process in which both parents would need to become involved with. At last Moira was experiencing the very sweet taste of success with the doctors and partial success with her husband too. She felt victory was hers as the doctors were taking her serious by now. Her husband, despite there being no acknowledgement from him that there was a problem with Helen, had however allowed himself to become involved in the diagnostic process. He was like it or not forced into looking at the complications of their daughter's life. He was forced into looking at her milestones and at her general age appropriate abilities, or the very lack of them in Helens case.

Weeks later found Michael was not feeling too good about himself. Knowing that as a father he should have been fully immersed in every aspect of their childs life and with total acceptance of all of it, that he should have been supporting Moira at every step of the journey. Still struggling quite a bit, to make a full and open acknowledgement to his wife, that their daughter had problems, he was working on improving himself in that aspect. He was marginally coming around to expressing to Moira, the idea of things not being quite as you might expect them to be for a child of Helens age. Sounding a little flippant as he told her.

"So, I agree you've done the right thing in pursuing this Moira. However, I'm sure we are wrong in our thinking that there's a problem with Helens brain, but better that we have the experts tell us we are wrong which we both know they will do."

Sweat dripped profusely from Moiras hands. She grabbed a towel. She didn't feel too sure of its cause. Placing it into the anxiety Pidgeon hole, she felt would perhaps not be right at that time. She did not feel anxious but perhaps more a sense of relief. At last she was getting her husbands attention where Helen and her potential issues were concerned. There in that statement from him, was her very first glimmer of hope that he was on board her ship. His first-time to ever acknowledge, that he too felt something maybe was not quite right with their daughter's life. It was in his use of the words.

"I'm sure we are wrong" with the emphasis being on we.

*M*ichael in his statement to her had also used the word 'brain.' Moira was conscious that she had never suggested to him that there might be a problem with their daughters' brain. Michael having used the word brain in his response to her, felt like confirmation that he had been thinking about the whole situation. Throughout the weekend she continued to remind herself, how it was a 1st time for Michael ever making any degree of admission in terms of their daughters' differences. She was feeling quite elated and thought about how it was right to feel that way. On the other hand, she questioned her own thinking. Asking herself if thinking their daughter will have a lifelong problem was making her a bad mother, she then quickly dismissed those thoughts. Moira was smart enough to know, that problems need to be addressed in order for solutions to be found. She would then quietly praise herself for being so realistic. Michael surely knew that too. She hoped for some more acceptance and some more progress from him in the coming days and weeks.

*H*aving asked on several occasions for assessments to be done, eventually there they were all three of them sitting in the hospital room. Knowing how someone else was about to confirm that which in her heart Moira did not want to be confirmed, allowed her to see that for them moving forward in life, this official diagnosis could only be for the better good of their child and for the better good of all of them as a family. Having a diagnosis of something or other would not change the person whom Helen was, but would hopefully open up some doors for her as she would go through her many years in education. Despite not wanting to hear any diagnosis from them, my brother has shared with me how he *was feeling just a little relieved too. Being a doctor himself Michael quite rudely interrupted the speaker. Attempting to take over with the diagnosis once their psychologist and doctor had begun, Moira quickly shut him down. Perhaps her interruption was maybe a little on the harsh side for him but it was very necessary. She quickly thought how to that point he had not supported her at all, how he had not made any real acknowledgement of Helens issues. Now here he is in front of the people whose job this is and he's trying to take over. No, she was not about to let that happen. She told him firmly.*

"Can you take the doctor hat off and just be my husband and be Helens father and let the professional people speak and do their job. We need to hear this together Michael."
Apologising to his wife and to other people present, Michael then sat quietly whilst taking hold of his wife's hand. Eventually he shared with everyone in the room, how he was feeling guilty in terms of how he had kept such a closed mind. His tone was very soft. It was gentle and full of compassion as he looked towards his wife.

"I'm so very sorry Moira I should have listened to you. Your persistence has proved to be beneficial. I can truly see that now."
Squeezing his hand gently she too had a soft and gentle tone in her voice.

"It's done. No more needs to be said. We move forward now with a decent plan in place."

$\mathcal{M}$oira had been quite a fast learner. Already having made the good educated guess herself that their daughter was most likely on the autism spectrum, she had been putting quite q few things in place for Helen. Understanding that she

would have to bring their different worlds together was something which she at times found relatively easy. At other times she had found it painfully and profoundly hard. She could at times be heard telling her husband.

  "It's too much Michael I can't do this. My instincts at times are to have the same expectations from Helen, as we would from any other child and it isn't fair to her, because her brain is wired up differently to ours isn't it"
Michael in so many ways was the husband any woman would want. Eventually showing a good degree of acceptance and understanding with compassion, to both the extra needs of their child and the needs of his wife, he pulled her close and hugged her tightly. His voice was kind and soothing.
  "Your quite an amazing woman Moira Kearns. You can do this. We can do this and you know I'm always right here with you. Seriously Moira you are not and we are not, going to get this right all of the time so don't let's beat ourselves up over it."
She acknowledged his compliments, his input and his caring response. At last having her husband's support with their daughter's dilemma, gave her a great sense that things were going to be all right eventually. That together they would give their child the best life which she could possibly hope for. That was their united aim. Moira hoped that it would be their attainment too.

Helen showing gratitude.

*H*elen Kearns was well under two years of age at the point of some further serious decision making in the Kearns family. To the exclusion of her diagnosis of Asperger's syndrome she was quite a healthy little girl. Michael and Moira wanting to give their child a sibling, had decided to go ahead with plans to extend their family some more. Suspecting she would have to wait sometime after removing the contraceptive pill from her daily intake, she was proved wrong. Moira was pregnant with their second child in no time at all. Getting through her pregnancy the second time round, was quite different to the first and was something of rather a tough challenge for Moira. Traditional morning sickness leading up to the usual twelve-week mark was different for her with this pregnancy. It had become an any time of day sickness and had extended almost throughout the whole of the pregnancy.

*U*sing quite an array of pictures to help their daughter Helen better understand what was happening in the family and especially in and with her mother's body, proved a little futile for the Kearns. Helen had experienced tantrum after tantrum in the weeks leading up to the birth. Going back outside to the use of the lavender bush Moira lived in the hope it would calm their daughters' anxieties. Sadly, for everyone involved *that showed itself to be futile too. Knowing there was very little else which they could do, the Kearns parents had to simply wait patiently and hope the baby's arrival might have a calming effect on their first-born child.*

Being able to give birth to their second born child at home, was something which Michael and Moira had dearly hoped for. Feeling fortunate for having had their wish granted and for having a problem free birth, it was an experience in which the parents were able to involve Helen in too. Excited to meet the new addition to the family, Helen stroked the tiny body with some fondness and deep joy. A baby brother for Helen would and was going to bring much happiness to the whole of the Kearns family. She bonded with her brother in a very short time period. The tantrums began to stop as she became mammys little helper. Involving Helen with daily care of the new baby, had been a smart decision and was working well. Moira had continued in her friendship with Frank and Jessica Geary. Having had their children over to play on occasions had been beneficial, in helping see some differences in the children. Their presence was especially beneficial in helping Moira spot some of Helens differences. Another christening was duly planned and subsequently occurred at the Kearns family home.

The small white envelope which popped through their letter box, brought a pleasant smile to the face of Jessica and Frank Geary. Again, they were invited by Michael and Moira Kearns to an event which would be taking place in their home. It was to be the christening of Dominic Kearns. Having opened up the envelope Marissa's mother Jessica informed their children of their family invitation. Seeing excitement on their face she was aware it would be unkind of them not to attend. To Michaels and Moiras delight the Geary family did accept on this occasion. Moira smiled to herself. It was now her opinion that she had achieved making the Geary's feel comfortable in her and Michaels presence. She felt very accomplished in that which had held high importance to her. Dominic's christening day went to plan, with Helen Kearns once again enjoying the company of Marissa Geary and her younger brother.

*W*atching and observing their young son Dominic over the next couple of years, found the Kearns parents not having too much concern. There was nothing about him which Moira or her husband could see, to cause them suspicion of any issues or problems like his sister was and had been enduring. Having been a part of that myself, it always felt like a privilege to be involved in their life's. Spending some time in their farm house out in Enniskerry, once again Moira poured out the tea. Extending her arm towards me she giggled as she handed me the mug.

"Here Martina get this down your neck. Have a scone too or maybe I should say have a rock cake. Trying my best never seems to be enough and I'm never really sure where I'm going wrong. They actually taste all right though. Get your teeth through the outer crust and that's the hardest bit over and done with."

Laughing together we both enjoyed her buttered scones with tea. Having a lot of involvement in the lives of my brother Michael and his wife Moira, I always felt that I too knew Helen pretty well. Struggling to keep herself still at the best of times, I could not help but wonder how she presents herself in the busy and maybe at times chaos of the school classroom.

"It has to be a challenge for the teachers Moira. Imagine the attention and amount of time which she takes away from other children."

Moira enlightened me of the fact that Helen has a classroom assistant, who mingles with others but is always primarily there for Helen.

"It works well Martina. Michaels got his head round it too at last so that's all good."

I was very relieved to hear that my brother was giving his support where required and no longer having his head buried in the sand. I had seriously struggled to understand Michaels resistance and him being a doctor too.

"That's good; it's actually very positive Moira. The more support that child gets the better. It'll make all of your life's easier and perhaps make mine a bit easier too."

Moira did acknowledge the huge input which I had in Helens life through my close association with her and my brother.

"You're a super aunt to her Martina, well to both of the children. Now that we have confirmation showing that Helen is on the autism spectrum, you should be involved in all of the planning for her. Make my job a bit easier and be some good practice and experience for you too."

Being unable to help wondering why my sister-in-law thought I might need practice and experience, I couldn't help but wonder, if she was thinking that Autism was going to run through the family.

"It's not a given you know Moira. If I ever have children they may or may not have serious life challenges. Don't be stressing or thinking about and concerning yourself about that which we don't know."

Confirming to me that my thinking was correct Moira agreed to pay heed to my advice. We laughed as we continued to chat, relax and somewhat unwind in the beautiful sunshine, which the universe had provided to us that morning.

This day at home was not going to be any different for the Kearns family. Their daughter flipped her long red curls across her face. She was in quite a determined frame of mind. Flipping of the hair was almost Helens landmark. She would demonstrate the action when she had seriously wanted to make things happen in her life. Feeling how it might be in her interest, but knowing that perhaps it might not be approved of by her parents or other adults in her life, she would then just hope. She was a very smart child for her age. All of that performance with hair flipping, was ahead of her yet again bounding down the staircase. She was taking the steps two by two, in what was her often robust and very clumsy manner. For Moira that two by two on the stairs despite her disapproval of it, was now reminding her just how much their daughter was like herself in that respect. It had felt to Moira as though history was repeating itself. It gave Moira quite a good insight into how her own parents Padraig and Grace would have felt, when she so often did the stairs two by two action. The vision of their daughter brought her mother out in a cold sweat. Anxiety would have been evident in Moiras voice as she shrieked at their child from the next room.

"*Helen will you slow down please. Use the stairs properly before you break your neck.*"

Moira always remembered her manners when talking to their young daughter. The fact that she was feeling frustrated or angry with their child did not impact on that memory at all. She could often be heard telling her husband.

"We have to teach her Michael. Kids with high functioning autism don't instinctively know how to respond to people. We need to be her teachers and that starts with the very basics of never forgetting our manners when speaking to Helen." Michael was not as attuned to their daughters needs as was his wife, however he was by this point prepared to listen and to be guided. Having some feelings of remorse, regret and some annoyance towards and with himself, he was not going to ever again repeat the behaviour which he had done in the earlier years of Helens life.

"Keep reminding me what I need to be doing Moira. I will forget and don't want to have you feel that you're doing this alone because you're not. I'm right in there with you." Acknowledging his desire to have the very best approach with Helen, Moira assured him that she would give him reminders should they be required.

Hearing her mother's words to slow down being called out, never ever made even the smallest difference to Helen in that type of situation. She had her mind focused and the sooner she got a response to having that need met, the better the situation would be from Helens perspective. This was partially due to her autism and partially due to her strong, somewhat defiant and very determined personality. The child was not and would not be listening to her mother. Helen's only thoughts and her only interests at that moment, were in the birthing cow which she knew was over in the barns at the McGinty's farm. Considering her young age Helen had a very keen interest in the animal kingdom. Tugging hurriedly at her winters coat eventually getting it off the peg, then her wellington boots and pulling them up as she spoke, she was clearly a girl on a mission.

"Mom can I go? I want to see if the calf is here yet!"

Helen was asking for her mother's consent whilst preparing herself at the same time, for a positive response from her mother. From my perspective it would have been interesting, to see how the child may have reacted to a negative response at that point. She mostly addressed Moira as mother. She may be a child with some differences in the way in which her brain is wired up, however she has a very good brain. Helen Kearns was and is smart. Thinking or actually knowing how her mother didn't like to be addressed as mother, she was smart enough to know not to use the word or the title as Helen called it in certain situations. Helen only ever used the word mom, when she was a little unsure of getting her own way with something which she highly desired to do. Moira had clearly made that connection too. She would therefore know that when Helen addressed her as mom, that her childs request was of high importance to her.

Moira was always a very tuned in, very understanding and accommodating mother. Maybe a little too accommodating at times. She had the knowledge that Helen would rarely be on the same wave length as herself and Michael. The woman also had quite a strong determination to fulfil those needs which she felt were important to her. It was very important to Moira, to ensure that Michael was brought around to her way of thinking with consistency, where their daughter was concerned. Feeling how she was already making progress with that task, once again Moira had felt quite accomplished.

*T*he McGinty family had known and been friends with the Kearns family for quite a few years. Their mutual feelings on that was more like, they had known each other for what had felt like an eternity. Flinging her arms in the air in a sort of 'whatever' type of gesture Moira put her childs mind at ease. Telling her that as they hadn't been there for a while that she felt how they were well overdue for a visit.

"C'mon then we can go together it'll be fun."
Pulling up her own wellington boots Moira then grabbed her daughters' hand with a good degree of gusto as she told her.

"Once outside I'll let go then I'll race you to the river. Can't have you getting a head start by running ahead when it's a race. This way we both have an equal and fair chance."

*S*etting off across the sludge laden field eventually getting to the river, Helen was first to get there. That was all in her mother's plan. Hoping the race would burn off some energy for her child she was left feeling quite disappointed. Moira quietly cursed at herself. She was aware that she should have known better than to have had that expectation. She was very aware that whilst children who are naturally hyper and become agitated quite easily, do generally speaking become tired out gaining some benefits from exercise. This had never appeared to be the case for Helen. She could and often did exercise for hours outdoors in the fresh air, running through fields or relentlessly trying to do some hand stands. That huge output of energy for Helen never made much of a difference to her overall energy levels. Struggling to settle to sleep almost on a nightly basis was common place for her. At times the childs parents had felt as though they were *becoming almost exasperated. They were often quite close to the edge of exhaustion and felt that Helen must be too.*

Having arrived over at the McGinty's farm and at the cow barns, Helen had a smile beaming from ear to ear across her face. Intermittent almost grunting like sounds coming out from the barn told her they were in luck. That there was still time before the cow gave birth. Helen jumped up and down in the air calling out to her mother. Her expressions were beyond joyful as she heard and saw that the cow was still in calf. Calling out to John McGinty in her sweet and at that time almost angelic sounding voice, Helen wondered if she could stay in the barn together with him.

"I'd love to see the calf being born. I've seen it happen on television but never in real life."

Initially feeling maybe a little dubious, Moira Kearns and John McGinty eventually both agreed that the child could stay. Deciding between them what a forward and curious little girl Helen was for her age, caused her mother to smile. Helen was coming up to five years. Pride in their daughter Helen showed itself from the glow in her mother's face. Both Moira and John McGinty were feeling quietly confident, that Helen would easily deal with the sight of any blood which might present itself. John promptly and gently took the childs hand leading her into the barn and down to where the cow was laying. With his rough and rugged Irish voice he told her.

"Come on then miss Kearns let's see what's happening down here."

John McGinty was a nice man who had raised a family of his own. He liked children. He enjoyed feeding their curiosity in whichever way a situation was presented to him. Meeting the need and helping to feed the curiosity of Helen Kearns on that occasion gave John the feeling of a job very well done.

Going inside the farm house Moira and Eileen McGinty put the world to rights. Both ladies being very sociable with an insatiable appetite for memories of times gone by, they pulled up two chairs by the fire. That's where and when they reminisced. Moiras eyes opened wide as the tray was brought in from the kitchen by one of the McGinty's teenage children. Refreshments were there on the tray in abundance as was always the case in both of their farm homes. Both ladies had kept up with some of the old fashioned traditional Irish ways in the kitchen. Soda bread baked on the open turf fire by Eileen McGinty, containing fruit and treacle and saturated with home-made butter, was served with some piping hot tea. Very many other Irish traditions had also been upheld by both of those families. That the old traditions would be enjoyed by their children, was their wish and their hope for many generations to come.

Moira was remembering the day when their daughter was given the diagnosis of Asperger's syndrome. Speaking about it at length and with some passion in her voice she told her good friend Eileen.

"Feels like a lifetime ago now Eileen. So much time was wasted while I fought the system for Helen and in some ways, I had to fight Michael too, in order to get us there to that day of her diagnosis."
Eileen could sense some degree of anger, almost like a taste of bitterness in Moiras voice. Wanting to console her friend a little, she was quick to jump in with some praise for the man whom she knew Michael to be.

"Men can find it incredibly hard to accept certain situations Moira and furthermore to acknowledge them to others. Don't be too hard on him- please."

Appreciating her friends' comments and her wisdom Moira thanked her for her sense of caring too. She continued to share with Eileen McGinty, how she and my brother had felt on some levels as though they were in the pits of despair that day. Upon hearing those words from the specialist doctor she didn't especially want to have acceptance. Moira shared how she in particular was at times very confused by her own mixed feelings. She shared with Eileen, how on the one hand she had felt totally devastated hearing their childs diagnosis. On the other hand she had such a strong sense of relief, from knowing that at last someone else had seen in their child, that which she could see and had done so for such a very long period of time. She relived with Eileen McGinty, how Michael had become absorbed in the clinical aspects of the diagnosis, wanting to take over with some explanations from the specialist doctor. The women laughed. Both knowing that she would bring him into line as Moira so very clearly had done.

Eileen McGinty had held a first-class degree in psychology.

She was therefore able to draw on her own learning, in her attempt to support her friend with her thoughts. She was able to give assurance to Moira that her way of thinking was perfectly normal and to be expected. Eileen shared that quite a large volume of parents and perhaps more so mothers who were very tuned in to their child, would experience that sense of relief and then look to redress themselves for thinking that way. Sipping on her sweet tea Moira smiled, as she once again thanked her friend Eileen for her words of wisdom.

"You're looking in through educated eyes Eileen. I needed that bit of reassurance. Thanks again."
Moira too holds a first-class degree in psychology. Adding to her confusion were the facts, that she was not able to apply her knowledge from that learning to herself, in that situation around Helen. Eileen was able to offer her some support in that thinking too. She used many examples which she knew Moira was familiar with and that she would understand. The ladies embraced, with Eileen wanting to ensure that her friend did not feel inadequate in any way. Reminding her how.

"It's all about you this time Moira. Do remember the many times our chats have been all about me, so it's give and take. We 're always good for each other."

"Thanks Eileen and I know your right. Dam it your always right."
The ladies laughed some more.

Dominic Kearns was just under 2 years of age at the point of his sister's eventual diagnosis of autism. Comparing their children when she knew that she shouldn't, had been another tool in Moiras arsenal to highlight to them, some ways in which their daughter was different. Moira as we know had known from when Helen was around the age of nine months, that something wasn't quite right with their child. Not wrong with her either just different. She at times recalled in her own private thoughts, the feelings of intense disappointment she had felt towards her husband, throughout his long period of denial regarding Helens issues. Eileen was feeling curious.

"You're in deep thought Moira a Penny for them as the saying goes. She laughed."

Feeling it would be wrong and perhaps unfair to share her negative thoughts about Michael, Moira instead produced a large ear to ear smile.

"Nothing serious Eileen just visions of what might be going on at home at the minute."

Eileen – Wondering how young Dominic might be getting

on at home with his father, hoped the response was going to be a good one. She was not disappointed. Moira was quite confident in her response.

"I'm sure it'll all be good Eileen but perhaps maybe a bit of a challenge at the same time. Michaels really good with the children but you know how they can be and often are at this age."

She felt proud of herself for burying the negative regarding Michaels parenting of Helen. Moira continued to share that due to the child being just two years of age, he was at a point in life where everything which could be climbed onto would be climbed onto. She shared with Eileen how her son's curiosity was also typical for his age and how it knew no bounds. Both ladies acknowledging the positives in that, they equally felt how Michael would certainly have had his hands full that day. Eileen had her own views and openly shared them.

"Working in clinic and on the wards is a world which he is used to Moira. A world where staff respect his authority and behave accordingly. Dominic being a two-year-old child will certainly show his father another side of life. A side which he's maybe not all that familiar with."

The women laughed.

*H*earing how Dominic could be and often was quite hard work, yet he could be easier to manage in some ways than was his older sister, was not surprising information for Eileen McGinty. Remembering some tales from when their own children were around that age she shared those with Moira. Helen came running back and into the house at some speed. Interrupting conversation between the two ladies she called out for her mom. She was clearly feeling very excited as she told the women.

"It's here mom the calf's been born and it's all yucky and slimy looking and it's standing up. Come on come and see it quick before it lies down again."

Tugging at her mother's arm she got Moira into an upright position by almost dragging her from the chair.

"All right Helen calm down. We'll be there in a minute."

*W*alking over to the barn together to welcome the new life into the world, Moira wondered about their daughters' thoughts of what she had just witnessed. The situation lent itself to Eileen and Moira, thinking about new life in general and how fascinating the whole procedure of that birthing event is. Drawing some comparison between humans giving birth and the animal kingdom giving birth, the women could see very many differences. They expressed their gratitude for having pain relief readily available to the human world. They wondered about degrees and severity of pain in the animal kingdom and especially so for cows, as that had just been an experience for all of them. Seeing and watching the new calf in all of its glory, the women were feeling almost as joyful and as fascinated as Helen had been. Eileen and Moira returned back to the McGinty's farm house. Everyone had *agreed to leave Helen there in the barn with John McGinty. She was a young child who as we know had possessed an immense desire to be helpful to people, with a curiosity to match. She would help John do some odd jobs in the barns whilst the new calf got to know and suckled on its mother. Helen was enthusiastic in her tone as she shouted out to John.*

"I'm good at sweeping up I sometimes help my mom sweep the kitchen floor."

Johns smile spread across his face as he accepted the childs gesture. Having been impressed by Helens sense of eagerness to help and her insight to what she had considered to be her strength he smiled to himself. Visions of her sweeping up and mucking out in the barns, he considered was going to be just very slightly different to her sweeping up the kitchen floor. He placed a small broom with quite a short handle in the childs hand. It was one which his own children had some times used in the barns when they were growing up. Being a hoarder over many years was proving itself to be very useful to John McGinty at that time. Having had a small collection of barn tools in the loft overhead, he had brought down that broom with the short handle. John had often told himself that things just might come in useful one day. The broom was now proof of that theory to him.

Time upon them for Moira and her daughter to return back home, they each said their goodbyes to Eileen and John McGinty. Organising her own life as she had quite often tried to do, John had accepted the childs request for her to return back to see the calf the following day. That he told her would be pending her mother's agreement too. To Helen's joy and delight, she knew that her mother's smile was a consenting one. Helen held her mom's hand all the way home. It felt as though her curiosity had at least been satisfied for now and that maybe her hyper active mind had calmed down a little too. That might hopefully be good news for Michael and Moira in terms of them getting her settled to sleep that night.

Being a Saturday Michael would have been home all day.

Working week for him at the local hospital was Monday to Friday. Being very talented in the kitchen he would often use cooking as a form of relaxation. This Saturday was one of those days. Upon their approach to the front door Moira and Helen were filled with surprise. Air outside of their farm house gates, was saturated by the aroma of curry coming from their home. All of the Kearns family loved chicken curry and the hotter the better for the adults. Michael had made two of which one was a somewhat milder version for their children. Helen has on occasions expressed her appreciation to her parents, which in some ways has surprised me. This was one of those occasions. She pleased both of her parents with her sincere comment. Given her young age it was a good show of maturity and respect for her parents too.

"That smells great dad. I'm starving too."
Taking the compliment and wanting to know how the time at McGinty's had been, Michael checked in with the ladies in his life. Hearing about the birthing cow with all of the gruesome details, he wondered if perhaps his timing to ask the question could have been better.

"Sounds like it all went well then Helen. Dinners on the table now."
I'm thinking of what a great husband my brother is. I'm wondering where I went wrong in life to be in the marriage

which I have chosen. This story however is not about me so back to the Kearns.

Deceit in its lowest form

It was quite late summer time and what a good one it had been. To say it always rains in Ireland that theory had been blown right out of the water. Some might say how it now felt and looked more like autumn outside. Leaves changing their colours with many already on the ground it was an absolute scene of natural beauty. Having entered some photographic competition at school, Dominic was snapping away with the camera. Having entered previous competitions at the local youth centre and never with a win, he continued to pursue his hobby. He liked and was quite good at photography.

The Kearns family loved the many changes which had been brought about by the different seasons. In many ways they had held a huge advantage given to them from the fact they were living in the countryside. Helen and her brother Dominic both being older now, had good understanding of many of the implications of the changing seasons. Helen was often concerned there would be some confusion for wildlife. She loved wildlife as did the whole of the Kearns family. The children could at times be found arguing over who was taking the best care of their wildlife garden. Moira still retaining the lavender tree had given up quite a chunk of the garden to their children. Often being in the position of peacemaker she could be heard loudly trying to negotiate with them. That would be on occasions when the children wanted different things in their parts of the garden. On those occasions their mother would become the peacemaker, in what at times had almost become a psychical fight between the two of them.

"Yes, all right Dominic you can have a pond. You can have frogs. I don't want to see or hear that they are being taken out of the pond and it'll be your responsibility to look after it. You change the water you keep it clean and you don't try to involve your sister, or bring the frogs anywhere near her or near her part of the garden."

He was nodding in approval and acceptance of what she was saying. Moira was not sure that she was convinced of his sincerity. A slight raise in her tone would hopefully do it.

"Hope your listening Dominic. This will be a one chance only situation. You break the rule then the pond goes as will any and all occupants of it."

Considering she had been very clear with Dominic about the pond rules and about all agreements reached between him and his mother, she could only hope he would respect all which she had said. He would take the consequences if he didn't. Young Dominic collected all which he might need and then set about building the pond. Waiting patiently for the weekend, he desperately hoped his father might take him to the local reptile rescue centre. Having heard from school friends that they had an abundance of frogs at the centre, he thought how he might be allowed two or maybe three if his pond was large enough to accommodate that many.

His sister Helen hoped to create an area for wild birds and for some squirrels too. Moira and Michael agreed to the bird area, however they had some very strong reservations about attracting squirrels. Moira tried to explain the best way she could in fairly simplified terms.

"Yes, squirrels can be and often are very cute looking Helen. They can be very dangerous too though. Sometimes getting into the loft space in a house they can and have been known to cause untold damage."
Helen being her usual self she was not yet ready to give up the fight.
"But mom"
"Never mind but mom you need to listen to me young lady. Squirrels chew up electric cables. That creates a big expense for the home owner. That's why you cannot have an area or anything which might attract them to come in close proximity to the house. Hope you've got that and bring this chat to an end."

*W*ishing that she had left the 'close proximity to the house' words out of the conversation, Moira felt quite annoyed with herself. Knowing their daughter so well she knew that Helen would do what she needed to do in order to get her own way. Those words could be and perhaps would be used by Helen to manipulate her situation. Deciding to give more clarity Moira told their child.

"When I say close proximity to the house Helen what I precisely mean is, that squirrels are not to be encouraged anywhere in our gardens, neither front nor back. I hope that I've made myself clear."

*U*nderstanding and agreeing that yes it was clear, yet not wanting to accept what her mother had said, she did agree to abide by it. Having a ten-minute sulk in the kitchen and then in her attempt to make Moira feel like a bad parent, the child *explained her new plan to her mom. Being not especially or overly happy about it, Helen had agreed to create her bird attraction area, away from the hedges and away from all of the bushes. Helen reminded her mother, that there was no cause to tell her to keep away from Dominic's project and the obvious reason why, which was her immense dislike for frogs. Helen then in her own usual bossy way, reminded her brother Dominic to keep well away from what was going to be her bird project. Another argument almost ensued at that time between the Kearns children. Sending them both to their rooms for the time being, Moira wondered if she had made the right decision about the garden projects at all. Wrapping a coat across her shoulders to keep the evenings chill away, Moira then took herself outside to sit close to her lavender bush. Breathing in breathing out she quickly felt better. She was once again, ready to face the wrath of what ever their children might have to throw at her or throw at each other. That would be in the argumentative sense and not ever in the psychical sense.*

Morning began in the same fashion as it did on so many other mornings in the Kearns household. Feeling as though it was maybe a little bit on the chaotic side, Moira drew in a very heavy sigh. She did not deal with the growing chaos too well at all. With almost everything having its own place yet hardly anything in its place, was causing Moira to once again have some feelings of quite deep frustration. Dominic Kearns just like his older sister, possessed a life attitude that perhaps on some levels matched the condition of his mind too. Life to both him and his sister Helen was very precious as was their time. From a very young age they had both shown quite a strong appreciation of planning ahead and the benefits which that would and often did bring to their days for them. Time on their minds was for socialising, for their pleasure and for their enjoyment. That would be in the absence of much of a concern for your personal surroundings, or any chaos which might ensue from that. Having very little to no perception of how their chaotic ways were impacting on their mother, the Kearns children both continued in what you might describe as behaviour fairly typical of teenagers.

𝓐 very deep sigh was heard coming from the kitchen. As was pretty common place in their house it was from Moira. Promptly taking herself outside she sat on a tiny bench which was sited in close proximity to their large lavender plot. She buried her head in her hands and sobbed quietly. Quickly regaining her composure, she wiped the tears from her eyes. Moira loved the scent from their lavender bushes and had a great appreciation for its relaxation qualities too. She gave some thinking time to her dilemma. She wondered if there would be anything which could help her to lessen those awful feelings of annoyance with their children. If there was to be anything to do that job, Moira decided that this place in their garden would have to be it. Time spent close to the lavender bushes did immensely calm down her feelings of deep intense frustration. It however could not change her thinking process. She was more that aware that only she could ever do that.

𝓜oira holding or sharing the same view as their children or her husband, when it came down to their surroundings, she knew was something which was never going to happen. She had choices to make. She would deal with the chaos herself so giving the unspoken message to the children, that it was all right to be so disorganised and so untidy. Her second and in my view her better choice would be, that she would call the children to the kitchen to clean up their chaotic mess. Moira would know from past experience that should she call them with that instruction, that she would then have to deal with the potential arguments, which often have and would most likely again ensue from her instructing them to clean up.

Helen and Dominic would always be very quick to blame the other. The scene could get quite tense and often did so. That would usually be very much to the annoyance of their mother. Being a lady who had quite an organised mind, she constantly did battle with the chaos which their children had presented to them on quite a regular basis. Her husband was more laid back about the home situation. Sitting comfortably on the sofa in the midst of it all, with music playing softly in the background he could be heard telling her.

"Stop stressing Moira it's a bit of mess. It's our home not a show house."

Knowing the wisdom of his words and wishing she could think more like him where the home was concerned, Moira usually failed miserably. She often quietly wondered if maybe she too was on the spectrum. That possibility would certainly answer some questions for her. It would account for her lack of patience with the disorder of things and for her dislike of raised voices and noisy environments. Acceptance of her own raised voice at times felt like a conundrum to Moira. Keeping her thoughts secretively to herself she almost snapped at her husband in her response.

"I can't Michael it's not in my nature and you should know that. I like things to be organised. I need organisation in my

life and in our home. The kids have got to get that into their heads but how and when?"
Outstretching his arms towards her with quite a wide and delightful smile, Moira was responsive. She appreciated his gesture and his words. He spoke to her with compassion in his voice.
   "There that's a little better I hope."

Thinking how fortunate she was, being married to what was a very decent man with great kids, Moira went right ahead and shared those thoughts with her husband. She would then use those thoughts, in an attempt to try to put their chaotic living arrangement into some sort of perspective in her mind. Reminding herself that Michael was right, she would speak to the children again with some gentle reminders, instead of the usual banter she might have with them regards their levels of mess and untidiness. Being aware of the huge challenge she was setting for herself in doing that, Moira felt she would be successful in overcoming it. Then questioning herself again regarding why should she change the way she sees things, she answered her question without delay. She would not change. She should not change. She was trying to raise their children in a positive manner and would continue to do so.

Moira had a very strong sense of pride in her ability to achieve with a determination to match. She promised herself that she would not let herself down. On that occasion she was successful. On many others she failed miserably. She had a wonderful life ethos and a wonderful idea to share with their children. Deciding that when we want something in this life we earn it, she called Helen and Dominic to the kitchen table. That's where the deal was done. They want to be given a certain degree of responsibility for garden projects, then they first show their levels of responsibility, by not creating chaos within the home and then blaming each other when confronted about it. That was it. That was the deal. The frogs and the bird's area were temporarily put back on hold. Two weeks of compliance in the house then it could be and would be all systems go. It was all agreed and not to be negotiable. Let the house situation deteriorate again and they each lose their garden privilege. Moira had always been consistent with their children in every area of their life's. Dominic and Helen knew their mother well. Whilst not feeling overly happy with the new plans, they knew their mother well enough to know that she meant what she said.

The Kearns family home was quite old. Moira had been told by her cousin Alice, how it had stood there for almost three hundred years. At times Moiras thoughts wandered back to that weekend when she was a young woman and her visit out to Enniskerry. Her absolute shock to hear from Alice about the cancer and about her own inheritance of the house and farm land. All those years later the whole situation at times felt very surreal to Moira. She wondered what Alice would make of the chaos, which her children were often creating in the house. Hoping that she would be able to understand and relate to the situation, it still gave Moira concern. Making her mind up to speak to her mother she did that.

"You knew Alice pretty well mom. Would she be very upset to see the level of chaos which the kids create and then walk away from it?"
Grace hugged their daughter. She could tell she was feeling very distressed. She gave her some reassurance.

"No Moira Alice was not an especially tidy person herself. She hoped that you would care for the overall structure of the house and that's exactly what you and Michael have done and continue to do. That house will still be standing a few hundred years or so from now. Will it still be in the family is completely a different story."
Taking solace from her mother's words she thanked her for her insight.
"That's all good then. Knowing its only me who is upset and distressed by their behaviour, makes the whole scenario so much easier to deal with. I hope it stays in this family for many hundreds of years to come. Thanks Mom."

Michael and Moira Kearns had lived in that farm house since their wedding day back in 1985. Being modernised yet holding onto some of the characters of an old house, it had much to offer to the modern family. Having gained it as her inheritance as a very young woman, from a very rich and generous cousin to her mother, Moira had dealt with her inheritance admirably. She clearly had quite a mature head on her shoulders, with no desire to squander all of which had become hers at that very young age. She was at this point in life reaping many rewards from that financial maturity. The farm house and farmland comprised of almost ten acres of land. There were four small fields which were used for cattle grazing by their neighbours. There were a couple of medium sized areas put down to arable farming by Michael and his wife Moira. That is where sufficient potato crops were grown together with many other varieties of vegetables.

Helen and Dominic had shown quite a keen interest in the organic growing of vegetables. Often going there to offer *help with planting digging and picking of their crops, their parents appreciated that support. There would always be sufficient quantities being harvested to meet the needs of their own family plus their extended families. Occassionaly there would be surplus to the extended family requirements. That's when the Kearns would send their left over produce to the local shop. Neighbours would be delighted to make their purchase in the knowledge it was all locally sourced. Life for Michael and Moira Kearns was feeling pretty good. They were pretty much settled. Life out in Enniskerry was relatively good. That was the overall situation from Moiras perspective.*

Sunshine came beaming down through some tree branches.

Those mature trees had to be more than one hundred years old. Neighbours had occasionally grumbled about their height with some at times demanding their removal. Standing proud at the back of the farm house the trees provided shelter from the elements. Michael and Moira could not imagine their grounds without them. The children appreciated their value too. Being overall peaceful, friendly and sociable people, the couple attempted to liaise with their neighbours. Living in the hopes of educating them that the trees would be of benefit to everyone in the area, they had a very good degree of success. Securing protection of their properties in inclement weather conditions, was one amongst many other positive reasons for keeping the trees. The Kearns being such nice people, their neighbours found it quite hard to continue, with what they had eventually considered to be their unrealistic protests and unrealistic demands. Michael was very forthcoming with his views.

   "Another achievement for us Moira. Well for you really as you're the one who did most of the hard work with the

neighbours. My mind was already made up to keep the trees, regardless of local opinion. You made it all happen with their blessings."
Acknowledging her husband's praise she reminded him how fortunate they are as a family.

Michael and Moira were woken once again by the sound of birds tweeting outside of their bedroom window. It was quite a delightful picture to see how many birds would congregate around their family home. Winter times especially had brought many migrating birds to their windows and to the ledge which Moira and Michael together had purposefully built for them. Being a man with quite a good heart Michael Kearns could often be heard telling his wife, what immense pleasure it gave him to know he was providing breakfast and whatever other meals they had wished for, to the birds and whichever wildlife that may otherwise have gone hungry. Having set the coffee pot the previous evening it would then be ready for their arrival down into the kitchen by 6'o clock sharp in the morning. Michael and Moira were always early and good risers. They were very prompt on a daily basis.

There were many chores to be done in preparation for the day, ahead of their children joining them downstairs. Always feeling important to Moira that the chores would be done without the children's presence, she would tell her husband.

 "It's the only way I can get through the jobs Michael. I'm always struggling to cope when they're under my feet and despite them being older now I can't help still feeling that way. I think there's just more of them now and they're not especially helpful. It's as simple as that."

Michael was as was usual for him, very understanding of her way of thinking without expressing himself too much.

"There's your coffee Moira. Let's just use this hour to its very best advantage then."

Smiling, she wrapped her arms round his shoulders. Placing a soft and gentle kiss on his cheek, she knew that her husband was aware, that was her way of showing her gratitude to him for his never-ending show of understanding. Often secretly thinking that when they made Michael they broke the mould, but as she had no desire for him to get above his station, she decided how that would remain to be her private thought.

Michael was and always had been the calming influence in their marriage, especially where the children and their poor behaviours were concerned. Moira had quite often showed her appreciation to him for that. She appreciated how he could with not too much difficulty, persuade her to overlook many things she otherwise might and perhaps would and at times she did get stressed about. Michael set off as usual for work shortly after 7am. The journey to school for Moira and the children was usually a happy one, with the children now expressing their eagerness for the school holidays which were pretty imminent. Helen was forthcoming and much louder and more excited than was Dominic her younger brother. Moira did not relish the idea of the school holidays being imminent, in the same way as did their children. Having Helen constantly pecking in her ear sent her blood pressure rising. The child was using her sweetest voice hoping that would bring her the response she wished for.

"I saw the holiday books in your bedroom mom. Are we going on holiday soon?"

Not giving her mother opportunity to respond the child was hurriedly and excitedly asking again.

"Well, are we? I hope we are. I want to go in holiday. Jenny told me that she is going and Catherine said that they're going and everyone else is going. I want to go too."

Being almost 10 years of age, you might expect that Helen would have a better degree of self-control. She didn't! Persisting with her questions and time quickly running out for them to get through the school doors, the children went into their classrooms without Helen having any answers to her many questions, including the one about holidays. Moira thought about how much time was often wasted between herself and Helen, with Helen firing question after question with no real opportunity given, for a proper and fully informative response from her mom. Moira at times had secretly wished that her own and Michaels roles could be reversed. She wished that her husband was doing the school run. Yes, she quietly thought about how it would no longer be a secret. She would have a conversation with him. Persuade him how he would know how to handle everything being fired at him. Persuade him how he was so very good like that. Tell him how he would need to reschedule his working hours, to make himself available for the school run. She had it all planned out in her head.

Feeling very inadequate and almost leaning a little on the side of hopelessness, Moira felt as though she wanted to cry. She didn't like feeling that way. Kissing their children on the cheek she waved them off from the school gate.

"Go straight to class no messing around and see you both this evening."

Helen was still trying to pursue the conversation whilst being tugged along by her younger brother Dominic. At age almost seven and a half years Dominic Kearns was so much quieter and calmer than his sister. Despite him being a full two years below Helen at school, teaching staff on occasions would call upon him to utilize his calming impact on his sister.

"Helens so hyper today Dominic would you be a love and sit with her for ten minutes?"

Being almost like a mentor for Helen at times had made Dominic feel very special. Always happy to oblige when asked to do so, the siblings would sit reading together in a very small and quiet area close to the school office. Moira could and at times did draw some degree of solace, from the knowledge that teaching staff had also found Helens behaviour quite a challenge at times. Consoling herself with the thoughts that so many teaching staff are trained, in methods and ways of dealing with kids who present difficult behaviours and yet they struggle, she allowed those thoughts to raise her spirits a little.

Feeling somewhat less inadequate than she otherwise may have done, she took in a deep breath whilst she relished that feeling. Her lack of ability to always be able to deal with their daughter was having quite a significant impact on her health. Once back home Moira got on with her chores. Utilising her time to batch bake and batch cook she felt would relieve some pressure, on the days when she would be feeling less adequate. Yes, Moira had a good reality check on everything including herself. She was aware that there would perhaps be many more of those awful days, where she would experience feelings of inadequacy. Baking smells from the kitchen had created an appetising aroma throughout the whole of the house. She knew this would be welcoming to their children. Moira hoped for a quieter time that evening with fewer questions from their daughter. She was disappointed yet again.

Travelling into Dublin City from Enniskerry had always been something which the Kearns children looked forward to and enjoyed. Helen especially often had her own requests.

"Can we visit the wax museum mom. We all like it in there and especially like the house of horrors."
Not having been to the museum for more than a year the family agreed to have it on the agenda. Michael appeared to be especially keen.

"I'm sure it'll be updated since the last time we were there Moira so yep let's do it."
The museum visit combined with an evening meal at The Elephant and Castle restaurant in Temple Bar, rounded off the day very nicely for the whole family. Everyone was by now feeling relaxed and contented. Moira especially with her feelings of inadequacy from time to time, was very relaxed indeed. She thought how good life could be and was when she allowed it to be.

Peace and tranquillity of their home place, was balanced against the hustle bustle of such a large city as Dublin. They felt blessed through having both of those experiences to choose from in their lives. Having some colleagues and friends who were living in the suburbs of Dublin city felt like a great convenience. That was especially so for Michael. Being not too far from his place of work he would on occasional weekends, go to those colleagues or friends' homes as opposed to going back to his home in Enniskerry. Always calling Moira on those occasions Michael would remind her of his very busy work schedule.

"Always something to do and something new to learn Moira. You know how it goes from your own working days. I'll be home Sunday; Probably late afternoon."

He would end the call without hesitation or any opportunity availed to her, for her to be able to mention school life or home and family life. The feeling to her was almost one of him having no interest in what was happening at home.

Moira was a very genuine and fair type of person who did not especially like or want confrontation, however she was no pushover either. She would always once he was home express her thoughts to Michael, about him staying at a colleague's home over the weekends when free from work. His defence would usually be how they were each enhancing each other's medical skills. She wasn't altogether convinced. The thoughts of her husband having an affair had crept into her mind. She would then generally talk to herself, with reminders of how analytic she could be and often was of many life situations. She would often discover how her analysis was very wrong with a self-promise not to go there again. That was definitely something Moira Kearns failed to achieve. If it could be analysed it for sure would be analysed.

Another Weekend upon them and Michael had stayed away from home once again. Dominic and Helen were settled at a friends' home for an hour or two. Moira was by this point feeling almost abandoned by her husband. She paid a visit to her friend Eileen McGinty over at the McGinty's farm. Eileen just like Moira was very intuitive. Wrapping her arms around Moira the woman told her.

"Come on Moira I know you're troubled about something. Is it Helen? Spit it out. You want tea or should we walk?" Deciding to walk first the women then went to sit by the river. Watching the water as it flowed in and out between the large stones Moira thought about her marriage. Weather being good to them made everything seem and feel just a little bit nicer. Thinking how this was perhaps a good time to share her worries with her friend, Moira blurted out her innermost thoughts.

"He's up to something Eileen. Michael is up to something and I don't like the idea or the thought of my suspicions." Hearing from her friend how things have not been great at home between them recently Eileen too became suspicious. Hearing how that level of tension combined with his absence from home some weekends, Eileen was now quick to give her opinion. Her opinion had not been requested but she would offer it anyhow.

"He's having an affair Moira. I just know it. He has to be. All the signs are there and they're pretty clear to me. He offers you some pathetic reason for his absence and expects you to believe it."
Accepting her friend's opinion Moira sought out some further guidance, on what might be the best way to handle their situation. Eileen was clear with her advice.

"Confront him directly Moira when he gets home. You're a smart woman and it seems to me that he has lost sight of that fact. Let him know that you're not stupid and that you're not naive."

*H*earing the words from her friend which she had herself already guessed to be the truth, reduced Moira Kearns to tears. The lady's embraced. Eileen continued with her words of wisdom and support. Encouraging Moira to be brave she told her.

"Listen lady you've dealt with lots more than this in your life time. You will deal with this too. It's fine to have a few tears but now you wipe them away and you get your plan of action in place. You fight fire with fire and nothing less." Knowing her friends' words made sense Moira smiled.

"Your right I do need to confront him and I will."
The women embraced once more with Eileen then reminding them both it was time for her to return home. Hoping that if the children had returned home early, as they sometimes did, that they would have kept out of each other's way in her absence. She wasn't sure they would. Moira hurriedly made her way back across the fields to their farm house. Helen and Dominic were both home earlier than expected. Catching up on some homework they both appeared to be well on Moiras return back to the house.

*P*artially agreeing with her friends' sentiments, Moira knew she had quite a way to go in her mind, before she would be ready for that confrontation with her husband. Despite her agreeing with her friend Eileen in the moment, Moira was now having second thoughts. She was very aware that there were some other ways in which she could check out Michaels story. Grasping an opportunity to Pick up his phone with an impromptu decision to sneak a look at its content, she very promptly put that idea out of her head. Knowing how checking out his phone would have been one option open to *her, she put it back down quickly resisting that temptation. She had always held the view that honesty and trust had to be imperative at all times and in all relationships. Checking out his phone she had felt, would then be bringing her down to another level. That would be a level which Moira had decided she did not wish to drop to.*

Needing to hear some confirmation of her suspicions direct from Michael himself, Moira decided that she would confront him at the next available opportunity. Yes, despite not really wanting to know the answer she was not prepared either to continue allowing him to think of her as a fool. Moira sat in the garden head buried in her hands. Thoughts of the loving, caring man whom she had married consumed her. Thoughts of where he was in his head now also consumed her. Deciding that the Michael she had met, had known and loved was now gone, she did not like the person who had replaced him. She would ask him the direct question. Looking back over the few previous weeks and months, Moira managed to recollect quite a few unpleasant scenarios, which had been occurring at home between herself and her husband. Michaels temperament was not to be confrontational in the general manner or sense.

Those unpleasant times she was recalling had all been created by him. It was all starting to make sense to Moira now. Just a little bit like a jigsaw puzzle everything was starting to fit into place. Being very occupied with their children's life's over the last months, she had taken her eye off the ball where their marriage was concerned. He had clearly taken advantage of that fact. Struggling to see what it was, which might have caused Michael to become so distant to her, Moira couldn't find any real answers other than he was having an affair. Someone at the work place had probably taken his attention and she would have to hear that news from her husband. Sweating palms had visited her life once more. Having a lifetime of their association with her deep anxiety she knew what to do. Leaving their children home alone Moira wrapped up well. She went down to the river. Water slowly running over the small rocks were now in competition with the water running down her face. She got it all out. All of her anger and her disappointment in the current state of their marriage was screamed out where no one could hear. She had made her mind up. She was now emotionally in a stronger place and ready to challenge her husband on his arrival home that day.

Returning back home late that Sunday afternoon, Michael was once again quite distant towards his wife and somewhat distant towards their children too. On this occasion she was ready and prepared to make some observations. Moira was aware of and did notice his coldness, towards herself and towards their children like she never had done on previous occasions. Calling her husband to the kitchen and being a woman of her word, she told Michael she needs to hear the truth. That she no longer believes his stories about studying together with colleagues, regarding new aspects of ear nose and throat surgery. A sense of relief washed over her in the knowledge that now at last she was going to hopefully hear the truth.

Blood appeared to instantly drain away from Michaels face. He turned almost pure white and was quite grim looking. Beginning to lie to her again he then quickly changed his mind. Moira was not as swell prepared as she had earlier anticipated herself to be. Seriously who would be properly prepared for what she heard next. Muttering the painful words quietly almost under his breath he devastated his wife. Feeling quite stunned Moira thought about the young man, whom she had met in a hospital conference room so many years ago. How they had fallen in love to never be apart. Here they are now and she wants to be in disbelief. Thinking of how she had adored him for many years and thought he had adored her too, yet he had now ripped her life apart. Where had her judgement of character gone? Why didn't she read the signs better?

Stopping the questioning and the awful blaming of herself seemed like a sensible plan. So many thoughts running like a marathon in her head she tried to calm herself down. Not wishing for their children to see the sadness and distress on her face, Moira promptly took herself outside to the garden and to the lavender bush. This was the bush which over the years had become her saviour at times of immense stress. It was a fact of certainty that she was immensely stressed at that moment. Having heard the information direct from her husband about the other woman, we can assume that Moira was left feeling quite shell shocked and feeling perhaps more than devastated.

Suddenly the reality of their situation had hit her. Somewhat as though she had been hit by a sledge hammer. Knowing that their marriage was in crisis mode she was experiencing quite intense emotions. Those emotions had at that time become virtually impossible for her to control. Michael had followed his wife outside to the garden. Her attempts at keeping the volume level low gave her husband the wrong impression. His idea that she was calm and collected quickly proved him to be wrong. Moira let her anger be known to him together with many other emotions too.

"So, you're telling me that you're having an affair. Oh my god Michael your having an affair and you've been so sneaky and deceitful about it too. Why oh why? Am I no longer good enough for you? No don't answer that. Get out of my sight now! In fact, I almost want to tell you to get out of the house but unlike you I will consider the bigger picture. I will consider the needs of our children as well as or maybe even rather than my own needs."

Moira shocked herself by her use of quite a few expletives in her outburst and description of her husband. Her only relief at that point was the fact that their children were both engrossed in a movie. Having wanted to see E.T. come home, for what had felt to the children like an eternity, eventually there it was on national television. They were engrossed and would be so for the following two hours. That at least she thought would give her some uninterrupted thinking time. Wiping away any further tears Moira put on her brave face ahead of going back inside. Hearing the children invite her to join them was not conducive to her remaining too calm. With a struggle to maintain her composure and a slightly raised tone in her voice, their mother told them.

"It's your movie not mine. Enjoy the story together with the popcorn and coke. I will enjoy what I need to be doing." *Relieved by their total lack of protests Moira sat down at the kitchen table. Not being much of a drinker the thoughts and consideration given to bringing out the brandy bottle, were all high up in her mind but with caution. Feeling unable to trust herself with its consumption if she started, and as usual considering the needs of their children as her priority, she decided it would perhaps be best not to. Placing the bottle back inside the cabinet, she knew that had been the safest decision to make regards the brandy. Deciding to take a power walk instead, she grabbed her shoes. Saying goodbye to their children, Moira then took herself away to the quietness, the serenity and the natural beauty of their local woods.*

Walking back inside of the house shock and surprise totally encompassed the mind of Michael Kearns. The realisation of what he had potentially done to his marriage and had done to his family, felt like much too much pain for him to tolerate. He was overwhelmed with emotion. He was very aware that it had to be overwhelming for Moira too. Knowing how he had turned their lives upside down he felt ashamed of his actions. Having quite a strong awareness at that point, of where he wanted to be and whom he wanted to be with, he once again hoped that it wouldn't be too late. The other woman no longer was a feature of any importance in his thoughts. She no longer mattered. She was no longer of any significance at all to him. Having that instant remorse in his thoughts for the actions of his affair, he hoped it would not be too late for him to reconcile with his wife. Michael was smart enough to know that attempting to share those thoughts with Moira, would not be beneficial or in either of their better interests at that time. Taking himself upstairs to a spare bedroom, he told their children how he was suffering from quite a severe migraine. He then bade them goodnight.

Recovering from the news which she had just heard, Moira Kearns knew she had some potentially life changing decisions to make. Would she let it all go and tell Michael to move out, or would she fight for her marriage? Was her marriage even worth fighting for? Praying silently to herself for Helen and Dominic but especially Helen, not to ask any deep questions that night, Moira's wish was granted. Calmly and very quietly approaching her mother, almost as if she was aware that there were marital problems; Helen told her.

"Dads had a long weekend at work now he has a migraine. He's gone to the spare bedroom so you don't disturb him with light."
The child wanting to make it more plausible had added on her own bit about the light. Moira smiled.

Acknowledging what her daughter had shared to be the truth Moira took a deep breath in. Spending the evening alone with their children was quite a daunting thought for Moira Kearns. She had felt unable to trust her own emotions so she made her decision. A trip back home to her parents in Dublin was something which was well overdue. She already knew that Helen and Dominic would be happy to visit their grandparents. Being with their children but away from the family home in Enniskerry, Moira had felt would perhaps be an easier way to manage her difficult situation. Having some other distractions, she could send the children off in different directions, thus eliminating too many daddy questions to her from Helen and Dominic.

"Come on kids we'll go see gran and gramps. Surprise them with a takeout for dinner. Leave your father in peace to deal with and recover from his migraine."

Helen and Dominic loved those visits to their grandparents in Dublin. Both felling excited about the imminent visit the kids gathered together some books and a board game.

"*Just in case it gets boring mom. You know us. Always a plan in place to fall back on.*"

Impressed with the forward thinking of their children, Moira felt how they had got her genes in that department. Wanting to give reassurance that all was well on the marital front, she joked with them in a humorous way about their father and his lack of planning skills. The journey from Enniskerry to Dublin whilst feeling quite fun for the children, had felt a little tedious for Moira. Stopping to collect a small choice of meals and drinks from her parent's local Chinese takeout, Moira found the distraction helpful. Padraig and Grace Reilly were both surprised and delighted to have their grandchildren and their daughter visit.

"*I know your both busy people Moira but It's really been too long. Great to see you all and where's Michael?*"
Helen being quick off the mark to share the news about her father's migraine, had worked very well for Moira. Wanting to praise her daughter for her quick response she decided not to. This left her not needing to give any further explanations which would duly concern her husband. That was a situation which Moira was very relieved about. Not having to mention his name at all that evening would have to be the very best scenario for her.

Hoping that some time away from their family home out in Enniskerry might occupy her thoughts, Moira Kearns was not disappointed. Enjoying the food which had been provided by their daughter, Padraig then requested they participate in a board game.

"Remember our monopoly days Moira. Can we play again for old times' sake?"

Laughing their way around the streets of London, Moira had temporarily forgotten the painful and quite deep feelings of devastation, which she had the awful experience of earlier that afternoon. Requesting to get the photo albums out Helen and Dominic had a refusal largely due to their time scale. Their mother was adamant.

"School in the morning so we can't be late tonight. Let's do it another time."

Saying goodbye to her parents and to the grandparents of her children, brought a silent tear for Moira. She surprised herself by her ability in the art of denial and lying.

"Sorry mom it's just that's it's been such a long time. We have to get back here more often."

Climbing into their car the Kearns set off for their farm home back in Enniskerry. The children loved to sing when travelling and this time would be no different. Liking the old Irish Rebel songs, they both gave a rendition of 'The wild Colonial boy' and 'Sean South of Garryowen'. Those being some of Moiras favourites too she declined their invite to join them.

"Sometimes kids it's just nice to listen and to be entertained. That's my preference right now so carry on please."

Singing the whole of the homeward journey was yet another bonus for Moira that evening. Pulling onto their farm house driveway, she reminded Helen and Dominic how it was time for them to go direct to bed. Not being good with dealing with change in her life Helen protested a little. Having to take a shower first was what she had to do. Despite it being late

Moira knew that to refuse would be futile. Telling her child to be quick and then direct to bed, her wish was granted.

Moira often wondered what she had done in life to have been fortunate enough to have received her inheritance. She was not a person who had ever felt entitled to anything in any aspect of her life. Thinking about her Moms deceased 1st cousin Alice, Moira considered how the woman must have seen something good in her, otherwise she would not now be living on that farm in their Enniskerry home. Having thoughts of a negative nature about herself was understandable at that time. Any woman who has ever been cheated on or any man too, will have a full understanding of what the feeling is like and it isn't a great one. Moira would have the sympathy of all who knew her, if only she had shared her experience. Eileen McGinty would be the person she would go to as she did at the weekend. Calling Eileen from the privacy of her car, Moira confirmed their worst fears.

"*Yes, Eileen I confronted him and guess what you were right. Hearing the words coming from his mouth I wanted to kill him. God I'm so angry and I'm so devastated too. Got to go. I've left the kids inside and don't want to risk them creating anything chaotic this evening. Catch up later in the week and thanks for being a friend.*"

Reminding Moira how the friendship road runs two ways the ladies ended the call.

Monday morning felt quite tough in the Kearns household. Michael was up and out for work at the hospital by 7am prompt. Moira changed her early morning routine. Knowing how she would not wish to or be able to be in the same room as her husband, she had decided to wait until he left for work.

Hearing the door shut quietly behind him she descended the stairs. Ensuring the children's daily routine was unaffected her brain must have gone into robotic mode. Breakfasts completed, lunch boxes made up, coats on and out the door at 08.25 sharp as was usual for them.

"C'mon you two we need to hurry."
That's a statement which was usual for them too, so no clues given away regarding their mom's marital situation. Arriving at the school gates just as they were about to close, was not very unusual for Helen and Dominic Kearns either. Waving them off from the car Moira then drove herself back home and directly back to her bedroom.

That's where she sobbed till she couldn't sob anymore. Till there were no more tears left within her body. Knowing how getting through the day was going to be quite a challenge for her, she decided to take things as they came and not to be overly worried about mundane household chores. Not having slept great the previous night she decided to break her own rule. She returned back to bed, with an alarm set in time to be up and ready to meet the children from school. Helen resented her mother walking them to school and many times informed her of that fact. She could be and often appeared to be quite abrupt when she spoke to her mother. She would often be heard protesting about the school run.

"I'm not a baby I can go alone. Walk Dominic to school if you have to."

Many arguments at school with Helen's involvement had begun, due to her inability to make her needs known in the regular sense. She would appear to be rude and abrupt when that had not been her intention. Her brain being wired up differently to those of us who are not on the spectrum, had created many tough situations in life for Helen. However, she was and is a warrior and a fighter. Socially being quite limited and much in need of routine, Helen gradually discovered that life wasn't always like that. That we cannot always adhere to our basic routines. Struggling to cope at all with any degree of change in her life, Moira had some bad feelings and some bad vibes, regarding how Helen would cope with the absence of her father.

The house phone rang out. It was Michael. Moira felt quite surprised to hear her husband's voice and did not especially want to hear it either. He sounded passionate in what he had to say to her.

"Please don't hang up Moira hear me out please. Its awfully important."

She did not feel even slightly interested in or concerned about what was important to him. Telling Michael she was busy she then replaced the receiver. The phone repeatedly rang out to the point of where she eventually picked it up again.

"What? What do you want Michael?"

Hearing a deep sigh of relief from him Moira listened calmly. He was requesting that they have a chat without Helen and Dominic present. He wondered if he could drop them at his parents' home for an overnight camp out that night. Moira wasn't too sure. It was short notice for the kids and everyone was aware that Helen needed time to digest any upcoming event. Time to process what had been shared with her. She didn't like change of any description. Already having put a plan in place to see their neighbouring farmer that evening, Helen might and most likely would be agitated if she couldn't go. Moira with a strong degree of reluctance agreed to give the situation some thought. Later she would let her husband know their decision.

After much consideration and thought Moira agreed that it would be best the children were absent whilst the parents had their discussion. She would give Helen the choice. Having it presented as a choice as opposed to an instruction, it would still be difficult for their daughter but perhaps less so. Helen and Dominic Kearns had throughout their lives, both enjoyed what they had always referred to as their camping nights. It would be a small tent in mine and Michaels parents back garden. It had always put a new definition on the word camping but the kids were happy and contented. Preparing herself for the divorce conversation and how they might split up their assets, Moira agreed to have the meeting pending their daughter's agreement for that night. She had made up her mind. She would try to keep the discussion as calm and as amicable as could be possible. Thinking how there would be no point in having feelings of animosity between them, Moira decided that would be the most productive road to follow. At the end of the day they had two children together and they had to be their priority. She would keep everything calm in the better interests of Helen and Dominic. She was ready.

Helen came bounding down the stairs again taking them two by two. It almost looked as though she was a participant in a leaping competition. Moiras anxiety levels were suddenly raised. She wiped the sweat from her own hands and from her brow as she heard her daughters' footsteps. Thinking how one day this was going to potentially end up having a bad outcome, she did all which she could do. She called out to their daughter. Helen and her brother having gone into the kitchen to find out what their mother wanted, they found Moira to be quite firm but not angry in her tone. She spoke only to Helen.

"There's no excuse for how you use the stairs Helen. You've had reminder after reminder yet that rarely makes a difference. Your trip to Dublin to spend your birthday money is now put on hold and that's an end to it."

Tears began to fall from Helens eyes as she pleaded with her mother. She made some more promises there would be no more running on the stairs. Having been in that situation on many previous occasions Moira was aware that she needed to stand very firm this time.

"Listen to me Helen. I've told you and told you and you've promised and promised but here we are yet again in the very same situation. Its simply sheer good luck that you've not had a serious fall. Here's what I need to see happening from you from now onwards."

Interrupting her mother whilst wiping away her own tears Helen then told Moira.

"All right I'm ready to listen and I'm sorry, really sorry." Putting a new plan in place an agreement was then reached between Helen and her mother. That was also the point when Moira gave their child a choice for that evening. Helen choose to go camping.

School day for the Kearn's children had felt quite exciting.

End of term being imminent, there were very many nice activities in place. Moira knew that she could probably relax if only the other marital stuff wasn't hanging over her shoulder. Feeling determined in her attempt to place the affair to one side, she would find it easier to get through the *evening conversation with Michael. There would be no more questions asked. Moira was determined not to be the hysterical wife. She would accept that he no longer wanted her in his life and sort out the practicalities of it all. Michael was home much earlier than usual that evening.*

"It's only 4pm why you home so early?"

Telling her he would discuss everything once the children had gone to his parents' home, Michael then instructed Helen and Dominic to collect their belongings. Giving them reminders to take all of their school belongings which they required for the following day and to say goodbye to their mother. Michael promptly loaded up the car. Waving goodbye to their children a then quite solemn looking Moira took herself to the top of the garden once again. Sitting once more next to the lavender bushes she began to relax a little. She was preparing her mind and her thoughts for the upcoming talk about the sharing of their finances. The house was hers so there would be no concerns there. She wished her husband to come back home quickly- get it all over and done with.

Michael on his return back home joined his wife outside in the garden. Feeling full of trepidation, he began by informing her how he now realises just how stupidly he had behaved in terms of the other woman. Moira was shocked as that was not the conversation she had been expecting.

"Can't believe what I've done Moira. Despite there being many weekends, which genuinely took me away from home for work practices, there was just one of those where I got tangled up with her. Oh my god I behaved so badly I was so stupid."

Interrupting his dialogue Moira informed her husband that trust had been broken, so why would she now believe his pathetic attempt at trying to minimalize his very abhorrent behaviour. Lunging at him with clenched fists she shocked herself by her angry outburst. This anger was not in her plan. It had appeared to have come from nowhere. Taking hold of both of her arms he tried to prevent any further onslaught of violence towards him.

"*This is not you Moira. You have every right to be angry with me. However, I know you so well and know that violence is something you would be very remorseful for once you've calmed down.*"

Letting go of his grip on her arms he then fell to his knees.

"*I'm begging you Moira for forgiveness. It really happened once only and directly after having shared that information with you, I realised what an absolute fool I had been. Not excusing my behaviour as there really is no excuse, but will tell you, that I was well plied with alcohol at the time. All other weekends away were genuinely spent with a group of surgeons, where we all learned from each other.*"

Being a very reasonable woman she listened to and absorbed all of which he had said without any further interruption. Michael continued to tell his wife, how many times he recalls the day their eyes first met, across the table in the conference room. How many times he has considered that being in her life and having her in his, has been and still is an absolute joy.

Tears dropped from Moiras eyes and from Michaels too.

What she had just heard from her husband was very different to that which she had been expecting to hear. Gathering her composure she firmly told him.

"*I'm really confused now. I was expecting to hear a request for divorce from you not a request for my forgiveness. Am I right in saying that I'm hearing that maybe you want to address your behaviour and hopefully resolve the marital issue whatever it might be?"*

Moira felt quite astounded by confirmation that yes that was exactly what she was hearing. She had also analysed their situation more that she realised. Knowing how there would be no advantage to Michael in telling her the truth about his cheating ways, she was compelled to share those thoughts with him and then see how the land was lying.

"Your telling me this was a single act of betrayal Michael. Just shows what you know about the reality of what you've done to me, done to us and done to our family. Let's just look at the many things you've done. Look at the many acts of deception involved in your torrid affair."

Interrupting his wife in a calm manner Michael really made a bad decision.

"Your doing it again Moira. Your analysing again just like you over analyse Helen and her life."

Her face showed him that was a bad decision. Her quite firm words were confirmation of that.

"You know it's wrong to bring another person into this conversation. Let's leave Helens life where it belongs and don't you dare attempt to accuse me of wrong doing. Now you can listen and I will speak. There's no permission from me for you to interrupt, so just don't and I will be as analytical as I feel that I need to be."

Moira wanted her husband to be aware of the many levels in which he had betrayed her. Wanted him to know how it wasn't simply he had cheated with another woman. She told him how his act of deception impacted her emotionally on so many levels. Outlining to Michael the facts that he had met another woman in a place where he should not have been.

He left that place together with the other woman instead of going home. He took the other woman in his car instead of Moira being in it. He took the other woman to quite a secluded place in order to conduct his one-night stand. She told him how it didn't matter whether he cheated once or cheated on her multiple times. She reminded her husband how the other woman had been victimised too. Michaels face was the face of a man who was feeling mortified by all which he had just heard.

"Oh my god Moira there's nothing I can say in defence to all of that. Your right on every level. Maybe I don't deserve you. Maybe I should leave."

With no response she walked away to sit down quietly and think. She had certainly put her husband in his place by her tarrade of words and why not. Wasn't it the right thing to do? It can be so very easy to cheat on your partner and not appreciate the awful impact which that has made on them and on their life.

Moira Kearns had always had a very mature outlook on life. Understanding that some people can and do make some mistakes in their life, she decided how that was probably the situation with Michael. Remembering how he had otherwise been a very good husband to her and a very good father to their children, she felt their marriage was worth fighting for and working on. Having agreed to talk about it at length and look deeply at why he thought that extra marital behaviour was all right in the first instance, they agreed to have some marital counselling sessions. Moira would arrange for that to happen and it would be with a private councillor. As Michael had created the situation he would therefore provide the funding for the counselling sessions from his own personal money.

School called. Hoping to speak with either Moira or Michael they would never be disappointed. Always being available for school phone calls they were both equally involved with their children's education. Moira took the call. Informing her how their daughter had been reprimanded wrongly and then given detention, they wished to offer their apologies. Details of Helens autism and her ADHD diagnosis which was clearly shown on their computing system, had not been read by a supporting teacher. That feels inexcusable in my opinion. All supporting teachers are scheduled extra time ahead of taking their class. That would be purely for the purpose of learning of any extra needs their students might have. Having asked Helen to describe what and how two particular characters in the story which the class had just read, were feeling, Helen had shrugged her shoulders. That response had then been perceived by the teacher, as Helen was not paying attention and was being rude. Helen did not understand feelings or emotions. She did not display empathy either. It was simply a part of her condition. She was clearly distressed by the fact she had been punished for that which was not her fault. Something which she was not guilty of.

Moira expressed her thanks to the school head for calling with the information. She shared with Mrs Donnelly how very disillusioned she was feeling, regarding the incompetence of their staff member.

"I'm hoping that the person concerned will be appropriately dealt with. I'm thinking how perhaps there should also at the

very least, be an apology from the teacher to our daughter. Helen at the very least deserves that."

Moira was given an assurance from Mrs Donnelly that both of those things would happen the following morning. I'm thinking how much restraint Moira demonstrated and just how tolerant of the situation she had been. Had it been my child I would have been demanding that the said teacher, not only apologised to Helen but spoke to the whole class too. Admitting his or her own lack of knowledge and insuring the class were aware, that Helen had done nothing wrong, are the only scenarios which would have satisfied me.

Collecting their children from the school gate that evening, Helen went over to her mother looking very subdued indeed. Dominic getting to speak ahead of his sister, appeared to be delighted by being able to share her bad news. He told their mom.

"She was in trouble at school this morning and had a whole lunch time detention."

Feelings of almost shock but certainly surprise were by now consuming Moiras mind. She was taken back by the apparent delight which their son was taking from his sisters' mishap. Firmly reprimanding him for the above she also pointed out to Dominic, that people should arm themselves with facts ahead of making judgements. Turning to their daughter Moira informed her about the call from the school head. That information brought a smile to Helens face. She then showed her sense of grace.

"I'm glad someone defended me mom can we forget about it now."

Agreements reached between Helen and her mother that yes, they could forget about it now, they then spoke about the possibility of having yet another camping out night with their grandparents. Both children had very much enjoyed the more recent experience of camping in the Kearns back garden. They had both shared the desire to do it all over again. Moira agreed she would talk to their father and take things from there.

"I don't want to hear any more about it now. We'll see what your dad says and thinks and what grandma and gradad think too. Ok that's an end to it."
Skipping ahead of their mother the children raced each other back home. Moira gave some deep thought to her marital position and how any break up of it, might or would have impacted badly on their children.

Weeks into counselling found Moira being able to know and to understand, how her husband had got himself into what he considered to be at the very least, that awfully regrettable situation. He gave her some assurance as much as could ever be possible, that he would never be repeating that behaviour again. Knowing herself that she was a pretty good judge of character, she was feeling convinced that they would never be met with that situation in their marriage ever again. The therapist had also shared his view.

"You've worked quite hard on this Michael over the past six months. You've realised what was really important to you and you've fought hard to keep it. You've worked hard to ensure you can both go forward together as a happy couple, leaving your mistake behind you. You've worked very hard too Moira. You've wanted to gain some understanding of

how those awful situations can happen within a marriage. It's clear to me that you both want the same outcome. I'm therefore confident in the view that now is the time to bring our meetings to an end. It does however need to be your joint decision and not mine. I will be happy to offer further sessions should you both or one of you feel there's a need for that."

Michael and Moira having already had discussions about this at home ahead of their meeting, agreed this should be their final meeting. Wishing their therapist well the Kearns left his office feeling the happiest they had been for a very long time.

Blast from the past

*H*aving been a stay at home mum had given Moira Kearns heaps of pleasure over the years. Working the arable farm in addition to raising the children had always kept her incredibly busy. The children both at Secondary school now, she felt it was time for her to re think her work versus home situation. Some farm hands could be employed freeing up some of her time. From her financial perspective going out to work would not be especially viable. Considering the financial aspect, she then discussed it with Michael. Looking at how it was not just about finance, but was more about some stretching of herself intellectually, she had hoped that her husband too might see it from her perspective. He did. Moira was a highly educated woman. She did not wish to and was not prepared to let that education go to waste. Having two degrees would have to be a bonus for her in any work interviews which she managed to secure.

*T*he raising of two children of whom one has some special needs, would also make Moira a strong asset for any line of childcare work. Combining that with her degree in psychology and her previous work experience, she hoped would make her a strong candidate in any potential interviews. Childcare work was where her interests lay. With Michaels blessing and his agreement (not that she needed either of those), Moira put in her application to Tusla. Her application was to be for a child psychologist position on a part time basis. The applied for position was open to someone for three days per week. It was advertised as a job share.

*W*aiting patiently for a response it had felt to Moira like an eternity, since she had put her application in the post box. Eventually after some weeks the long awaited for phone call came.

"Its human resources at Tusla here Mrs Kearns. How are you today?"
Moira responded with a very short almost abrupt response
"I'm good thank you."
She wished they would cut out the pleasantries and get to the important point of the call. Her only interest was in whether she had secured an interview or not. Thinking how it might be best she didn't say that she then quickly changed her tactic slightly.

"All's good here thank you and you?"
Picking up on Moiras tension they woman told her to relax.
"You're in. Your application was successful."
A very delighted Moira expressed her thanks. Plans were put in place for a formal interview to take place. Post interview Moira was offered the position which she had applied for. She was eager to hear a mutually agreeable starting date. That agreed the ladies then bade their goodbye's.

*S*haring her news with Michael and their children that evening, was an exciting moment for Moira Kearns. A glass was raised to congratulate and wish her well in what was going to be her new role in life. Timetables were drawn up in the Kearns kitchen. Everyone in the house was a contributor to the mess being made on a daily basis. Moira insisted how *everyone would then contribute to the clearing up of that mess. Excuses for not following the rules were not going to be tolerated or be acceptable. Reminding their children and herself and Michael too, that a person's actions always have consequences, she hoped would be sufficient of a deterrent to all of them not to break the rules. Moira Kearns planned for their home to run like clockwork and largely she got her wish. A young man had been hired to take over Moiras share of the farm work. Life was looking very good indeed.*

Her returning back to work date upon them Moira was out of bed not too much after dawn. Thoughts of the day ahead excited her. Having her caffeine intake was as always her first priority of the day. Saying a chirpy goodbye to Michael as he left for the hospital she then called out to their children. Michael doubled back and into the kitchen. Wondering what he might have forgotten on this occasion, Moira was quite taken by surprise by her husband's statement.

"It's you Moira it's the star within you shining bright and shining through. You haven't seemed this upbeat in the mornings for a very long time. Work has put that spring back in your step. I just had to tell you that."

A beaming Moira thanked her husband for his kind words. Michael then left the house for the 2nd time that morning and left his wife feeling good about herself. No sign of either of their children yet Moira did a rethink. Having provided both of them with an alarm clock each was not appearing to make much difference. Excuses flowing from Helen and Dominic too, at times were often in abundance. Their excuses would range from something like.

"It didn't go off mom. It's not loud enough mom, or I heard it but was too tired to get out of bed."

She considered how very creative their children could be with their thinking process, when they choose to be.

$\mathcal{E}$ventually with everyone ready to leave the house, Helen

and Dominic set off to walk their route to school. Moira got in her car for the drive into Dublin city. Putting her foot on the accelerator her feelings of freedom were immense, as the early morning sun shone brightly and a slight breeze blew through her hair. Helen having a fabulous sense of adventure and being something of a rebel at times, she could see faster ways to get to their destination.

"C'mon Dominic we'll cut through the fields and out at the side of McGinty's farm. We'll get there in half the time and no one will know."

Having no interest in his sisters' rebellious ways the lad continued with his journey along the roadside. He was quickly joined by Helen who as we know enjoyed an adventure but not by herself.

$\mathcal{B}$ack at the work place on a part time basis felt quite good

to Moira Kearns. She was starting to realise just how much things had changed during her years of being absent from the office. Introductions to colleagues eventually over and done with, she was then shown to what would be her desk. A hefty load of case files sat on the corner in the in tray. Upon seeing them Moira took a deep breath in. She was informed how the latest part time employee had resigned some weeks previously, hence the large pile of work. Moira was advised to read through the files one by one ahead of attempting any work on any of them. She could then pick out five files which she felt had the greatest sense of urgency. That would then be her allocated load of work. Seeing the coffee maker in the corner, that had to be and was her first port of call. Having some coffee would serve her with a double purpose. Relieving her need for caffeine and showing the friendly and sociable side of her character, she enquired.

"Anyone want one. I make them pretty good."
Enjoying the coffee and the banter which bounced back from her offer, Moira then settled back down at her desk.

𝒩ot having seen Frank or Jessica Geary for what had felt like an eternity, did not mean that Moira had forgotten about them or their children. Speaking to Michael regarding the family, he acknowledged how it had to be at least two years since the two families had enjoyed some time out together. They both recalled the day with clarity. Having taken a picnic which she had sourced from their land and her own culinary skills in the kitchen, the families had met up in Dublin city. All children having held an interest in sea fare, they duly took a boat trip around the cliffs of Moher. Having enjoyed the trip and enjoyed the picnic, the families then went their separate ways. Frank and Jessica were especially grateful for the day out and wanted to show their gratitude.

"Thanks Michael and Moira. We're in very different situations in every aspect of life and that obviously includes finance. Without your generosity we would not have been able to experience what we all did today. Thanks again and hopefully we'll all catch up soon."
Waving their friends off the Kearns then travelled back to their home out in Enniskerry. That was Moiras last time for her seeing the Geary family.

ℬeing back behind the same desk where she had done her training at, had felt both bizarre and quite strange to Moira

Kearns. Sharing with the student present in the room how she had begun her career in that office, whilst shadowing a senior psychologist, the young woman asked if she could shadow Moira. Wow- what a start to her return back to work. Not personally having a problem with the young woman's request, she did point out a few potential issues. The fact that it was her first day back to work after an absence of very many years, could potentially be a big hindrance. Then there was the small matter of having it agreed by the team manager.

"*Look give me some time I'll talk to the team lead. See what she thinks. If she's happy then yes it can probably go ahead.*"

Thanking her the girl went back to her desk. Moira thought about how the girl at least had her own desk and didn't have to share one, like she had done in her training days. She was remembering her own training days of shadowing someone and remembering just how grateful she had been, to have been given that opportunity. Moira had been informed that her team manager was called Jenny Dolan. Speaking to Jenny the person she believed to be team manager, Moira was about to ask the question on behalf of the young lady when she was interrupted. She was shocked to hear the woman's comments.

"*The teams split in two Moira. I lead on the days I'm here and I'm not usually here on Mondays. I've come in today purposefully to meet you. Your reputation precedes you. I wanted to see why for myself.*"

Moira had temporarily forgotten her request from the young student present in the office. Their eyes then momentarily met which was a reminder for Moira.

"Oh, Jenny I was almost accosted earlier and that's why I've come to speak to you. Louise has asked if she could shadow me. Obviously, I told her we would need to speak to the team lead.

"Moira if you want the job then team lead is your position on the days which you will be at work. You have all of the credentials required for it. We would be sharing all responsibilities. Take some time to think about it. It can be very demanding and often has a habit of following me right back to my kitchen table. You getting the message?"

Yes, Moira was getting the message loud and clear. Feeling almost speechless yet honoured at the same time, she was struggling to compose her words.

"Wow-It's an awful lot to take in Jenny. Can I have a few days to think about it and let you know and by the way thank you. Your vote of confidence in me means so much."

The broad smile on Jenny Dolans face confirmed to Moira that yes, she was feeling quite happy to leave it there for the time being. Giving Moira time to consider all of her options would hopefully bring the response which Jenny had hoped for. The offer which had been made to their new colleague would be duly announced to the whole room. Jenny Dolan informed everyone that Moira was considering take up of the management role. She was giving it her consideration. Louise secretly wishing that Moira would accept the offer attempted some encouragement for her to do so.

"You'd be a great manager. A fabulous person for someone to shadow. Some of our training sessions refer to you. They look at the way you stood up to and challenged authority when you were a student. You've inspired me and very many others too."

Moira Kearns did not often find herself speechless. This was now the second time in one day for that to happen. She was floored but knew she had to somehow find an appropriate way to respond.

"Wow praise of the highest from you Louise. Thank you so much. I am as Jenny explained giving the role some serious consideration."

That information being the second shock and surprise of the day for Moira, she wished for the day to end ahead of any further unexpected surprises which might travel her way.

Kearns home being a relatively happy and contented one everyone had adhered to the timetable. Still being early days, it nevertheless appeared that things were ticking along like clockwork. Michael had given lots of timely reminders from the past and encouragement to his wife.

"Remember our first meeting Moira and the way in which you challenged people in authority from that meeting. Don't forget that Marissa Geary was returned back to her parents care, due to your hard work and your input. That insight and that ability to fight for what is right has never left you. You would be a great asset to the management team. You should seriously consider taking up the offer."

Looking back on her life to her student days Moira held her husband tightly.

"I too remember our first meeting. The handsome brute which you were and still are. Been through such a lot since then and come out the other side. Love you more now than I did then."

Their relationship was now on a very secure footing despite his mistake many years previous.

Moira having made the decision to accept the managerial role she called Jenny Dolan at the office.

"It's me Moira Kearns and yes I'll do it. I'd be foolish to turn down such a great offer."

Acknowledging her sense of relief Jenny shared how she had organised a meeting between them. They would be in the office together for one cross over day, in order to look at the most urgent families in need of Moiras attention. To Moira's surprise the Geary family were there on that list. Checking out through the files it became evident to Moira, that the young Marissa Geary had some involvement with some very unsavoury people. Marissa at the tender age of seventeen years had given birth. She had a child a baby daughter which had been removed from her at birth.

Taking in some deep breaths a then quite upset Moira had to quickly try to regain her composure. She guessed that Jenny Dolan had not been aware of the potential outbursts of anxiety which she sometimes suffered from. Hoping this would not be the time for that discovery to be made, Moira wiped the sweat from her hands. Momentarily wishing she was back home she thought about the lavender tree and how it would help her at that moment. Reflecting back on her friendship with the Geary family and not having had contact for quite some time, Moira was able to accept that situation without feeling bad or the experience of any feelings of guilt. Struggling to understand why Frank and Jessica Geary had not stepped up and supported their daughter by looking after the baby, she continued to plough her way through the file. She was soon to uncover the awful truth. Making the awfully painful discovery that Marissa and her brother had lost both of their parents, sent Moiras head in a spin. Due to their previous friendship, uncertainty regarding her dealing with Marissa's file initially consumed Moiras head. Thrashing it all out in her own mind ahead of speaking to her co- manager, Moira had hoped Jenny would share her view. She did!

Taking up the case of Marissa and her baby girl, Moira discovered how some months ahead of the baby's birth, the Geary parents had been involved in a car crash in Dublin city. Having improved their lives immensely by a return to adult education, both parents had secured good jobs. They had both been doing much better than in earlier years. Improved financial circumstances for them had helped provide them with a car. Being involved in a head on collision which was not their fault had resulted in the untimely death of them both. Marissa and her brother both being under the age of eighteen were taken into the care of Tusla. Marissa was already pregnant at that point with no other family members to offer support. Moira wiped away her tears. Regaining her composure, she made appointments to visit both children at their foster homes. She felt how Marissa had gone full circle now that she was back in the care system again. Moira reserved her opinions in relation to what if any support she could offer, from the perspective of Tusla and then perhaps from a more personal perspective.

Sharing the news of the demise of Frank and Jessica Geary with her husband, Michael too was distressed to know about the accident.

"It's just too awful Moira. Can't imagine how the poor kids must have felt. Its hardly surprising to know that Marissa

went off the rails. Hope it was quick for Frank and Jessica. Life can be so cruel."
Wrapping his arms tightly around his wife and pulling her in close, Michael could feel and hear her gentle sobs. It was the chance she had needed to let it all out.

"I'm devastated for them Michael. I'm not sure now if I am the best person to work with the family. Not sure if I could be objective enough."
Advising his wife how it would be best not to make any rash decisions at that point, she very much appreciated and agreed with his input. Having the weekend to spend together felt just perfect to the Kearns. There was lots of thinking time for Moira. Spending some of that time with lots of reflection on their past relationship with Frank and Jessica Geary, The Kearns were able to appreciate how much they and Moira in particular had helped Marissa's parents over the years.

Remembering how she had helped Marissa with the return back to her family from the care of the local authority, Moira felt proud. Her mind was suddenly made up. She had done it before. She could and would do it again. She would continue with the Geary children's file in a very professional manner. If an injustice had been served to Marissa on this occasion then Moira would root it out. If there was no injustice done then she would support and work with that decision too. Returning back to her office the following week was a good feeling for Moira. Being shadowed by the young student allocated to the team, brought back so many memories for her. Memories of having fight and spirit in her bones. Now she would create that fight and that spirit again. She would search for and investigate Marissa Geary's file and those of her child and her brother too.

*H*aving decided that a meeting with Marissa Geary's foster carers, would perhaps be the better place to start, Moira went right ahead and made those plans. Meeting up with the carers at her office ensured the privacy required. She was deeply saddened to hear what they had to say. Having then had a meeting with Marissa separately to the carers, Moira could clearly see that the baby would be at risk had she not been removed from her mother's care. Attempting to have a discussion with Marissa proved itself to be quite futile. She was clearly a user. There were needles on her bedroom floor with many areas of both arms abused with very little space left for injecting. Moira had previously been told by the foster carer, how very gradually over a period of a few months, Marissa had changed from being a regular teenager, into the drug addicted young woman who now stood before her. Help had been put in place all to no avail. Moira heard how very sadly, Marissa was not yet ready to accept that help. Despite having the knowledge that her baby would be removed, she still wasn't able to get herself out of the messy situation she had found herself in. Baby's father was also an addict and considerably older than Marissa. The baby was now being put forward for adoption. There were some families already identified as being potentially a suitable match for Marissa Geary's child.

*T*his news lay heavy on Moiras conscience. Remembering her and Michaels friendship with Jessica and Frank Geary, her Initial level of thinking was quite painful and maybe a little erratic. She felt that she had a duty of care to them on some level.

"They would be devastated Michael to see what's become of their daughter."

Hearing all of what Moira had said he did share his wife's sentiments; however, he could not see how himself or Moira could be of any assistance. He was clear with her that she needed to be objective. Needed to take a step back and let the adoption teams deal with this one.

"I've seen many situations at work Moira of young women in Marissa's shoes. Only they can bring about change as and when they feel ready and able to do so. There's nothing we can do. Jessica would surely understand and I'm sure she would agree with that if she was here."

Knowing how he was right, Moira was aware she would have to find some way to distract her own thoughts from the Geary family, other than on a professional level.

"Thanks Michael you've helped to put it all in perspective for me. Don't worry I'll find a way to sort myself out and remove myself emotionally."

Absorbing all of that news about the Geary children, about the demise of their parents and the potentially now imminent adoption of Marissa's baby, had impacted the Kearns quite badly but Moira in particular. Michael and Moira expressed a deep sense of gratitude for their own lives and for the wonderfully balanced lives of their own two children. They both felt and acknowledged to each other, that despite being on the spectrum, that their daughter Helen had made some amazing strides in her life. Dominic had made some amazing strides too. They hoped that life would continue to be good to all of them. Knowing that we need to work for that which we achieve in life, Moira took great comfort from the knowledge of how the Geary parents had sorted their issues out some years ago.

Moira and Michael held the hope that as Marissa was genetically joined to Frank and Jessica Geary, that she would one day find that same level of strength like they had done. In the knowledge that there was nothing more which she could do to bring change and in the interest of her own well-being, Moira made the decision to pass over the Geary family files to her colleague Jenny Dolan. Her decision being accepted by her co-manager gave Moira a great sense of relief. She had the awareness that Jenny would seek the best possible for both of the Geary children. She would seek the best adoption outcome for Marissa's baby. Leaving her office for home that evening, Moira Kearns had the feeling it was a day's work well done.

New adventures for the Kearns family

Fridays were always quite routine and much appreciated by the Kearns family. Being the end of their working week, they would look forward to their upcoming plans. Persuading their teenagers to leave what they called their pits had become something of a challenge in itself. This weekend was going to be quite different to others. Michael didn't know that yet. His family didn't know that yet. When you think about how your life is sorted, to then discover that a cat is going to be placed amongst the pigeons, it's time to brace yourself for whatever is coming your way. For my readers who are maybe not very familiar with the term, the cat and pigeon's thing is an old English expression. Its widely used when things are going to become a little controversial in one's life, or when new but quite pleasant or perhaps unpleasant information is about to be bestowed upon them. That could be information which may change the course of one's direction in life.

Michael had gone to work as usual. The clinic was busy. He was therefore very surprised when he then got summoned to the office at Drumlin hospital by his superiors. His curiosity levels were going off the radar. Wondering what he could possibly be wanted for he quickly finished off his lunch. With some degree of trepidation, he set off walking down the long corridor to the office which was situated right at the end. The man had a good spring in his step. Remembering how Moira had always told him, that when in stressful situations or when in unknown territory, that he should stop and focus on his breathing. That's exactly what he did. Taking a final deep one ahead of entering the office, Michael had felt surprised by his own over reaction. Thinking how it was quite unusual for him to be unnerved, by any request from people who were higher up the ladder than he was, he dismissed those thoughts as he entered the room. Having met many people over the years who had expressed their high levels of stress endured when going to unfamiliar places, he considered himself to be quite fortunate. Michael was grateful for his own familiarity of the office which he had been summoned to. He was soon to discover the purpose of that meeting.

*B*eing presented with a surprise opportunity to share his vast knowledge and to hopefully acquire some more from colleagues elsewhere in the world, had felt like a dream come true for top Surgeon Michael Kearns. He was left with feelings of deep joy and excitement, which he had not felt since the days of his meeting with Moira Riley. The idea of moving out to an ear nose and throat hospital in Russia for two years overwhelmed him. Michael had clearly been told that should he decline their offer, they would still hold him in the same high regard. His superiors told him that he was a highly respected member of the surgical team at Drumlin and how that would never change.

*D*isplaying any degree of excitement in the work place was quite unusual for Michael Kearns. He was usually considered to be almost sombre at all times. On this occasion his level of *excitement was demonstrated right there in the office. Punching the air three times Michael then requested his display should be ignored. That request being denied he was informed of their pleasure from seeing his reaction. Advising Michael to take time to digest the information he had just received, he was made aware there was a two months deadline for his reply. No pressure from them but they hoped he would take up the offer.*

"*Your such an asset to this hospital Michael. You have the ability to learn and bring even better things to us. Our Russian counterparts are very excited by the swap prospect too.*"

Closing the door quietly behind him as he left the manager's office, Michael went directly back to his clinic. Feeling ten feet taller than when he last sat in that chair, he had to and did prepare himself for his next patient.

Asking himself the question could he possibly take this opportunity he did not have an accurate answer. Thoughts of the many implications of his acceptance swamped his mind. Thinking about the children and how they might hear the news gave him some concern. Would the ask from his wife be too big of an ask, or perhaps it might actually be something which may excite her too. He wasn't too sure of the answer to that one either? Michael decided there could be only one way to find an answer to his questions. Setting the scene in his mind he would then carry that through. Calling Moira to ensure she was aware he would be providing their evening meal, left her a little confused.

"*Something wrong Michael? You cooking dinner on a work night feels odd?*"

Assurance given there was nothing amiss. Just a nice gesture on his part, Michael then remembered their agreement for honesty and the truth regardless of its circumstance. Feeling bad at the thoughts of breaking that agreement he suddenly changed his mind in his response to her.

"*I do have something to share with you but truly its nothing to be worried about. It's something potentially exciting for all of us as a family. Just be sure the kids are not around as it's not for their ears at the minute.*"

Dominic and Helen would on occasion have a takeout treat for dinner. Not wanting to be disturbed or overheard by their children, Moira decided this could be one of those evenings for a takeaway. Knowing how that would keep them in their bedrooms, she also knew they would not be an issue to their parent's privacy.

Arriving home at six thirty prompt Michael was armed with some ingredients for one of their favourite meals. He took the evening from there. Waiting with a display of great patience for her husband to share his news, Moira had the idea that it had to be something special. Perhaps a decent pay rise was in the pipeline for him. She thought how deserving he would be of that. Knowing how her inheritance of thirty thousand pounds was almost still intact was a good feeling of financial security for Moira. This had scarcely been used for anything other than for some home maintenance. She felt very proud of the man whom she had married. Eventually with dinner on the table the Kearns sat down together to eat. Michael looked a little on the nervous side. She knew he was feeling nervous from the give-away twitch from his eye.

$\mathcal{E}$ating in almost silence she wondered what it was he was going to share with her, which would cause him to feel this nervous. Deciding it could not be a pay rise Moira kept her thoughts private. Eventually placing his cutlery back down on an empty plate Michael pushed the plate away from him. He shuffled a little on the chair. Moira's patience was beginning to run out. With a little humour in her voice she told her husband.

"Oh, for god's sake Michael get on with it. Tell me what you need to tell me before I explode."
Taking in a deep breath he then shared with Moira.

"It's mind-blowing Moira. I'm still struggling to get my head round it, so I'll fully understand if you blow the idea right out of the equation."
The questioning look on her face told Michael that she was by now feeling quite confused.

"What idea Michael? Talk about putting the horse behind the cart. What on earth are you talking about?"
The following thirty minutes or so were spent by her husband, giving her some clear explanation of what had happened for him at the hospital that morning. Hearing of the opportunity to work and live in Russia for a short period had a great deal of appeal to Moira. Michael was not disappointed with her reactions.

"What an honour to have bestowed upon you. Your clearly highly thought about as an experienced surgeon. It feels like an exciting prospect for us but needs lots of thought ahead of you giving them your decision."

$\mathcal{F}$ollowing that evenings discussion and many other serious and lengthy ones with his wife, they both decided to grasp with both hands, that opportunity which had been offered to Michael. Their oldest child Helen was almost eighteen. She would be given a choice of what to do. For Dominic it would have to be quite a different story. Being under sixteen he was still under the umbrella of their local education department. Dominic would need to remain in Ireland and stay with some family members. He would then be given a choice of what to do post his education years. Both Helen and Dominic were delighted to hear of the prospect of their parents going to live in Russia.

*H*earing of her choice to either stay with extended family in Dublin or travel over to Russia with her parents, without any hesitation Helen made her decision. Feeling excited by the information she had heard she took in some deep breaths. She then told her parents in the usual for her almost abrupt manner.

"Hell, NO I'm not stopping here. I've wanted to travel for a long time now but obviously was too young to go it alone. This is my chance this is it mom and if I don't like it or can't settle down then I can and will come back."

Well that was it. That was Helens choice made. There would be no questions to be asked at that time. Michael and Moira had done the ground work. Being able to share a plan for Dominic was slightly more challenging. The story was quite different to that of his sister. Suggestions were made that he could choose which grandparents to live with. Both families were fit and healthy and would be happy to have him stay with them. All were happy to support him with transport to and from his school in Enniskerry and to any extracurricular activities which he may wish to attend.

Lots of phone contact would be planned between Dominic and his parents. Michael and Moira would also do his parents evenings over the phone with Dominic's school. Grandparents would attend in person, for all of his other school meetings including parents' evenings. Dominic was very satisfied with the plan. He was a young person who appeared to have had an old head on his quite young shoulders. At times being given the description of being like an old soul, on this occasion he could fit into that category. He told his parents with quite a firm yet very caring and somewhat humorous voice

"You really need to take this opportunity dad and you too mom. I'll work hard to get where I want to be in education. I will not let you down and I will not let myself down either. I'm sure Helen will be a pain unless your both very firm with her." Moira and Michael both wondered how their son got to be so grown up. Dominic found it humorous yet a little serious at the same time.

"It's happened right under our nose Moira and Helen too. Both very grown up and are young people any parent would be proud of. Let's hope that after Dominic's comment about his sister that another scrap is not ensuing."

An applause came from the living room from both of their children. Dominic was very expressive. He could not resist a little humour when he told their parents.

"Great to see you both appreciate the fact that we are grown up with minds of our own. Now we need to live them as you need to live yours and just don't forget to keep Helen in check."

Was he pushing it with his sister? Nothing further to be said at that moment the parents retired for the evening.

"You two don't forget to lock up and turn out the lights and don't be too late going to bed."

Helen and Dominic had spent some time that evening looking at their life's. Looking at how very financially fortunate they had been by comparison to many of their school friends. They did not especially believe in Catholicism. They did however believe that there is a god. Both expressing they're thanks to their god they too then retired for the night.

Accepting their daughters' plan to travel to Russia with them, Michael and Moira then duly shared what expectations they would have of her. They would both expect Helen to be seeking employment almost immediately upon their arrival in Pullman near Moscow. Michael could be a little on the over sensitive and the over lenient side. He could potentially be persuaded by Helen in her attempts, to make him see and to make him agree that she did not need to uphold their work expectation. Moira Kearns is a very strong-minded woman. She would be right there insisting that their expectation be met. Despite being more than comfortably well off financially, she would still be expecting Helen in her better interest to contribute to their financial pot. Michael was now questioning that decision.

"She needs to have a sense of value Michael and a sense of how far money goes, or does not go as the case might be."
Helens father was still trying to be a little more lenient. His only saving grace was that he had that conversation with his wife in private, away from the ears of Helen and Dominic.

"She's still so young Moira with a world full of stuff for her yet to discover. As we can easily afford to keep her Isn't it a little on the mean side requesting she finds employment."

Moira was anticipating she would be having an unwanted battle on her hands. She was very firm and very clear in her explanation, that their own financial comforts, should have no impact on their children. She reminded Michael how all children have to learn to be financially independent. He listened and he then agreed. Together they felt they held quite a good balance on their parenting skills. Sharing his decision to move to the hospital in Russia with colleagues and friends at the Dublin hospital where he worked, was a very poignant moment for Michael. The news brought reactions and actions which he had not anticipated would happen. He was humbled.

A clinic and ward party was arranged where he was greeted by management, by secretarial staff, by colleagues and also by nursing staff. Michael was soon to discover how he had been revered by everyone who knew him. They said their well wishes and their final goodbyes. Michael was due some annual leave. He would take that ahead of his departure to Russia from the country which he loved. Knowing that it was going to be what they had considered as quite a short-term secondment, Michael was able to ensure everyone that he would be back in the blink of an eye. Arranging and organising Dominic with his time to be shared between both sets of grandparents, was much easier than contemplated by Michael and Moira.

Their farm house was rented out to a young colleague of Michaels and his wife. Having moved up to the Dublin area from county Kerry, they wanted somewhere temporary to live for a twenty - four-month period. The farm house out in Enniskerry would be the ideal position for them. Grace and Padraig Riley would oversee, that all and everything went smoothly with the house rental. Their farm land had been taken over by Eileen McGinty and her husband John. The arable aspect of the farm land would be kept up to scratch by Eileen. John would take care of the rest and would keep quite a keen eye on the new tenants too. Everything was in place and had gone so much smoother and easier than either of them had anticipated.

Two weeks or so ahead of the Kearns family departure most things were in place. Helen having had very little knowledge of the country which she would be travelling to, had picked out what she considered would be required for their trip. Her luggage bags were heavy. Going over the weight limit, Moira had informed their daughter how she may struggle with the chaos of a busy airport and there would potentially be fees to be paid at airport departures. Helen didn't care! She almost shouted at her mom.

"I've got strong arms and I've got money mom so if it's over weight then it's over weight. It's my problem."
Whilst not being overly happy with their daughters' attitude Moira kept her mouth zipped. Knowing how Helen would find out the hard way, her mother considered that may well be the most effective way in the learning of the lesson.

Their son Dominic had already left their home some days previous to their moving day. With a happy and smiling face he told his parents in a jovial manner.

"It's for the best that I go now. Then you'll know that I'm well settled with gramps before you desert me."
Knowing how that was his humour Michael and Moira helped their child with his belongings into the waiting car. Dominic's rejection of their attempts of a display of affection was more acceptable to his father than it was to Moira.

"He's fifteen Moira. I wasn't into hugging my parents at that age either. Let's just wave them off down the drive."
Wiping the tears from her eyes she agreed to her husbands request. Suddenly as the car fled out of sight Michael and Moira Kearns realised how that was it for two years. Having immense trust in Dominic they hoped that trust would never be miss placed.

Closing up their farm house on the outskirts of Dublin City, packing sufficient clothing to see them through their period away, was a little harder than Moira Kearns in particular had anticipated. Arrival of their new tenants was expected some four weeks after the Kearns had moved out. The morning for their departure arrived. With a degree of trepidation, the Kearns family pulled shut that door behind them. They didn't even take a backwards glance. It would all be for the best Michael had decided. Travelling by taxi into the city of Dublin, the family arrived at the airport, some three hours ahead of their take off time. Struggling a little to keep up pace and to manage with her luggage too, Helen sought some support from her parents. That being their first rejection of their *daughter in terms of the airport and the flight, Helen was left feeling a little confused.*

   "I don't understand. The cases are heavy and you won't help me?"

   Moira was quick off the mark to respond. Reminding their daughter how she had advised her of the potential weight issue, how not to bring so many belongings and reminding her of the duplicate reasons for that advice, Moira now had to remain firm as did her husband.

   "You didn't listen Helen. You told me stop worrying and if there was an issue that it would all be your problem. Now you have to figure how to deal with that problem and you need to hurry up too."

A hard and quite expensive lesson was then learned by a sulking Helen Kearns. She had to make a very large financial payment for her excessive luggage weight. Her further appeals to her parents for support with that fell on deaf ears. Taking a one-way flight from Dublin airport to Vnukovo international airport in Moscow, the Kearns were delighted to at last be on board the aircraft. It was to be a first-time flying experience for the whole family.

   Being a very long flight with quite a lot of turbulence on route, to say they felt uncomfortable would be something of an understatement. Helen had brought some of her own reading material, in addition to all else which she had taken on board with her. Sharing her books with both parents they were both impressed by the level of material which their daughter was reading. Arrival at their Russian destination held a great sense of relief for the whole family. Progressing through passport control and luggage collection, they then summoned the use of a taxi car. Travelling out through the Russian countryside to their new place of residence, held some excitement for them. That was perhaps especially so for Helen.

"Wow mom it looks beautiful. Can't wait for us to see the apartment."
Whilst on the one hand wishing that their daughter might be silent, Moira didn't want to discourage her enthusiasm. Agreeing with the comment, she then reminded Helen and Michael how they were almost at their final destination. The buildings housing their apartment was very tall. They thought how different it all looked to their place back in Enniskerry.

It was summertime and was the families favourite time of the year. It was almost the middle of August to be precise. Blue skies had held some sunshine which came beaming down and in through the windows of the Kearns 2nd floor apartment. They liked their apartment on some levels but mostly due to its modernisation. In other ways they were feeling quite lonesome for their homeland and for their family and friends back in Ireland. Living in what they were considering to be almost concrete city in comparison to what they had left behind, the Kearns family still felt very blessed. Knowing how they would have their own place to return to at the end of Michaels secondment period, was the catalyst to help keep their feelings of loneliness submerged and to keep their spirits up. Michael commenced his new position on the 4th of September in the year 2014. Working in a hospital in Pullman whilst living in that same area had felt like a good plan to the Kearns family. Being around 9 miles from Moscow City was something of a bonus too. The city would be easily accessible should they ever wish to go there.

*T*ravelling out to the hospital that morning Michael thought about how the weather was holding some semblance, to that which they had left behind them in Ireland. A phone call from Moira Kearn's back to her parents' home in Dublin was much appreciated by everyone. The Riley parents were delighted to give updates on Dominic and how well he was managing in his parent's absence. Having confirmation of that from Dominic himself was quite reassuring for Michael and Moira. Dominic and his grandparents were eager to here all about life in Russia. They were impressed by what they heard but not so regarding the cold winters.

*M*ichael and Moira had done their research on the country which they were moving out too. Having the knowledge that January was going to most likely be their coldest month, it would usually be around -4, they had lots of time to prepare. Shops were already heaving with very many suitable items of winter clothing, including quite a few items of thermal wear. Michael and his family would not be leaving anything to chance. Trawling through the shopping arcades of Moscow in their anticipation of goods becoming unavailable, they quickly filled their wardrobes in good time. Being joined by their daughter Helen on those shopping trips, she began to grasp the value of hindsight. Having not paid much attention to or listened to her mother back in Dublin she now wished she had done. Helen thought carefully before making her statement. She was especially hoping to gain her father's support.

"The clothes here are lovely mom but I already have so many. Maybe you and I could share some of mine then I can have some new ones Wouldn't that be a good idea dad."

Moira was not about to be brow beaten. Reminding their child how she had stated, that if there were any problems then it would be her problem. She then told Helen to get on with it and wear her own clothes. Throwing his hands in the air Michael shared his memory of the plan, that it would be between Helen and her mother. Nothing to do with him. Helen was a young woman who could sulk for Ireland should she choose to. On that occasion she did make that choice. Wandering away from her parents in the shopping precinct gave Helen the hopes they would compromise. Well that her mother might compromise. One thing which Moira had learned from her psychology training, was that it would never be a good idea or a good plan to allow yourself to be manipulated by anyone. She had been putting that learning into practice almost for the whole duration of Helens lifetime. She was not about to change her ways. Spotting her parents some time later Helen re-joined them. The family returned back to their apartment with the parents laden with shopping bags full of icy cold weather clothing. Helen clutched a small shopping bag. It contained just a few small bits of thermal underwear. She was humble in what she told her parents.

"Thank you for allowing me to come to Russia with you both. Yes, I should have listened to you mom. I'll know better for the future."

Understanding how hard it would have been for Helen to say those things to her mother- Moira felt quite proud and she felt accomplished too. Extending her open arms to their daughter the women embraced.

Living close to the Pullman area of Moscow was initially something of a challenge for Michae,l Moira and Helen

Kearns. Having heard many stories about the dangers for foreigners living in Russia, Moira decided that some further investigation would be a necessity. She had heard about its negative reputation by Western media. The family were relieved to discover how that was not especially the case. The Kearns were somewhat relieved to learn, that crime in general was quite low and not very common at all against foreigners. Having left their small farm home in their native Ireland some two years previous, they were still settling down to a very different way of life. They had by now become foreign nationals living and working in Russia. With the passing of each day their journey had gradually become an easier one. Michael Kearns aged 52 years is a specialist ear nose and throat surgeon. Being a tall and very handsome man with slightly greying red hair and very Irish green eyes, he stood out in appearance, at the hospital where he worked in the midst of his Russian colleagues.

Moira is a very well-educated lady who holds 2 educational degrees. Her 1st being in sociology and the 2nd in psychology. Moira had applied for and secured a position, working within one of the prestigious health clinics in Pullman. Her position there would generally be working with young women who had prostituted themselves, in other areas of the country and in Moscow too at the time when prostitution had been legal. Moira was a sprightly smallish 50-year-old lady with a very healthy lifestyle. Part of her method of working with clients was that she would meet them at the local park. That's where she would arrive with her red hair tied back, wearing sports trousers and trainers. A very different look to the one which she presented at the office. Power walking or running through the park for 30 minutes would give those women the *feel-good factor. Give them the strength which they required to get through their day in a very positive fashion. That would hopefully inspire and motivate them sufficiently till their next meeting with Moira. Those meetings, informal chats and runs in the park with Moira Kearns had helped the women to walk away from and leave prostitution behind them. That's where the majority said they had felt it belonged.*

These women were carrying many emotional, psychological and in some cases psychical scars too, from their previous way of life. A very high percentage of these ladies had no longer wished to continue with what had been their chosen career of prostitution. They were trying to seek support to either get out of, or to stay out of what they at that point had considered to be their unsavoury ways. Sharing with her husband that prostitution was now illegal in Moscow, Moira found that whole conversation quite distressing. Sharing how the girls had at times been going to some underground dark places, with many going to dark clubs, quite often for the whole purpose of seeking work reduced Moira to tears. She was also very saddened as she discovered, how back before the Soviet Union had crashed in the early 90s, that there had been prostitutes on virtually every street corner in Moscow. It felt very pleasing to her to have the knowledge, that Moscow is now a much cleaner and well-respected city by the rest of the world.

Coffee percolating away in the machine was a very good start to their day for the Kearns. A common denominator within the family was their need for a caffeine fix, first thing in the morning every morning. The house would generally be in silence till at least one mug full each had been consumed.

It was the weekend and the family were all home. Despite their plan being a temporary one they still considered it to be home. Helen would at times make her protests telling her parents.

"Enniskerry is my home my only home and always will be so."

She would be enlightened or reminded by her parents, call it what you will, that home is where ever you lay down your head. They had the old-fashioned ideas and Helen could accept that or she didn't. She did not lack acceptance of what they had said but she did not understand it either. She was confused. Despite now being an adult, the wiring up of her brain had never changed and of course it never will change.

Michael much to his surprise took a call from Crumlin hospital that morning. It was those higher up the ladder as he liked to think of them. Being given news of a change to his contract in Russia he was at the very least surprised. Initially having gone out there on a two-year period of secondment to Moscow that could now be extended to four years, if Michael and his family wished for that to happen. Their arrangement could be changed and would be considered under 'The Fixed Term' work rules of 2002. Despite there being so very many differences to their way of life and the challenges which they were still enduring, the family had experienced virtually no regrets to that point regarding their move. Michael had been informed once again that he did not have to do the extra two years. It would be for him and Moira to decide. Their only issue for them now with the increased time period would be their son Dominic. Knowing Dominic already had a plan in place to take a year out from education, made the new time frame a sweeter pill for them to swallow. He could and they

felt quite certain that he would join them in Russia at some point. Having their own annual leave planned too they would return back to Dublin for two weeks per year.
Camping was high up on their agenda as a possibility for that weekend and then they had a change of mind. They choose to be entertained instead. The camping idea could happen at some other time.

The Kearns had made the very pleasing to themselves discovery, that many Russian people have quite a similar thinking process to Irish people. They learned how Russians had set and kept their bar very high, in terms of them placing value on friendships and on family. Eventually they all set off from their apartment. Taking a lengthy bus ride into the city of Moscow was quite a pleasurable experience in itself. There being lots of street entertainment for them to look at they were happy with their choice. It was especially productive for Helen. Seeing and listening was easier for her to comprehend, than it would perhaps have been for her trying to understand the written word in the Russian language.

Discovering that there's quite a large variety of festivities happening all year round was a pleasant surprise for the Irish family. There were street theatres, some outdoor concerts and some other type of celebrations just to mention a few. Putting all of those facts together helped them to conclude, that Moscow surely has to be a great place to live. Being Roman Catholics the Kearns had searched for a Catholic church. Attending Mass at the Cathedral of the Immaculate conception of the Holy Virgin Mary, was overall quite an enlightening experience for the family. They learned how the cathedral had been closed down in 1937 by the communist authorities and reopened again in 1999. The Kearns were by now discovering lots of new information about the country in which they had chosen to make their temporary home.

A whole two years into their new life found that the Kearns family had returned back to Dublin city for a four weeks' vacation. Joy on the face of their son Dominic on their arrival was as Moira had described it "A sight to behold." Staying at Michaels parents' home had been their choice whilst Helen stayed with Moiras parents together with her brother Dominic. Chats around the kitchen table in both their homes, enlightened the parents just how well their son had managed in their two years absence. Dominic's school reports had shown excellent behaviour at all times, in all areas of the school premises. His academic achievements were matching in their comments. Calls between Michael, Moira and their sons teachers had always been very positive.

Dominic had aspirations to one day in his adult life become a marine scientist. He confirmed his parents' thoughts that he would take one year out from education ahead of going to university. He had decided that during that one-year period he would pay a visit to his family in Russia. He hoped to see what all the fuss was about out there. Almost four weeks had flown by and suddenly it was time for the Kearns to leave Ireland again. They had chosen not to visit their home out at Enniskerry. Driving them over to the airport, Michaels father reminded the family just how proud they all were of their ongoing achievements. Dominic whilst saying goodbye to his parents and his sister, assured them he would be knocking on their door one day in the not too distant future. He would not give any further information regarding his plans. The Kearns family went through airport departure lounge being a little tearful this time. Having seen how much Dominic had grown in their absence had surprised them. They had left Ireland just over two years previous leaving a child behind. They were now leaving behind them what was quite a young man.

Waiting for their flight back to Moscow had felt just a little tedious this time. Everyone being overly tired was not and never would be conducive to a relaxed flight. Eventually being on board the aircraft, the family settled down in the hopes of catching some sleep. Arrival back in Moscow was faster than anticipated. A taxi car was taken to their apartment. That's where and when Helen released all of her pent-up emotions. Hearing the sobs coming from her bedroom Moira suggested they should give her some space.

"She'll come out when she's ready Michael. It had to be hard for her leaving her brother and grandparents again. Then add into the equation the fact that so many plans were changed when we were in Dublin. There's no surprise really that she's emotional at the minute."

Michael agreeing with all which she had said, expressed his compassion for the extra difficulties their daughter would always be faced with, throughout every aspect of her life. They then drew the line on that conversation. Eventually that evening and after having slept a while Helen emerged from her bedroom. Looking something a bit like she had done ten rounds in the boxing ring with Mike Tyson her parents kept their views to themselves. Michael smiled as he asked her.

"Tea Helen or a cold drink?"

Declining his offer, the girl graciously told her parents how she was taking a walk in the local park.

"Blow away the cobwebs and the thoughts of saying goodbye in Dublin last night. Back in time for dinner. "

And she was gone. Again, yes, you've correctly guessed the vision on the staircase and the front door scenario. Michael checked the door for dents. Being rented accommodation there would be potential implications for any damage which was incurred. Taking a sigh of relief Michael shared with his wife that on this occasion all was intact.

"Jeez Moira it's only a matter of time. One of these days it's gonna happen unless we can find a way to stop her fiery behaviour."

Deciding to leave that thought right there the Kearns took themselves outdoors for a walk. Taking in the beauty of nature surrounding them was the therapy they both required.

Dilemma for Helen

*T*heir daughter Helen was once again as was usual for her, up and almost ready to leave for work at 7 am prompt. Quickly arranging her long red wavy hair into a bun, the young Irish woman thought about how it made her look more sophiscated. Sophistication was very important to Helen yet you would not see that in many of her behaviours. Calling out goodbye to her mother she ran down the very long staircase and out through the front door. Almost taking the door from its hinges as she left was pretty common place for her. Yes, she had also once again taken the stairs two by two. That was Helen. Heavy and rough handed at almost everything which she did in life. Moiras lifelong warnings to their daughter regarding the stairs had always fell on deaf ears. Moira had at last come to accept there would now be no change in that department.

*B*uses and most forms of public transport were usually very efficient and not too expensive in their area. Helen was quite smart minded. Discovering that making a travel purchase in bulk would be financially productive she knew what she should do. She would often purchase several rides maybe at least twenty in one go. That would then provide Helen with a well reduced travel price on her individual bus rides. Being an Irish colleen from Enniskerry, she was rapidly changing her mind on where and what she considered to be home. Still not *understanding the concept of 'home is where you lay your head down' Helen was nevertheless in her head making some choices. She appeared to certainly be finding and attempting to build a life for herself in Russia.*

Grabbing a coffee as she waited for the bus Helens thoughts were focused on the day which lay ahead. Working in such a highly prestigious environment as she did, she was feeling very fortunate to have secured her position there. Eventually arriving at the library for foreign literature she hung up her jacket and scanned the large room. Helen always took a light weight jacket when going outdoors. She would take precautions regardless of how hot or dry the weather might be. It was one of her quirky ways. She quite rightly had little regard to another's point of view on her doing that. She was not a people pleaser and hoped how that situation would never change for her.

Sitting down quietly at her desk Helen Kearns adjusted the level and the height of her chair. Being one of those quite posh leather chairs, you could shift it up and down depending on a person's personal preference. She had taken the chair to its very limits that morning. Depending on what her needs were at any given time, would always be the catalyst for Helen to decide, which level or height to have her chair set to. Wanting to have a totally good view throughout their very spacious room, she decided it needed to be quite high. She was thinking about the many people who had filled up the area which was now surrounding her. Helens piercing green eyes scanned all the way across and around the vastness of that room. Just like her father she had very beautiful green Irish looking eyes.

Taking a few short moments to think about what she could do, in alignment with what she might do, Helen took a deep breath in. It was not going to be an easy decision for her. Her desire at that time was to bring improvements to her working environment. She was hoping to and wanting to improve on what she had considered to be the chaos, directly there in front of her eyes. She was a people watcher who loved to set herself a challenge. Helen would try in her mind to figure out and discover what a person did for a living and then if they appeared to be friendly, she would check with them upon them leaving the library. She would make notes from any success which she might have achieved. Helen made notes about most things in her life. They would always have to be hand written and filed away carefully in her locked diary. Writing by hand was something which she had done from a very young age. Bringing change of any description to her life would cause her raised levels of annoyance, of anxiety and of stress. She therefore continued with the hand writing right into her adult life. Michael and Moira often thought about how well Helen had adapted to the change of living in a different country. Their only conclusion could be and was that as it was something which initially excited her and that her brain was ready to accept the challenge.

Helen whilst being chronologically very young she was aged 20years, plus 3 weeks and 2 days, she often appeared to be much older. She was very particular about getting her age just right. In fact, getting almost all things in her life just right was very important to Helen. She was and is as we know on the Autism spectrum. Having a diagnosis of high functioning autism has allowed her to do very well academically, however it has created issues in other areas of Helens life. Her biggest and most profound problems were probably and always would be, associated with her differences of not being socially correct and available in her communication skills.

She is a young woman who in so many areas of and aspects of her life and of her thinking process has quite old-fashioned ideas. Often thinking about and considering how technology would always have a place in life she decided that it definitely did not have a place in her notebook. She loved to try to mix up her hand writing skills and styles, with each attempt trying to improve on the last one. She was trying to be the best version of herself which she could be. Helen had felt that her attempts at handwriting, would be as good as any for a place for her to begin that journey of her own self -improvement.

Silence was suddenly shattered within the library as one of her regulars came crashing through the doorway, letting the doors slam close loudly behind him. Delighted to see the young man Helen once again attempted to remind him of the rules.

   "We have to be quiet in here Akim."
And then instantly she felt bad. Helen reprimanded herself for being thoughtless. Quickly remembering that her young Russian customer Akim was permanently living in a totally quiet and silent world, she felt the need to offer her apologies to him. Helen understood how he would not have known the serious level of noise which he had created, as he let the doors slip away from his hands. Being profoundly deaf from birth had been and always would be the life experience of Akim Ivanovich Typreheb. He appeared to be a young man who was not too perturbed or impacted too badly by his very

hidden disability. Helen would then recall her own feelings regarding autism. Being aware how it impacted her far more than she would ever let others be aware of, she wondered if perhaps the same could be true for Akim.

*W*anting to apologise for what she had considered to be her sheer lack of thought, Helen approached the small desk in the corner where the young man was sitting down. Akim was by now sat quietly reading a book. She was amazed by the fact that he was actually reading an English book, despite him being of Russian nationality and being disabled too as she saw his situation. Helen squared her shoulders back as she stood tall in front of her customer. She looked him directly in the eye. Akim could lipread and was very good at it. Telling her not to be concerned for that which she had said, he then took Helen very much by surprise. In addition to lipreading Akim had also been taught by his parents and his teachers how to speak. He shared with Helen how his younger years had been spent at the bilingual school for deaf children in Moscow and how that is the only school in Russia where sign language has equal status with written and spoken language. To say that Helen was shocked and amazed beyond belief is an understatement.

*L*eaving the library some two hours later Akim approached the young Irish woman who was still sat at her desk. His request to her to meet him later that evening for a meal and some drinks, was something of a surprise for Helen. With very little thought and consideration she graciously accepted the invitation from Akim. Helen felt a little anxious throughout the day. She thought about how communicating for a short period in the library was one matter but having an evening *out together would have to be something else. She wasn't feeling sure! Reproaching herself with hindsight she felt that perhaps she had acted in haste by accepting Akims request. Now she would have to see it through.*

Arriving home early that evening Helen ignored her parents and went direct to take a shower. It was a sunny evening. She liked the sunshine except for when she burnt and that was quite often. Having typical Irish skin, she would turn a deep shade of red quite quickly, whilst everyone else would be getting their dream tan. Usually being quite careful to apply her sun protection, it didn't always seem to be enough. Having brought a good supply with her from Ireland, the just in case scenario, she probably had enough for the whole 4-year period.

Deciding what to wear for her date was a bit of a dilemma for Helen. Seeking out her mother's approval which came as quite a surprise for Moira, she eventually choose a brown stripy dress which hung slightly above her knee. She choose some matching brown strappy sandals and her light weight jacket. The couple had a plan to meet up outside an Irish restaurant and pub. It was called Mollies and is situated in the very centre of Moscow city. Telling her mother how she was planning to meet a female friend in town caused concern for Helen. She had feelings of guilt for having told a lie to her mom. Given Helens many social issues her parents would always feel delighted, if and when she had an evening out with a friend. If the friend's gender was of any importance to the parents Helen would not know about that. She had never put that to the test. She left the family's apartment in time to pick up the 5 pm bus into town.

*W*aiting outside of Mollies she had a glimpse of Akim as he walked down the street. Thinking of how handsome he was looking in his smart brown trousers, cream shirt with his top button undone and a jacket flipped over his shoulder, she greeted him with the spoken word. Akim did what was 2nd nature to him. He used his voice whilst signing along at the same time. Then remembering that Helen would not be able to understand sign language, he made some strong attempts to drop the sign. Despite the obvious language barrier, the young couple appeared to get along quite well. Enjoying a meal from the selection of traditional Irish food on the menu, Helen was very impressed by Akims level of thought shown by having taken her to an Irish pub. The evening having come to its end he walked her over the road to her bus stop. Helens bus making its appearance she heard a very quick and almost abrupt.

"Till the next time Helen."
He then placed a kiss on her cheek and he was gone.

*C*limbing on board the bus she thought about how scruffy looking it was. How scruffy and dirty looking the seats were. How dirty the windows were. Helen thought about anything which she could muster up a thought about, which might be of help to her. She was seeking distraction from her other thoughts and from her evening out with Akim. It wasn't that she didn't like the man she actually did and a lot. She liked him however she didn't want to make that acknowledgement to herself. The situation would be all to difficult for her with their poor level of communication and with him being Russian too. That was all in addition to him being a member of the Orthodox church. What would her strict Irish catholic *parents have to say to all of those facts she wondered to herself?*

Back home in their apartment in Pullman Moira Kearns was still awake and up waiting for their daughter's safe return from their night out. Trying not to interrogate the young woman, to Helens absolute delight Moira asked her very few questions. Bidding a fair goodnight to her mother and after using the bathroom Helen went direct to her bedroom. That's where she cried silently into her pillow. She rubbed her tears away as they fell quick and fast from her beautiful green Irish eyes. Quite unusual for her Helen said a short prayer to god, asking him to give her strength. The strength which she would need in order to say no to Akim. She knew he most likely would ask her for another date. For many reasons she would have to be able to say no.

Dominic Kearns had completed his school education and had taken his leavers certificate. Next steps being a year out for the purpose of travel and enlightenment. That would be ahead of taking a degree course in university. Dominic was ready to surprise his parents. Making his plan together with his grandparents he left Dublin airport on a one-way flight ticket for Moscow. The doorbell ringing out at 5 in the morning woke the Kearns household. To say that Dominic's idea of surprise was effective would be something of an understatement. Discussions around getting the most from his two weeks in Moscow he declined their offer for him to stay longer.

"I want to see other parts of the world too. Coming here had to be and was my priority and it'll be great."

Accepting their sons wish Michael and Moira arranged to show him the sights whilst keeping his interests in mind. Two weeks went by very quickly. In the blink of an eye it was time for Dominic Kearns to step on the next leg of his journey. His parents attempts to ensure he was financially stable for the year were heavily rejected by their son. He was acting like an independent young man and gained much pleasure from doing that.

"It's fine. I've planned for this for quite some time now and want to do it on my own two feet."

He continued to remind his parents how he had worked a lot of weekends for the past three years and had saved up almost all of his earnings. Michael and Moira were left feeling impressed yet they checked again for some certainty of his finances.

"You only have to say the word and we'll transfer some to you Dominic."

He began to look a little annoyed. Having supportive parents was great, but the need to be independent from them was great to their son too. Hoping this would be absolute clarity of his financial situation he lovingly but firmly told them.

"I've got more money than I'll need and Ill probably do short work stints in some countries too. Stop worrying please."
Placing a kiss on their cheeks he reminded them it was time to go. Being driven to the airport by his parents together with his sister Helen, that's where the family said their goodbyes. Estonia and Latvia both being next on the list for Dominic he wasn't certain of his destinations after that.

"Enjoy your time in seeing the world. Wherever you are, just know that we are no more than a simple thought away."

*W*atching their child go through the departure lounge the Kearns parents were left feeling sad yet very proud. Michael had a slight quiver in his voice.

"Our baby Moira only he's no longer a baby."
Helen having a look of sadness of her face. She was quickly reassured by Michael and Moira.

"C'mon on remember how you felt when we first left Dublin. You were beyond delighted to have that chance to see a bit more of the world. That's exactly what your brothers doing right now."
Expressing her gratitude to her parents for their insight Helen suggested they should all spend the day in Moscow. Unlike her brother she surely did not have that desire for financial independence. She was also thinking of any potential dates with Akim and how a new outfit to wear could be nice.

"You could treat me to some new clothes after we've had lunch. We could go to an Irish restaurant. There's one called Mollies and it's in the city centre."

*B*eing impressed with their daughter's knowledge of the Irish restaurant, an agreement was reached that the family would dine there.

"Sounds great Helen. All this time living in Russia and we've never discovered an Irish restaurant or an Irish pub. Can't wait to see what's on the menu and how traditionally Irish it actually is."
Walking back to their car in the airport car park Helen almost had an anxiety attack. She recalled how Akim had shared with her, the fact that deaf people are often remembered due to their method of chatting with each other. She recalled Akim using some sign language in Mollies on their date night.

Not for the purpose of communicating with Helen but to show her the meaning of certain words and signs. That memory then gave her the unpleasant worry that she might be remembered by some staff. That having the potential of leading into some comments being made about the young man she had been there with previously. In her head the risk was too big a risk. She had to quickly come up with a reason not to go to Mollies. Being aware how there could be no way in which her parents could identify her dishonesty, Helen calmly told them.

"Sorry mom and dad I've suddenly got the worst migraine ever. It's come from nowhere with no warning. Can we just go home?"

Knowing how her parents would accept her statement she also knew this meant there would be no new outfit for her. Well not on that occasion anyhow. However, Helen was a smart young woman. She would create some opportunities to have her parents pay for some new clothes of her choice on a later date. Thinking how manipulative she was behaving and planning to behave did not feel good to her, yet not bad enough to cause her a change of mind. Needs must and all of that was starting to become her motto.

Michael and Moira were now looking forward to their time in Moscow coming to its natural end. They were at the start of the process, of making plans for a return back home to Ireland early the following year. Having the knowledge their son Dominic had secured himself a good education ahead of him travelling the world, they could see a good future for him. Hopefully he would on his return to Ireland pursue his desire to become a scientist. Michael and Moira Kearns were very happy to support any further education their son might require, in order to follow that career path. They wondered about Helen and what she might do once she returned back to Dublin. Encouraging her to bring her friends over to their apartment left Helen feeling quite mortified about the idea. Getting the facts right she only had one friend. She did not consider that Akim would continue with his wish to remain friends, once she declined his request for another date. Yes, that was her plan and she had strong feelings of uncertainty, regarding how he might respond. She however was leaning towards the side of he would be declining any further contact with her.

Akim arrived at the library some weeks after their first date.

The usual thunder storm had occurred as he walked through the main doors. Helens heart had missed a beat as she heard him ahead of seeing him. Trying to deny herself in her mind the attraction which she had felt towards Akim, Helen failed miserably. Approaching her at the desk the young man was looking a little nervous. In fact, he was looking exactly how she was feeling. Hearing his request for another date Helens resilience had very quickly disappeared. Thoughts of any and all potential issues, which could be raised as a result of her dating him also disappeared quickly from her mind. Helen graciously accepted his request. Making their plan to meet up back at Mollies again that evening, he then said goodbye. Akim had gone to the library, for the sole purpose of seeing the person he struggled to remove from his thoughts over the past few weeks.

Their second date was very revealing about this young deaf man. He spoke to Helen about how he had previously gone through education and had left with some good results. Akim had secured some qualifications. Those qualifications were quite enough to successfully help him to secure his current employment. Akim is a teacher. Upon hearing that news there was a look of surprise on Helens face. He was teaching sign language studies to children aged between twelve to fourteen years. He was working in a boarding school for the deaf in Moscow. He explained how sign language was being taught alongside the use of oralism too. Sharing with Helen how many parents did not appreciate the idea of any levels of oralism, being taught to their deaf children in schools, Helen did not feel she could comment.

"I'm sorry Akim I don't know anything about deafness as a disability, but I'm confident that as a profoundly deaf person yourself that you're doing what's right."

He felt respected by Helen and that his opinions were being respected by her too.

"Thanks Helen. Many people through their ignorance and through their lack of education, consider that I'm not good enough to be a teacher. I appreciate your kind thoughts."

She assured him that kindness on her part did not come into the equation. That she's an outspoken type of person and that she speaks as she finds.

The woman was in awe of all which Akim had achieved in his life despite his disability. She did however struggle to grasp or understand how a profoundly deaf person could be so well educated. That of course was ignorance on Helens part. Sharing with him information about herself and about her condition of autism felt good for Helen. Akim had little understanding of the sheer complexity of her condition. He was however interested and wanted to discover more. Again, their night had come to its natural end, with Akim on this occasion taking her in his arms and gently kissing her on the lips. Helen had felt a little surprised by his action. She was however at the same time very pleased. She kissed him back giving Akim the message that she perhaps liked him too.

Many more dates with successful communication occurred between Helen and Akim over the following months. Communication had become much less of a barrier between them. That was partly due to him having taught his girlfriend how to use sign language. Taking Helen to meet his parents they were left feeling thrilled. Knowing that such a very nice young woman, who had a genuine interest in Akims methods of communication had entered their son's life gave the man's parents some feelings of deep joy. Many situations were often discussed between Helen, Akim and his parents. This was all to the exclusion of religion or anything which had a religious connotation. Helen was already aware that Akims whole family belonged to the Orthodox church and how they were all regular attenders. They were however very open and very broadminded about everything in life. Akim gave lots of assurance to his girlfriend, how his parents would not see her being Catholic, as being anything of a problem or a barrier to their relationship. Helen had craved for parents who would hold that view of all religions in the same way in which Akims parents did.

Michael continued to enjoy and to learn from his experience at the hospital. He had been given some new roles within the same hospital for the remainder of his time on secondment in Russia. Through some further self-reflection, he was pleased that he had taken the initial opportunity of moving over to Russia. The hospital there had availed him many new ideas, opportunities and many new ways of dealing with situations. He would be excited to bring his new learning back to Ireland in the future. Being moved over to the hospitals new wing for adults who were suffering from hearing loss, was becoming a great experience for Michael too. He was in awe of the many patients who were living their lives in such very challenging circumstances. In addition to his keen interest in medicine, he had always been blessed with a technical mind too. Wanting to somewhat improve the lives of his most profoundly deaf patients, Michael had created an idea in his head. He made the decision that perhaps talking to his family about his innovative ideas, could be beneficial for everyone. To gain the perspective and the opinions of another person or persons would be invaluable to him. Having peoples input regarding his ideas ahead of speaking to colleagues was important to Michael.

Moira continued to enjoy her life and her new lifestyle living in Russia. She had gained some great pleasure from her many positive results, with the young women to whom she had been assigned. She often reminisced about her time spent as a young child growing up in the leafy suburbs of Dublin. She would remember her parents and at times remember the young man whom she had loved and lost. That was some years ahead of meeting her husband Michael. Moiras parents who were by now into their senior years had been very strict from a religious perspective. Their very old fashioned and quite prominent in Ireland in those days, ideas of you marry into your own religion, was as we know the catalyst which had caused the separation for Moira and her then boyfriend Charlie Cunningham. Moira despite being from a different generation and despite initially not agreeing with her parents views on religiously mixed marriages, she somehow became tangled up in that type of belief. Moira throughout her life after her meeting with Michael Kearns who was a Roman Catholic like herself, began to think that her parents were right. That you should not become involved with someone from a different religious background. She then held on to those strong and very strict views.

Helen was very aware of what her mother had lost in her relationship with Charlie Cunningham, due to Moiras own parent's religious views. She was also aware of her moms' own feelings regarding mixed religious relationships and how they now mirrored those of her parents. Helen was very cautious in her thinking. She at times wondered about the strong possibility of herself and Akim ever getting serious and what view her parents take on that might be, but especially what her mother might say or think. Despite regularly seeing Akim and having been his girlfriend for the previous nine or ten months, Helen was not yet prepared or ready to let their relationship be known, to anyone outside of Akims family. For those religious reasons and concerns Helen had kept their relationship totally secret from her parents.

Postcards arriving over the previous months to the Kearns apartment, gave his parents great assurance that their other child Dominic was exploring and enjoying life. Having arrived from countries as far apart as Sweden, Norway and Slovakia, they could see that he was continuing with his grand tour of the world as he had called it. What appeared to have the greatest interest through Dominic's eyes, was the vast areas of forestation which he loved to explore. He wrote vividly to his parents from time to time.

"The peaceful and serene views are just fabulous. To pitch a tent in the forest under the setting sun, is one of the very best feelings and one of the best experiences of my lifetime. I'm so happy here."

Dominic had loved wildlife ever since he was a very young child. There would be no limit to how many different varieties and different species which he would encounter in the forest. Moira wondered if he ever thought about his part in the wildlife garden with his frogs. Parents were delighted to read all of those statements from their son. Michael was sincere compassionate, calm, and very caring in his tone.

"We've done something right Moira. You just know that when your off-spring stand up on their own two feet and go off to explore, then yes you know you've done it right."

She shared a smile which gave confirmation that she agreed with her husband.

Michael Kearns was feeling very excited as he shared with his family, his thoughts for making things better and bringing many long-awaited improvements to the life of a deaf person. Drawing up his ideas at the kitchen table he enlisted opinions from both his wife Moira and from their daughter Helen. Helen initially was a little confused regard why her father was having such a strong interest, in the needs of deaf people and especially so deaf adults. Due to her relationship with Akim she was having feelings of almost paranoia. Questioning her father about his new role, she initially had a great sense of relief.

"Thought you were a kid's doctor, a paediatrician in the ear nose and throat department."

Being assured that's exactly what he was Michael was also able to explain about his new role.

"It's a temporary opportunity for me Helen for the rest of our time here in Russia. It's in the adult's ear nose and throat department, working with deaf adults. There's the hope of bringing some improvements to their lives. Let me explain about my own thoughts and ideas."

Considering Akim was a working member of the population, Helen assumed he would no longer be involved with the local hospital. She was satisfied he could not cross paths with her father in any sort of knowing way. She listened as her father continued.

My own idea as per this drawing is to create a small device, which would connect to musical outlets such as radio and television. It would also connect wirelessly to a person's own hearing aids. It would allow sound to travel direct from one source to another. This he felt would have to give more clarity to the hearing aid user. Moira and Helen too were feeling very excited about the possible innovation. Helen of course was considering how this idea would be something amazing to help improve her boyfriend's life. She wondered when it might be implemented. Hearing from her father that his idea was still in the stage of its infancy, he could not be accurate when if ever it might become available. Moira praised her husband.

"Not only are you a medical doctor you're now becoming an inventor too."

Michael laughed but yes that was the reality of what was potentially happening. Again, expressing his excitement at the idea of his considered product becoming a reality, his family felt proud. Moira offered her encouragement.

"Take it up the ladder Michael. I'm sure they'll be delighted. Not just by your talent for creating this but also for the fact

you've put that much thought into your new role with adults. Who knows it could potentially work for deaf children too, get them to look at some funding for you to progress with the project."
Michael appreciating that level of support from his wife and daughter he decided to go ahead. Her would see and speak to someone on his return to work the following day.

A̶kim arriving early at the library to collect his girlfriend for lunch, maybe hadn't been the best idea he ever had. Leaving together they had been seen by Michael Kearns. Recognising Akim from the ear nose and throat clinic Michael was clearly surprised to see him together with their daughter. It was obvious to Michael by their body language that they were a couple. He did not make his presence known to them and Akim did not see Michael. That's kind of like a side effect problem for deaf people. Their eyes being their ears means that quite often their visual focus is purely just around them and perhaps not taking in the bigger view. Sharing what he had seen with his wife Moira that evening, they decided to speak to Helen regarding her secrecy and what was in their words obviously her boyfriend. Helen had been deeply engrossed in and concentrating on what Akim was sharing with her. She therefore did not see her father either. The conversation back home was something of a shock for Helen.

F̶eeling as though she was being interrogated just a little like the Spanish inquisition, she did not like the situation very much at all. Helen became almost introvert towards both of her parents. Listening to their many questions being fired at her, she had to be very swift in her thinking. She had to think on her feet as it were. Wanting at all costs to avoid their many questions and answers about religion, she choose not to answer any of their questions. Helen took herself outside of their apartment and down the road to their local coffee shop. That's where she sat for the next seventy minutes. Yes, we know it was seventy minutes as Helen always was and is so particular with everything she does. She carefully records her movements in her small diary with great accuracy. She needed some thinking time away from her parent's presence. Helen had decided that she also needed to see her boyfriend Akim. She needed to share some important information with him and wasn't sure how he would or might react. Many potential scenarios of Akims reactions felt like a roller coaster spinning around in her head. Helen had not felt this confused since the day she watched the McGinty's calf being born. Her confusion then was associated around how the calf had got into its mothers' belly in the first instance.

Michael and Moira had begun to feel defeated. More than an hour from leaving their apartment, their daughter had not returned back home. That was out of character for Helen. She would usually say when she would be back home or call her parents with updates. Wondering if their approach had been to heavy Michael could see that possibly yes it had been.

"We've gone too far this time Moira."
She nodded and continued to tell him.
"Possibly yes we have but it's the secrecy and the dishonesty I hate Michael."
Again, he was nodding in agreement, however Michael felt the need to remind her of her own younger years. Remind her of her secret boyfriend Charlie Cunningham and the reasons why he had been kept secret. Remind her about the levels of stress which she had endured back then and how that's

probably the same level of stress which Helen would most likely be feeling in this current situation. Moira looked reflective but remained silent. Breaking that silence, they both acknowledged that their daughter's happiness was of most importance to them. Moira however expressed that should there ever be an attempt on Helens part to make that young man a serious boyfriend, then that would not be very acceptable to her. She encouraged her husband to have the same line of thought.

"I know it's difficult Michael but let's face it- that boy is not going to be Roman Catholic. We just know that!"
Michael already having knowledge of the boy's religion from his medical records, he knew he could not share that with his wife. Not wishing to appear to be dismissive of her view, he choose his words with caution.

"Look Moira Helens not here now so let's put this to bed until tomorrow evening when we could try talking to her again."
Agreeing that his idea was perhaps for the best Moira found herself a book in which to lose herself and to absorb her many painful thoughts.

Travelling up to Akims parents' home Helen was feeling full of trepidation. She climbed the steps up to the front door in an almost frenzy. Reminding herself that she needed to calm down ahead of speaking to Akim, the girl practised her deep breathing. Helen had been taught breathing techniques as early as when she was a 1st class student in her local school back in Enniskerry. She often had anxiety attacks in those days largely due to her inability to socialise effectively due to her autism. She knocked gently on the door. Akim was feeling surprised to see his girlfriend standing there. It was evident to *him that she had been visibly distressed. Inviting her to step inside he then enquired about what was wrong and why she had been distressed? Sharing with him how her father had seen them together Akim was surprised. He was equally delighted as now the door could be open for him to meet her parents. Despite him knowing how they would disapprove of him due to his religion, Akim still hoped to meet and get to know them. He had a strong side to his character. Thinking how it would be of benefit to him in that situation with her parents, he confidently reassured Helen.*

Reaction to him hearing how she was two months pregnant with his child, showed through the happy looking smile on Akims face.

"Oh my god Helen I'm so happy. We're going to have a baby together"
He looked at her anxiously whilst firing questions.

"You do want the baby too? Your happy about the baby? You looked very stressed when you arrived here."
Helen was reassuring that yes, she was happy and yes, she too wanted to keep the baby. She shared with him how she was however feeling a little confused as they had used contraception. She reminded him of the very many questions which she had endured from both of her parents. She assured him how that was the only reason for her fierce levels of stress. A look of relief spread across Akims face upon reading those words. They fondly embraced.

No one could have been more pleased or happier than Akim was about the pregnancy. Relief for Helen from his reaction was immense and then there was the surprise. Akim getting down on one knee proposed to his girlfriend. He asked for her hand in marriage. Loving this man in a way which she had never imagined to be possible and knowing how he had felt the same way about her, Helen was beyond delighted by the opportunity to be his wife. From her perspective there was now just the problem of her parents to address and especially that of her mother. Akim gave her some reassurance that together, they could and they would conquer all obstacles presented to them in life. That was to include any obstacles presented from her parents too. She felt supported and was appreciative and very grateful for the man in her life.

*H*elen returned back to their apartment later that evening.

Hearing the key turn in the door was a good feeling. Michael and Moira had a sense of relief that she had come back.

"We've been very worried. Knowing you left in anger and distress and with us having no idea of where you'd gone to or where you were, was quite hard for parents to deal with." Helen was attentive, respectful and responsive to what her parents had just shared with her. She apologised in the best way she knew how.

"I know now that I was wrong not to say where I was going and I'm sorry. I couldn't cope with all the questions and didn't know what else to do. I'm going to bed. Catch up tomorrow evening after work."

Immediately going through to her bedroom and closing that door tightly behind her, Helen had given Michael and Moira no chance to ask any further questions. Not especially liking their situation they knew there was no other choice for them. They too retired for the night.

*M*oiras position working with young and some quite older women too was coming to end of contract. Forward thinking *she would need to find something to occupy her time, for the months which were left on Michaels secondment. Being a woman who could not sit around doing nothing, Moira duly approached a local food store. Having a vacancy for a part time assistant which was offered to her, she felt fortunate. Being an Irish woman living and working near Moscow, had shown Moira many new experiences for which she was very grateful. This new position at the food store would hopefully bring many more people into her life.*

Moira thought how life felt very good to the exclusion of potential issues surrounding their daughter Helen. She then again thought about the reasons, why it would be a problem for Helen to have a young Russian boyfriend. Knowing her own mind so well Moira was very aware, that there was no question about the fact that religion was the cat among the Pidgeon's. If Michael was right and it was what he considered it to be between Helen and the young man, then it would obviously be coming to its natural end soon anyhow. They as a family would be returning back to their home in Enniskerry and the young man would be left behind in Russia. Moira sat back in the lounger, her feet outstretched just like she did when close to the lavender bush in their garden at home. She had a lavender shrub growing indoors in their apartment. Ducking and diving from her parents had become habitual for Helen Kearns, as she waited for the following weekend. She and Akim would share all of their news together with her parents at that time. Helen had a multitude of feelings in relation to that upcoming disclosure. She however had strong faith, full trust and belief in her boyfriend. She knew he would stand up to her parents in an assertive yet in a very polite and respectful manner.

Akim had been very reassuring to Helen that they would do that job of talking to her parents together. He called in at the library daily ahead of the family meeting. Wanting to be sure and certain that Helen was doing well he could see she was a little anxious. Helen had inherited a degree of her mom's reaction of sweaty palms to anxiety. There was nothing she was aware of which might or would settle that down for her. For Helen it was a matter of resolve the problem and that in turn resolves the anxiety. Sitting in a quiet corner within the library on her lunch break felt the safest option to them both. The risk of bumping in to Helen's father again was too great should they have gone outside.

Family Revelations

*T*ime sneaking up real fast, it would soon be time for the Kearns family to leave Moscow and return back to their home in Enniskerry. Michael had made some very close friends at the hospital. Two were surgeons like he was with another being a gentleman who worked at the Ear nose and throat reception desk. Michael had bonded with those men through common denominators. All four of them had a child on the autism spectrum. Despite knowing that they shouldn't do it, their comparing of notes and life achievements of their children went off the scale. Michael being at that hospital on secondment and soon to return back to Ireland, the others being from Russia and permanently resident in that area, they decided to throw a small dinner party for Michael and his family ahead of him leaving.

*A*kim going over to the Kearns apartment the following weekend was something of a surprise for Michael and Moira. Knowing how that was their plan, Helen had then kept a low profile from her parents throughout the whole week. She had wanted Akim by her side to support with the answering of any awkward questions. Helen had felt that there would be an abundance of them and especially so from her mother. Having decided to not even mention he would be visiting, she did question the fairness of that decision making on her *parents. Everyone up in the Kearns household the doorbell rang out early morning. Helen had advised her boyfriend to arrive around half past nine. Parents might be going out and did not want to miss them. That was the morning when Akim was formally introduced to Michael and Moira Kearns. Showing himself to have some quite unique resilience to life, her parents were left feeling highly impressed with their daughter too and her ability to use sign language. Taking a deep breath in Helen decided to be open and honest with her parents. She did it in Helens way. No subtilty- Just direct and almost abruptly she shared their news. Firstly, hearing that she was about to get married and then that they were about to become grandparents, was initially all a bit too much for her parents to hear.*

Michael Kearns with his head initially buried in his hands raised it up and then shocked everyone in the room. Telling Akim what admiration he held for him as a deaf person who was getting on so well with life, how very inspiring he was to others, he then asked Akim for his help. Using his daughter to help with communication Michael stated to the young man in front of him.

"There's a unit at the hospital I work in back in Ireland. It needs the support of someone like you to encourage other deaf families, or hearing parents with deaf children. There's a job with your name on it if you would agree to take it. You and Helen could live together on our farm if that would be suitable to you both."

Moira Kearns hugged her husband telling him how proud she was of him and proud of herself too. She had once and for all buried her religious feelings. She was prioritising their childs happiness. A shocked yet delighted Helen hugged her parents with a special hug and message for her mother.

"I've always known that you felt the same as Grandma about religiously mixed marriages. This is yet another way of you showing your love for me and I appreciate it."

Welcoming Akim into their family they all looked at plans for their almost imminent return back to their homeland. A second house would be built on the land which could be a home for the young couple if they wished to go to Ireland and to stay on the farm. That was yet another shock for Helen. She had her parents' blessings to stay behind in Russia if that's what would make her happiest. She was delighted to hear and see how they were treating her respectfully for the mature young woman which she was.

Plans in place for Michaels leaving dinner party-It was to be held in quite a small intimate looking restaurant just outside of Pullman. Helen and Akim were both invited by Michael to join her parents for the evening. Off spring of his colleagues and friends were grown and settled down in life with families of their own. Their evening went well. Again all being parents to a child on the spectrum, Helen was far more than they had anticipated that she would be. Everyone was very impressed by her communication abilities and how well she had settled into life in a foreign country. They were highly Impressed with her social skills and her ability to use sign language with her boyfriend. They were keen to hear all about her educational experiences growing up in Ireland. Drawing comparisons to the Russian system it appeared there were no comparisons. They shared how there's a lack of expertise in their country, to know how to help support and best educate the child with high functioning autism. And it gets worse. When he child reaches their 18th birthday they supposedly no longer have autism. They are then given the label of a mental health disorder such as schizophrenia. The Kearns family expressed some gratitude for their systems in Ireland.

Hospital colleagues were highly impressed by Akims level of talent and by his fluent use of oralism combined with sign language. Sharing information with the group in relation to his education as a deaf child, Akim went down memory lane. Education and socialising had not been the greatest of experiences for him in the earlier years. Things however did improve as he went through his senior school years. Akim was and is a profoundly deaf from birth person. Using his bilateral hearing aids has brought immense progress to his ability to use the spoken word. He was impressed by Michaels attempts to create a device, which would hopefully work between the hearing aid and the radio for example. Michael once again showed his acceptance of Akim.

"It's been great to be in your company Akim. Knowing you from the hospital clinic is really not knowing you at all. I've learned an awful lot from you tonight. See you soon."
Akim acknowledged the man's appreciation and returned the compliment. The idea of Michael Kearns being his consultant at the clinic was blown out of the water. It was something which they both felt wouldn't work very well at all. Helen also had some input to that scenario.
"Promise you'll sort it dad. Be too embarrassing otherwise."
Akims suggestion was heard by Michael.
"Might be easier if you swap some of your case load Michael including me. Management would then have to provide another surgeon to me."

Decisions were made that Michael would sort it on his next day of duty at the clinic. Their evening ending and all having said their goodbyes Michael would give Akim a lift back home to his parents' house.

Sharing information regarding their future plans with Akims parents gave Akim and Helen great Joy. His parents were delighted too. They had never been outside of Moscow. That was now going to change.

"We'll be coming over to Ireland to meet our grandchild and to attend at the wedding of our only son."
Two months later the Kearns family together with Helens boyfriend Akim, all boarded an aircraft which was destined for Dublin airport. Moira Kearns had been in touch with Eileen McGinty. Their farmhouse out in Enniskerry had been vacated the previous week. Eileen had taken charge of the house keys. An array of dairy products and some foods from their farm land had been provided by Eileen and left together at the house. It was autumn time with many days of warm sunshine. The house would be a sight to behold for all of them but perhaps for Akim in particular.

An airport taxi car was summoned for their journey out to Enniskerry. Akim was in awe of what he called the beautiful green grass of the countryside of Ireland. A welcoming party was present at their farmhouse. Dominic Kearns had returned back to Ireland from his year out. Delighted to see his parents and to meet and hear all about Akim gave Dominic pleasure. Instantly attempting to seek out information on Irish sign language, Akim shared how what he knows would not be of much help. Explaining how different countries will perhaps use signs meaning something different, in the same way as the spoken word could have a different meaning. It would be a learning curve for all of them who wished to learn Irish sign language. Dominic was keen as were his parents, Helen and their farming neighbours John and Eileen McGinty. Enquiries would be made the following morning for classes local to them perhaps in Dublin or in Wicklow. Having spent the day walking around the farm and enjoying the serenity and peace of their back garden, Helen was tired. Bidding goodnight to her family she and Akim retired for the night. Agreements reached that now Helen is an adult and about to be a mother herself, she would share one of their large bedrooms with Akim. Moira was forthcoming with her suggestion.

"*Best you two take the biggest of the spare rooms doing otherwise would be a bit hypocritical of all of us.*"
Helen was appreciative of the new found open mindness her mother had found.

"*You know mom you're the best you really are and I love you forever*"

Despite having welcomed Akim into their family and into their daughter's bedroom, Michael and Moira Kearns were not completely at ease with their situation. Talking privately with their good friends Eileen and John McGinty, they confided the news of Helens pregnancy. Moira was a little upset as she told them.

"*Won't be long till she's showing Eileen. I'll have to tell the family soon. Dreading telling mom and dad as we know what their concern will be and we know that it won't be Helens psychical or emotional well-being.*"
Eileen as reassuringly as she could, reminded Moira that in this world we all serve one god. That there is only one god. That regardless of how as individuals we show that respect

and honour, our prayers always go to the same place. Eileen put herself forward to speak to the Riley parents, also to the Kearns, should Michael and Moira feel that could be helpful. Agreements reached that Helen and Akim should be excluded from those conversations.

Plans were put in place for the weekend with both sets of parents and any siblings who wished to, were all invited out to the Kearns family home in Enniskerry. Michael and Moira Kearns were feeling quite tense. Plans had also been put in place by Eileen McGinty, for Akim and Helen Kearns to visit an old school friend of Helens for the day. Assurance of that visit happening, was secured by John McGinty driving them out there early morning. He would be collecting them both later that evening. Having the young couple removed from the equation would allow the family to speak openly. This would be ensuring that there would be no fear of causing offence or distress to either of them. Helen was excited and looking forward. Showing off her Russian boyfriend and her skills at sign language communication, would both give her a great deal of pleasure. Unsure whether they would speak of the pregnancy or not was how that was left.

Gerald and Bridget Kearns were first to arrive together with Michaels brother and his wife. They were bearing some gifts of home-made soda bread, with treacle, sugar and dried fruit all included in the mixture. Delighted to see their son back in Ireland for good, they had many questions about Russia and his time working at the hospital over there. Moiras parents Padraig and Grace Riley arrived shortly after Michaels. Her youngest sister Catharine and her husband were together with Moiras parents. Again, bearing gifts of the same nature as the Kearns both families laughed. Michael was quick, to have everyone enjoying a piece of their parent's hard work in their kitchens that morning. Taking in a deep breath Moira called their son Dominic to join them in the garden. She was holding out the hope that due to him being of similar age to his sister Helen and to Akim, that Dominic would come out in support of their relationship.

Eileen and John McGinty could be seen over the fields in the far distance. Being on their way to Moiras she reminded everyone how they would be joining the party. The McGinty's were not empty handed either. Carrying a tray of some freshly made scones, Eileen requested that Dominic brought out the butter, jam and some more plates. She would refresh the teapot. The Kearns and Riley parents both had a look of surprise, at the manner in which Eileen had made herself at home. Tuning into their thoughts and their feelings, she told them with a smile.

"You know we've been friends for more than twenty years now with Michael and Moira. There isn't much we don't know about each other's families. I'm delighted to be here today and as for you Michael, enjoy this. It's not a rock cake as you usually say Moiras scones are."

The mood had been slightly lightened by Eileen's comment. Moira hoped to lighten it some more but was interrupted by her mother's questions regarding Helen. Moira decided to bite the bullet. She was politely assertive.

"Mam and everyone we do have some lovely news about our beautiful and amazing daughter Helen. There's going to be no secrets. She's a young woman entitled to do whatever she wants to do with her life and she is doing just that. We're

hoping that you all agree but if you don't, well that's a great pity on your behalf but it'll make no difference to us."
That's when Moira was interrupted by their son Dominic. It was as though he had sensed his mams apprehension in sharing further information. Deciding how he would share it on her behalf, he proudly told his family.

"Helen has a regular boyfriend. They have a commitment to each other. He's Russian and he's called Akim. He's here in Ireland with her and is staying here in our farm house."

Michael and Moira had prepared themselves very well for the onslaught, of how their parents would protest that this could not be allowed to continue. They were very pleasantly surprised by people's reactions. Everyone chirping in with their view of how she was old enough to have boyfriends- and then began the twenty thousand questions. Eileen McGinty could sense that their friends were starting to struggle, in giving answers to the uncomfortable questions coming from both sets of parents. She decided just like their son Dominic had done that she would intervene.

"I think what Michael and Moira are trying to say is, that Akim is not a Roman Catholic, that he is a member of the Russian Orthodox church. Does that really matter? Doesn't one god serve all."

The garden then fell into total silence. Michaels eye began to twitch. There was the clue he was feeling anxious, stressed and feeling as though enough was enough and he had surely had enough of their parents with their religious stigmas. This was already a difficult situation for himself and Moira. They did not need to be having their parent's disapproval to deal with. Michael began to speak again. He shared with everyone how proud he was of their son. Dominic had met Akim. He knows that Akim is a bilaterally profoundly deaf young man. He has not let that disability define him and has proved that by not sharing with you that Akim is deaf. Michael continued to speak to a silent audience.

"Look, Akim has been offered a top-notch job here in Dublin in the hospital where I'm working. I'm delighted to say that he has accepted the offer. I also need, no, we need to tell you something else."

At that point Michael took hold of his wife's hand.

"Helen is pregnant. She and Akim are getting married once the baby is born. We're building a house here on the farm land. It will be there's. Till that time, they will live here in this house with us."

Their only response came from Dominic Kearns, who expressed his delight that a new life would be coming into their family. Michael and Moira both again felt proud of their son. Looking to the group congregated in the garden Eileen McGinty expressed her deep and bitter sadness. Ahead of doing so she firstly expressed her apologies to her friends Michael and Moira for what she was about to say.

"You've all been told that you're going to be grandparents, cousins and an Uncle. That a precious life will be entering this world and entering this family. The only reaction is from Dominic showing his lack of ignorance and his huge amount of compassion for the human race. Your bigoted ways and ideas feel shameful to me. You should all be supporting your children and your grandchildren. Not deriding them. Shame on you"

*M*ichael and Moira both thanked Eileen for her compassion and for her level of support. Suggestions were made by them that perhaps their parents and siblings, should all leave Enniskerry at that point. They should Return back to Dublin to their respective homes and examine their own conscience. Michael gave an ultimatum to Gerald and Bridget Kearns, that either they graciously accept Akim in to their family and all which accompanies that, or he breaks ties with them. Bridget shed some tears, as did Grace Riley when the very same ultimatum was given to her and Padraig and to their extended family. There was no verbal response. The Kearns and the Riley families duly departed from Enniskerry.

*H*aving done and endured that battle with their parents, only served Michael and Moira to strengthen their own level of acceptance of Akim. It had helped them to better understand, that what's important is how a person lives their life, how they treat others and not which building they go to in order to worship their god. Saying goodbye to their friends John McGinty then fulfilled his agreement. Collecting Helen and Akim from her friend's home he found to be a deep joy. Reminding Helen of the time when she was under five years of age and how badly she had wanted to see the calving cow, Helen recalled the whole event with clarity.

"Mom raced me to the river that morning. I didn't think she would let me go to see the calving cow, so I was super nice to her in the hopes that she would. I remember helping you to sweep up in the cow house too with the small brush you got from the loft."

John McGinty was impressed by how much Helen had remembered. Bidding goodnight to her and Akim he congratulated them on their forthcoming marriage and on the forthcoming birth of their child. Wondering if her grandparents had been told about the pregnancy and their different religions, John with great reluctance stretched the truth. Advising Helen that he wasn't sure, he also advised her that their opinions on the situation would be irrelevant. That it was her life to do with whatever she wished. Waving him off from their front gate Helen and Akim retired for the night.

Helen and her parents had all shown something of an interest in learning about the Russian Orthodox beliefs and how they may differ from Catholicism. Akim was able to enlighten them to a certain degree. Knowing how the Orthodox and the Catholic church split in 1054 he was not knowledgeable of the reasons why. He could only see humour in the fact, that there was a complex mix of religious disagreements between the two Churches. One of those disagreements being whether it was acceptable or not to use unleavened bread for communion. Explaining how Orthodox believers reject the infallibility of the pope made Akim think hard about the religion which he had been raised with.

Having been witness to the Kearns and the Riley's extended family's attitude towards Akims religion and towards the new baby coming into the family, this laid quite heavily on Eileen McGinty's shoulders. Feeling very empathic towards Michael and Moira and towards the young couple too, she would try to help some more. Eileen made further enquiries around the Dublin area. Discovering that there was quite a small Russian *community in Dublin, with a Russian Orthodox church, she had a sense of excitement. She wondered if it might hold any interest for Akim and perhaps for Helen also. Sharing that news with Michael and Moira a decision was made. Eileen would speak to their daughter Helen in relation to it. Helen and Eileen had always enjoyed a very good and strong relationship. That relationship was also applicable to the inclusion of John McGinty and Helen Kearns. Where religious rules were concerned and despite her now being an adult, Helen was still more likely to listen to the McGinty's than she would do her parents. She heard from Eileen how Permission for the young couple's marriage would need to be sought from and approved by a Catholic Bishop. They could then marry in the Catholic church if that was to be their desire.*

Padraig and Grace Riley spent some time reflecting on their own lives. Reflecting on the religious rules which not only had they adhered to, but had also strictly imposed upon all of their children. Discussing the religious aspect of the lives of Akim and his parents was very enlightening for Padraig and Grace. To say they felt humbled would be an understatement. Moving forward on the last chapter of their lives, Padraig and Grace Riley both surprised their children and their extended families. Organising an evening out at their local restaurant they expressed their delight at the idea of getting to know Akim. For him to hear from Helens grandparents how much they admired his parents outlook on various religions, was touching for Akim. For Helen and her family it felt like a dream come true. Having the blessing of her mom's parents for the wedding meant everything to Helen. In her usual outspoken and almost abrupt manner she then told her father.

"We have to speak to your parents soon. Share Akims family view with them and share how it has changed moms' parents thinking."

Quite unexpectedly Akims parents and his extended family travelled over from Russia to Ireland. Helen took the phone call from his mother. She identified the woman's voice almost immediately.

"It's me Helen. We're in Dublin and thought it would be nice to meet everyone."

Helen getting over the surprise informed Akim of his family's presence in Ireland. Plans put in place for a large gathering turned out to be very successful. That's where Michaels parents were introduced to the open mindness of the Russian family, also to the knowledge that Helens grandparents now see religion in a much wider manner. Bridget Kearns was first to make comment on the Riley's openness to religions apart from Catholicism.

"We've known many people in Dublin throughout our lives who are not Roman Catholics the same as the Riley's have. Really good people who've helped and supported me and my family throughout life. I too am happy to share the view of Akims family where Religions concerned. At the end of the day there's one god. How about you Gerald?"

Bridget and all in the group were delighted to hear how Gerald Kearns was also prepared to change his lifetime view. Showing their appreciation to Michaels parents Helen and Akim individually expressed their happiness. Akim then surprised then whole group including Helen.

"When our baby joins this world, I don't want any conflict in any area of our life's Helen. For that reason, I'm becoming a convert. I want to join the Catholic church."
The room fell into almost silence. There was the occasional gasp from people who were feeling uncomfortable and not knowing how to respond. Akim helped them out.
"There's been no pressure on me to do this from anyone. There's nothing spectacular about the idea. It's simply to be on the same page in every area of my life with Helen."
A round of applause was heard from all in the group.
"To Akim and the wonderful man he is. To Helen and the great life which you will experience with this man. To the yet to be born baby we love you already."

𝒫lans put in place for Akim to join the Catholic church with his induction having already begun. People learned how he would continue for approximately two years of attending weekly class ahead of being baptised, then taking his first communion and finally his confirmation. That's when Akim would then eventually be initiated into the Catholic Church. Again, people applauded Akim for his assertiveness in establishing what becoming a convert would involve. Having taken up the position offered to him at the hospital where Michael Kearns is employed, Akim thought about how good life was being to him. Progress of building of a house on the farmland in Enniskerry had not yet begun, other than on the drawing board. Moira and Michael spoke to her parents but to Grace in particular. Having never spent any of the money which Moira had received in her inheritance from Graces 1st cousin Alice, was no surprise to Padraig and Grace. Moira now wondered what their thoughts might be, in using some of the money to provide a home for Helen and Akim. Half *would be reserved for Dominic too. Decisions were made to go ahead. All agreed that Alice would be totally approving of those decisions. That she would feel honoured to know that another young family were bringing a little bit of Russia, to what had once been her farm land. A huge applause and a glass was raised in honour of Alice and her husband Edward.*

Some changes were rapidly occurring within the Kearns household. Their son Dominic was now studying at Trinity College in Dublin. Being a college which is highly competitive to get into Dominic was beyond delighted to have secured a place there. Having changed his thoughts regarding a career choice, he had now begun studying medicine. Wanting to follow in his father's footsteps his hopes were to one day become a paediatric surgeon. Akim and Helen were married in Dublin some two years after becoming very proud parents to a healthy but deaf baby boy. Helen was by now pregnant again with their second child. Living with Moira and Michael for the first year of their baby's life had brought many untold benefits to the couple. Eventually moving into their new build on the farmland, a house warming party was arranged in honour of Alice, the lady who had provided them with all of this. Eileen and John McGinty the long-time neighbours and friends to Michael and Helen also both raised a glass to Alice.

Michael and Moira had their own surprising news to be shared with everyone excluding the McGinty's. That was a conversation which they already had with their friends. Eileen and John had offered their support, a wish that the Kearns should pursue and a promise to visit them in Russia. Michael had recently been offered and accepted a new job. It was back out in Russia in the hospital where he had been working whilst on secondment. The position was to be a permanent one. A rent-free house would be provided by the hospital to the point of his retirement. It would be at that point where he and Moira would return back home to Enniskerry to live in the farm house. Michael explained to the group how tenants had been secured for their farm house. It was with the understanding that Dominic would remain there for as long as he choose to. Their son had recently met their new tenants. He was aware of and happy with the house sharing situation. Moira had also secured some part time self-employment within a children's safeguarding unit in Moscow. She would be working in the role of children's guardian, as and when t families were being presented in front of the courts. Whilst the role would be one of self-employment she would be kept busy.

Wishing her new position commenced after the birth of her second grandchild, Moira was astute enough to understand the need for her pretty urgent presence in Russia. A shortage of safeguarding clinicians who were connected to the court systems, had created quite long delays. Many children's cases were heavily delayed, in securing their place to get before the courts. Moira's passion in the work place being around the safeguarding of children, she knew she had to go. Saying goodbye to their farming friends Eileen and John McGinty, was somewhat eased by the knowledge the McGinty's would be visiting them out in Russia. Eileen and John were also in almost the step parents position with Helen and Akim. Eileen when speaking to Helen regarding her parent's departure, was firm yet compassionate in her tone.

"You're a great mother and a great wife to Akim. You need anything you know where we are."

Appreciating their kindness, the couple assured Eileen they would be at her door should they have a need. Dominic too was aware of the McGinty's support in addition to that of their grandparents.

For the Kearns the prospects of their own parents ever attempting that journey out to Russia was a non-starter in their minds. Reassuring both sets of parents how they would return yearly for a holiday, Michael and Moira were taken by surprise by their response. Hearing from the Kearns and the Riley's how they would all have to see for themselves what Russia is like, there was a huge applause from everyone present. Moira hugged her parents and then Michaels too. Everyone saying their family goodbyes their parents departed back to their Dublin homes. Soon It was the weekend. The day for leaving Ireland behind them was now upon them, Michael had enlisted the support of their farming neighbours. Arriving with some home baked scones, Eileen McGinty had organised a small tea party in the Kearns home. Helen, Akim and their toddler child, together with John McGinty and the Kearns own son Dominic, all gathered around the turf fire.

Despite her wanting to do this upcoming journey Moira shed some tears, as did Helen and Eileen McGinty. Decisions were then made and agreed that there would be no formal goodbyes. Their parting would be viewed as though it was going to be a trip into town till the next time. Sometime later that morning, a laden car was driven out of their farm house gates heading towards Dublin airport. The parting was then treated by everyone present as per their agreement. Leaving their pregnant daughter behind them, highlighted to Michael and Moira what an amazing young woman Helen had become. Remembering how due to religious discrimination within their families, Moira had ended her own relationship with Charlie Cunningham all those years ago.

Moira once again felt the whole of the Riley and the Kearns families had achieved an enormous accomplishment. A person's religious practice would from that point forward, no longer hold any sense of discrimination for any of them. For that they owed thanks to Akim and to his parents. Using the art of distraction from one's worrisome thoughts, Moira focused on and began some written preparation, for her new role out in Moscow. Placing his hand over hers Michael encouraged his wife to rest and relax. Settling back into the aircraft seat as much as was possible they both agreed to look forward. Arrival at their new home in Pullman was the beginning of their new lives. It was not and never would be the end of their Irish lives. That evening they were joined for a celebration by Akims parents. Again, a glass was raised to Alice and to the sincerity of her endowment to Moira and her siblings.
"Here's to Alice and here's to Enniskerry and all within it."

Go dti an chead uair eile- Meaning- "till the next time."

About the Author

Beatrice Finn was born into an Irish farming family in County Mayo in the West of Ireland. Her classroom education was pretty basic and did not commence till the age of around six to seven years. Beatrice is happy to stand corrected on this, as it may have been closer to six years. Her broader education came from life experience growing up on the farm, to the age of fourteen years. That was the point in life in which Beatrice went through emigration, together with her parents and her siblings.

They found a new and better life in Leicester in the United Kingdom. Beatrice has lived in Leicester ever since. She makes occasional trips back to Cloontia County Mayo. A marriage, divorce, two children and four grandchildren, have all contributed to shaping her into the person which she has become.

Beatrice throughout her lifetime has worked in many different environments. The career which she has mostly enjoyed is her current one. Working with and fostering children and young people over the past twenty-two years, has brought many different experiences to her. Her second career is writing. Hopefully there will be many more tales to tell.

Printed in Great Britain
by Amazon

78736326R00187